HERO'S RETURN

Also available from
B.J. Daniels
and HQN Books

A Cahill Ranch Novel

Renegade's Pride
Outlaw's Honor
Cowboy's Legacy
Cowboy's Reckoning
Hero's Return

The Montana Hamiltons

Wild Horses
Lone Rider
Lucky Shot
Hard Rain
Into Dust
Honor Bound

Beartooth, Montana

Mercy
Atonement
Forsaken
Redemption
Unforgiven

B.J. DANIELS

HERO'S RETURN

HQN™

ISBN-13: 978-1-335-47786-6

Recycling programs
for this product may
not exist in your area.

Hero's Return

www.HQNBooks.com

Printed in U.S.A.

No one knows how to fish walleyes better than friend, fishing buddy and fellow *Twilight Zone* fan Mike Larson. This one is for you and your lovely wife, Elizabeth. We enjoy having the two of you in our lives.

PROLOGUE

The old footbridge creaked and groaned under her weight as she made her way in the darkness to the center where the water would be the deepest. She could hear the roar of the creek rushing beneath her, but she tried not to think about what she was about to do.

The Montana spring air had a sharp bite to it tonight. She shivered but kept walking, the bundle in her arms cradled protectively against her chest. The creek was much higher than the last time she'd been here and running much faster. She felt another shiver, this one from fear.

She'd forgotten the distance from the bridge to the creek's surface. The water would be icy cold, stealing her breath away, as if that was the worst of her problems. For a moment, she looked downstream. All she could see was darkness. Large old cottonwood limbs leaned out over the stream, casting even blacker shadows over the inky water.

Tucker Cahill was late. Maybe he wasn't coming. She wished he wouldn't, but she knew this cowboy. He'd come. They always did.

Reaching the middle of the bridge, she stopped to wait.

The wind was strong here. It swept her long blond hair into her eyes, but she didn't dare let go of the bundle in her arms to brush it aside.

Instead, she stood, buffeted by the tempest of her emotions more than the rising gale. She knew that if she wasn't careful she could lose her balance and be pitched into the water below before it was time. There was no railing on the footbridge. One misstep and she would be over the side, falling for what would seem like forever before she struck the powerful current and was swept away.

She glanced toward the opposite end of the bridge. What if he'd changed his mind about meeting her tonight? He was already suspicious. One clear thought surfaced as she waited. She didn't want to do this anymore. Couldn't. It had to stop— and it would—tonight.

Sensing Tucker, she glanced toward the shoreline and saw movement. She watched as seventeen-year-old Tucker Cahill made his way along the creek bank. The big handsome cowboy moved in long, determined strides. Of course he'd come, because he didn't want to let her down. He was already that kind of man at seventeen. She felt a mixture of shame, anger and disgust. He knew what kind of woman he was meeting tonight. Why had he let it go this far?

A part of her wanted to warn him off, to send him back, to let this one go. But there would be consequences downstream if she did. No, she had to finish this.

When he spotted her in the dim starlight, she saw that he was immediately alarmed to see her teetering so close to the edge of the bridge. He called to her, telling her not to move, as he strode, long legged, along the creek bank and then up onto the footbridge.

"Don't come any closer," she warned him as she hugged the bundle tighter and told him how he had ruined her life.

The emotion in her voice made him hesitate, but only for

a moment. The bridge swayed as he took a few tentative steps toward her, his boots echoing on the worn wood.

She balanced on the razor's edge of the bridge before calling out another warning, knowing it wouldn't do any good. He thought he could save her from more than the strong current beneath her. He wasn't the first man to think that.

The wind pushed at her back. The bridge swayed. And yet she didn't jump. For a moment, she thought she couldn't go through with it. She looked down at the bundle in her arms. The tiny nose and mouth, the brown of the eyes shiny in the starlight. But ultimately, she knew she had no choice. There was no turning back now. She was in too deep; they all were.

"Please, don't move!" the cowboy pleaded and quickened his step as he kept coming.

The footbridge swayed crazily under her feet. Tears stung her eyes as she looked down at the water. She was so tired. She just wanted this to be over. No matter the cost, it would end tonight.

Tucker was gaining on her fast. If she didn't move…

She wavered for a moment on the precipice until he was almost to her before she jumped. As her head went under in the freezing cold water, only then did she let go of the burden in her arms and was quickly swept away.

CHAPTER ONE

Skeletal Remains Found in Creek
The skeletal remains of a woman believed to be in her late teens or early twenties were discovered in Miner's Creek, outside Gilt Edge, Montana, yesterday. Local coroner Sonny Bates estimated that the remains had been in the creek for somewhere around twenty years.

Sheriff Flint Cahill is looking into missing-persons cases from that time in the hopes of identifying the victim. If anyone has any information, they are encouraged to call the Gilt Edge Sheriff's Department.

"No, Mrs. Kern, I can assure you that the bones that were found in the creek are not those of your nephew Billy," Sheriff Flint Cahill said into the phone at his desk. "I saw Billy last week at the casino. He was alive and well… No, it takes longer than a week for a body to decompose to nothing but bones. Also, the skeletal remains that were found were a young woman's… Yes, Coroner Sonny Bates can tell the difference."

He looked up as the door opened and his sister, Lillie, stepped into his office. From the scowl on her face, he didn't have to ask what kind of mood she was in. He'd been expecting her given that he had their father locked up in one of the cells.

"Mrs. Kern, I have to go. I'm sorry Billy hasn't called you, but I'm sure he's fine." He hung up with a sigh. "Dad's in the back sleeping it off. Before he passed out, he mumbled about getting back to the mountains."

A very pregnant Lillie nodded but said nothing. Pregnancy had made his sister even prettier. Her long dark hair framed a face that could only be called adorable. This morning, though, he saw something in her gray eyes that worried him.

He waited for her to tie into him, knowing how she felt about him arresting their father for being drunk and disorderly. This wasn't their first rodeo. And like always, it was Lillie who came to bail Ely out—not his bachelor brothers, Hawk and Cyrus, who wanted to avoid one of Flint's lectures.

He'd been telling his siblings that they needed to do something about their father. But no one wanted to face the day when their aging dad couldn't continue to spend most of his life in the mountains gold panning and trapping—let alone get a snoot full of booze every time he finally hit town again.

"I'll go get him," Flint said, lumbering to his feet. Since he'd gotten the call about the bones being found at the creek, he hadn't had but a few hours' sleep. All morning, the phone had been ringing off the hook. Not with leads on the identity of the skeletal remains—just residents either being nosy or worried there was a killer on the loose.

"Before you get Dad..." Lillie seemed to hesitate, which wasn't like her. She normally spoke her mind without any encouragement at all.

He braced himself.

"A package came for Tuck."

That was the last thing Flint had expected out of her mouth. "To the saloon?"

"To the ranch. No return address."

Flint felt his heart begin to pound harder. It was the first news of their older brother, Tucker, since he'd left home right after high school. Being the second oldest, Flint had been closer to Tucker than with his younger brothers. For years, he'd feared him dead. When Tuck had left like that, he'd suspected his brother was in some kind of trouble. He'd been sure of it. But had it been something bad enough that Tucker hadn't felt he could come to Flint for help?

"Did you open the package?" he asked.

Lillie shook her head. "Hawk and Cyrus thought about it but then called me."

He tried to hide his irritation that one of them had called their sister instead of him, the darned sheriff. His brothers had taken over the family ranch and were the only ones still living on the property so it wasn't a surprise that they would have received the package. Which meant that whoever had sent it either didn't know that Tucker no longer lived there or thought he was coming back for some reason.

Because Tucker was on his way home? Maybe he'd sent the package and there was nothing to worry about.

Unfortunately, a package after all this time didn't necessarily bode well. At least not to Flint, who came by his suspicious nature naturally as a lawman. He feared it might be Tucker's last effects.

"I hope *you* didn't open it."

Lillie shook her head. "You think this means he's coming home?" She sounded so hopeful it made his heart ache. He and Tucker had been close in more ways than age. Or at least he'd thought so. But something had been going on with his brother his senior year in high school and Flint had no idea what it was. Or if trouble was still dogging his brother.

For months after Tucker left, Flint had waited for him to return. He'd been so sure that whatever the trouble was, it was temporary. But after all these years, he'd given up any hope. He'd feared he would never see his brother again.

"Tell them not to open it. I'll stop by the ranch and check it out."

Lillie met his gaze. "It's out in my SUV. I brought it with me."

Flint swore under his breath. What if it had a bomb in it? He knew that was overly dramatic but, still, knowing his sister... There wasn't a birthday or Christmas present that she hadn't shaken the life out of as she'd tried to figure out what was inside it. "Is your truck open?" She nodded. "Wait here."

He stepped out in the bright spring day. Gilt Edge sat in a saddle surrounded by four mountain ranges still tipped with snow. Picturesque, tourists came here to fish its blue-ribbon trout stream. But winters were long and a town of any size was a long way off.

Sitting in the middle of Montana, Gilt Edge also had something that most tourists didn't see. It was surrounded by underground missile silos. The one on the Cahill Ranch was renowned because that was where their father swore he'd seen a UFO not only land, but also that he'd been forced on board back in 1967. Which had made their father the local crackpot.

Flint took a deep breath, telling himself to relax. His life was going well. He was married to the love of his life. But still, he felt a foreboding that he couldn't shake off. A package for Tucker after all these years?

The air this early in the morning was still cold, but there was a scent to it that promised spring wasn't that far off. He loved spring and summers here and had been looking forward to picnics, trail rides and finishing the yard around the house he and Maggie were building.

He realized that he'd been on edge since he'd gotten the call about the human bones found in the creek. Now he could admit it. He'd felt as if he was waiting for the other shoe to drop. And now this, he thought as he stepped to his sister's SUV.

The box sitting in the passenger-side seat looked battered. He opened the door and hesitated for a moment before picking it up. For its size, a foot-and-a-half-sized cube, the package was surprisingly light. As he lifted the box out, something shifted inside. The sound wasn't a rattle. It was more a rustle like dead leaves followed by a slight thump.

Like his sister had said, there was no return address. Tucker's name and the ranch address had been neatly printed in black—not in his brother's handwriting. The generic cardboard box was battered enough to suggest it had come from a great distance, but that wasn't necessarily true. It could have looked like that when the sender found it discarded and decided to use it to send the contents. He hesitated for a moment, feeling foolish. But he didn't hear anything ticking inside. Closing the SUV door, he carried the box inside and put it behind his desk.

"Aren't you going to open it?" Lillie asked, wide-eyed.

"No. You need to take Dad home." He started to pass his sister but vacillated. "I wouldn't say anything to him about this. We don't want to get his hopes up that Tucker might be headed home. Or make him worry."

She glanced at the box and nodded. "Did you ever understand why Tuck left?"

Flint shook his head. He was torn between anger and sadness when it came to his brother. Also fear. What had happened during Tucker's senior year in high school? What if the answer was in that box?

"By the way," he said to his sister, "I didn't arrest Dad. Ely voluntarily turned himself in last night." He shrugged. Flint had never understood his father any more than he had his brother Tuck. To this day, Ely swore that he was out by the missile silo buried in the middle of their ranch when a UFO landed, took him aboard and did experiments on him.

Then again, their father liked his whiskey and always had.

"You all right?" he asked his sister when she still said nothing.

Lillie nodded distractedly and placed both hands over the baby growing inside her. She was due any day now. He hoped the package for Tucker wasn't something that would hurt his family. He didn't want anything upsetting his sister in her condition. But he could see that just the arrival of the mysterious box had Lillie worried. She wasn't the only one.

CHAPTER TWO

Tucker Cahill slowed his pickup as he drove through Gilt Edge. He'd known it would be emotional, returning after all these years. He'd never doubted he would return—he just hadn't expected it to take nineteen years. All that time, he'd been waiting like a man on death row, knowing how it would eventually end.

Still, he was filled with a crush of emotion. *Home.* He hadn't realized how much he'd missed it, how much he'd missed his family, how much he'd missed his life in Montana. He'd been waiting for this day, dreading it and, at the same time, anxious to return at least once more.

As he pulled into a parking place in front of the sheriff's department, he saw a pregnant woman come out followed by an old man with long gray hair and beard. His breath caught. Not sure if he was more shocked to see how his father had aged—or how pregnant and grown-up his little sister, Lillie, was now.

He couldn't believe it as he watched Lillie awkwardly climb into an SUV, the old man going around to the passenger side. He felt his heart swell at the sight of them. Lillie had been nine when he'd left. But he could never forget a face that adorable. Was that really his father? He couldn't believe it. When had Ely Cahill become an old mountain man?

He wanted to call out to them but stopped himself. As much as he couldn't wait to see them, there was something he had to take care of first. Tears burned his eyes as he watched Lillie drive their father away. It appeared he was about to be an uncle. Over the years while he was hiding out, he'd made a point of following what news he could from Gilt Edge. He'd missed so much with his family.

He swallowed the lump in his throat as he opened his pickup door and stepped out. The good news was that his brother Flint was sheriff. That, he hoped, would make it easier to do what he had to do. But facing Flint after all this time away… He knew he owed his family an explanation, but Flint more than the rest. He and his brother had been so close—until his senior year.

He braced himself as he pulled open the door to the sheriff's department and stepped in. He'd let everyone down nineteen years ago, Flint especially. He doubted his brother would have forgotten—or forgiven him.

But that was the least of it, Flint would soon learn.

After his sister left, Flint moved the battered cardboard box to the corner of his desk. He'd just pulled out his pocketknife to cut through the tape when his intercom buzzed.

"There's a man here to see you," the dispatcher said. He could hear the hesitation in her voice. "He says he's your *brother*?" His family members never had the dispatcher announce them. They just came on back to his office. *"Your brother Tucker?"*

Flint froze for a moment. Hands shaking, he laid down his pocketknife as relief surged through him. Tucker was alive and back in Gilt Edge? He had to clear his throat before he said, "Send him in."

He told himself he wasn't prepared for this and yet it was something he'd dreamed of all these years. He stepped around to the front of his desk, half-afraid of what to expect. A lot could have happened to his brother in nineteen years. The big question, though, was why come back now?

As a broad-shouldered cowboy filled his office doorway, Flint blinked. He'd been expecting the worst.

Instead, Tucker looked great. Still undeniably handsome with his thick dark hair and gray eyes like the rest of the Cahills, Tucker had filled out from the teenager who'd left home. Wherever he'd been, he'd apparently fared well. He appeared to have been doing a lot of physical labor because he was buff and tanned.

Flint was overwhelmed by both love and regret as he looked at Tuck, and furious with him for making him worry all these years.

"Hello, Flint," Tucker said, his voice deeper than Flint remembered.

He couldn't speak for a moment, afraid of what would come out of his mouth. The last thing he wanted to do was drive his brother away again. He wanted to hug him and slug him at the same time.

Instead, voice breaking, he said, "Tuck. It's so damned good to see you," and closed the distance between them to pull his older brother into a bear hug.

Tucker hugged Flint, fighting tears. It had been so long. Too long. His heart broke at the thought of the lost years. But Flint looked good, taller than Tucker remembered, broader shouldered, too.

"When did you get so handsome?" Tucker said as he pulled back, his eyes still burning with tears. It surprised him that they were both about the same height. Like him, Flint had filled out. With their dark hair and gray eyes, they could almost pass for twins.

The sheriff laughed. "You know darned well that you're the prettiest of the bunch of us."

Tucker laughed, too, at the old joke. It felt good. Just like it felt good to be with family again. "Looks like you've done all right for yourself."

Flint sobered. "I thought I'd never see you again."

"Like Dad used to say, I'm like a bad penny. I'm bound to turn up. How is the old man? Was that him I saw leaving with Lillie?"

"You didn't talk to them?" Flint sounded both surprised and concerned.

"I wanted to see you first." Tucker smiled as Flint laid a hand on his shoulder and squeezed gently before letting go.

"You know how he was after Mom died. Now he spends almost all of his time up in the mountains panning gold and trapping. He had a heart attack a while back, but it hasn't slowed him down. There's no talking any sense into him."

"Never was." Tucker nodded as a silence fell between them. He and Flint had once been so close. Regret filled him as Flint studied him for a long moment before he stepped back and motioned him toward a chair in his office.

Flint closed the door and settled into his chair behind his desk. Tucker dragged up one of the office chairs.

"I wondered if you wouldn't be turning up since Lillie brought in a package addressed to you when she came to pick up Dad. He often spends a night in my jail when he's in town. Drunk and disorderly."

Tucker didn't react to that. He was looking at the battered brown box sitting on Flint's desk. *"A package?"* His voice broke. No one could have known he was coming back here unless…

Flint's eyes narrowed as if he heard the fear in his brother's voice. "I thought maybe you'd sent it on ahead of you for some reason."

Tucker shook his head. "Apparently someone was expecting me," he said, trying to make light of it when the mere sight of the box made him sick inside.

"Well, I'm just glad you're back," his brother said. "Whatever it was that sent you hightailing it out of here… We'll deal with it as a family. I only wish it hadn't taken you so long to return."

"I'm sure you have a lot of questions."

"You think?" Flint sighed and leaned back in his chair. "I knew something was going on with you your senior year."

Tucker nodded, his gaze shifting to the box sitting on his brother's desk. He swallowed. "It wasn't something I could talk about back then."

"And now?" Flint's phone rang. He buzzed the dispatcher to hold all his calls unless they were urgent. "I'm sorry. The phone's been ringing off the hook. You probably haven't heard. One of the locals found skeletal remains in Miner's Creek."

"Actually, I did hear. That's—"

Flint's phone rang again. He groaned as he picked up, listened and rose from his desk. "That was the coroner. I have to run next door. Not sure how long it's going to take. Where are you staying?"

"I just got in."

"You're welcome to stay with me and my wife, Maggie. Or you can always go out to the ranch. I think your room is as you left it. Hawk and Cyrus have been busy running the ranch. No time to redecorate even if they had an inclination to do so."

Tucker nodded. "I'm looking forward to seeing the place—

and the rest of the family. So you're married. Congratulations."

"Thank you. I'm sorry I have to run." Flint came around his desk to put a hand on Tucker's shoulder again. "I'm glad you're back. I hope it's to stay." He looked worried. Not half as much as he was going to be, Tucker thought.

"I'll be sticking around."

Flint sighed. "Then we'll talk soon. You have a lot to catch up on."

As his brother went out the door, Tucker rose and stepped to the desk and the box sitting there. Just as Flint had said, it was addressed to him. He didn't recognize the handwriting—not that he figured he would. Picking up the pocket-knife lying beside the box, he still hesitated, afraid of what was inside, but unable *not* to open it to find out.

He sliced the tape across the top and carefully turned back the flaps. A faintly moldy scent rose from the box along with the rustle of newsprint. For a moment, he didn't see anything but wadded-up newspaper and what appeared to be pages from a magazine.

Hesitantly, he pushed some of the paper aside and blinked, unsure for an instant as to what he was seeing. With a startled gasp, he jerked back as though bitten by a rattlesnake. Heart pounding and sick with disgust, he reached in and removed the wadded-up paper until all that remained in the box was the tiny battered naked doll.

One dull dark eye stared up at him—the other eye missing from the weather-beaten toy. Shaking all over, his stomach heaving, he lurched around his brother's desk to throw up in the trash.

CHAPTER THREE

Flint stood at the edge of the autopsy room, trying to breathe normally. He'd never liked the morgue, especially early in the morning when the smells always got to him.

Today the morgue reeked of eggs and sausage. Sonny had been eating a breakfast sandwich when Flint had come in.

"Busy morning. They brought in a homeless man." He nodded toward the second table where the naked corpse lay, its chest cavity open. "Looks like a heart attack given the condition of the heart." He made a motion as if offering to show it to him, but Flint waved that off.

Sonny, making a "your loss" face, put aside his sandwich to move to the other table where the skeletal remains had been placed in the positions where each had once been when connected.

"Amazingly, she's only missing a few fingers," Sonny was saying. "But the deputy who brought back the earth she'd been found in is still sifting through it, so he might find them yet."

Flint merely nodded.

"You can tell a lot from bones. Like this fibula," Sonny

said, picking up the left leg bone. "The length of the long bones tells us about what age she was—early twenties. From measuring the femur, tibia, humerus and their radii, I can tell that she was about five foot six. She was medium boned. If you look at the state of the bones, you can get a pretty good indication of how long she was buried along the creek bank. Fifteen to twenty years, but closer to twenty years."

"You're sure it's been that long?" Flint asked, thinking how impossible it might be to identify the woman, let alone locate next of kin if they did.

"It's not an exact science. It takes a while for the body to decompose to the skeletal stage." Sonny started to put the leg bone back but held it up one more time. "Looks like she broke her left leg. It's an old break that was long healed before she went for a swim."

He put down the bone and picked up another one. "These bony ridges form where the muscles were attached to the wrist. She could have had a job where she used her hands, like a waitress." Putting that bone back, he picked up the skull.

Flint saw that tufts of long blond hair were still attached to it. "What about DNA from the hair?"

"Already sent some over to the lab. But look at this." He pointed at the teeth. "Not a great diet. She had cavities and not much dental work."

"So what killed her?" Flint asked.

Sonny shrugged. "The obvious would be drowning, right? But this is what I really wanted you to see. I thought you'd find it interesting." He turned the skull. Flint had to move closer to see what Sonny was pointing to. "Wood. See, some of the wood splinters are still embedded in the side of the skull. I'm betting that's what killed her."

"Wood?"

He nodded and began to walk him through it. "Assuming she either jumped into the river to swim or fell, depending on what time of year it was, her head made contact with a tree limb violently enough to kill her."

"Is it possible the blow to her head didn't kill her instantly? Her remains were found a dozen yards from the creek."

"She might have been able to get out of the water, but she wouldn't have been able to go far. She wouldn't have survived long with that kind of head injury. Certainly not long enough to hide herself under a pile of driftwood."

"So it appears to have been an accident, but someone covered up her death by hiding her body," Flint said.

Sonny gave that some thought. "Had that one a few years ago, you might recall, where the fisherman slipped on the rocks, fell and hit his head. Made it almost back to his car before he died. His wound wasn't as severe. I supposed she might have been able to get out of the water and crawl a few yards. Seems more likely someone helped her and, when they saw that she was badly hurt or dead by then, hid her body. At least she wasn't swimming in the creek alone."

"My brothers and I used to go fishing and swimming by ourselves all the time. Never even considered that we might fall and hurt ourselves badly enough to kill us."

Sonny shook his head. "Kids. But this woman was old enough to know better. I have to wonder why her companion tried to cover up her death. Must have felt responsible. Well, whoever it was, he's had to live with it all these years. Guess it's come home to roost now, though, huh."

"Maybe," Flint said, not as optimistic as Sonny apparently that justice would get done on this case. Fifteen to twenty years was a long time. The case was ice-cold. Not to mention the fact that the statute of limitations had run out for the crime of hiding a body.

He said as much to Sonny. "No hurry on this case since no one reported a woman this age missing fifteen to twenty years ago." He frowned as he looked at the coroner and realized what he'd said. "What makes you think it was a man who buried her?"

"No woman would cover up her friend's death," Sonny said with confidence.

"You ever meet my ex-wife, Celeste?" he joked.

The coroner laughed. "I have five dollars that says it was a man."

"You're on, but more than likely we'll never know."

"Oh, you'll find him. Want to bet that I'm wrong about her age?" Sonny asked.

"No. I'm not going to let you hustle me." Flint took one last look at the bones on the table. "What I don't understand is why someone didn't report her missing," he said more to himself than to the coroner. "A family member, a friend, someone. I've checked and there are no missing-persons reports that match up from that time period."

"Could be she wasn't from here. Or maybe family tried to report her missing. It was before your time as sheriff. Anyway, as you know, law enforcement doesn't get too involved when the missing woman is in her early twenties unless there is reason to believe it might have been foul play."

Flint knew that to be true. Often missing persons that age simply have hit the road and don't want their relatives to know where they've gone. Kind of like his brother Tucker.

"Could be, too, that she didn't have any kin looking for her," Sonny said. "Or they had some reason they didn't want the law involved."

As Tucker heaved up the last of his breakfast and wiped his mouth, he heard Flint's concerned voice behind him.

"Tuck?"

He turned slowly to look at his brother. All the years, all the fear and pain, rushed at him like a locomotive barreling down on him. "It's my fault," he said, his words coming out as broken as his heart. "The remains you found in the creek? I killed her—and our baby."

Minutes later, Tucker slumped into the chair his brother offered him. He pressed the cold can of cola Flint had gotten from the vending machine down the hall against his forehead. After a few moments, he opened the can and took a sip as he tried to gather his thoughts. He'd known this would be hard. But after seeing what was in that package…

Flint had looked into the box but hadn't touched the doll. Instead, he'd moved the package and the paper that had been inside to the floor beside his desk and waited.

"I don't know where to begin," Tucker said, although he knew his story began the moment he saw her. Summer, twenty years ago. He and his friends had taken a road trip. They'd stopped for gas in a small town in another county to the northwest.

"I got out to take a leak. It was one of those old gas stations with the restrooms along the side. When I came out, I saw her. She was coming from behind the building, crying and looking behind her like someone was after her. When she saw me, she stopped, wiped her tears and gave me this smile that rocked my world." He shook his head. "I was hooked right there. She asked for my help. I had some money, so I gave it to her. I could hear my friends loading up to leave. She asked if I had to go or if maybe I wanted to go somewhere with her. She offered me a ride home."

He looked up to see Flint's expression. "I know. I was young and foolish and she was…" He shook his head. "Mysterious. Mesmerizing. Amazing. She had long blond hair and these wide blue eyes that when I looked into them I felt as if I was diving into an ocean filled with things I'd never seen before. Things *no one* had ever seen before. She was captivating and yet so vulnerable. I'd never met anyone like her.

I couldn't have stopped myself even if I had wanted to. I fell hard."

"You couldn't have told me what was going on?" Flint asked.

"We had to keep it a secret from everyone, even you. Her father and brother... She said she wasn't allowed to date until she was eighteen. Her father was very strict. The day we met, she'd had an argument with him. She said she wanted to run away. She couldn't live in that house any longer and as soon as she turned eighteen... She said she'd graduated early, but he wouldn't let her leave until her birthday."

"So you were going to run away with her," Flint said.

Tucker shook his head and looked away for a moment. "I was going to marry her as soon as I graduated. But then she told me that she was pregnant. We didn't use any protection that first time."

"The day you met her."

He nodded. "I... She was my first. We spent that summer seeing each other every chance she got to sneak away and meet me. Three months in, she told me she was pregnant. I was determined to marry her right then and there, but she said her father would kill her if he found out she was pregnant—and he or her brother would kill *me*. She said there was only one thing to do. She would leave, get settled and send for me."

Flint groaned. "She asked for money."

"I scraped up what money I could."

"You sold your pistol and your saddle. When I realized that you'd sold those, I thought you had been planning to leave home for months before you actually did."

"I gave her the money with the understanding that she would contact me after she ran away and I would drop out of school and meet her. Months went by without hearing from her. I couldn't eat or sleep. Going to school was killing me.

When I couldn't stand it any longer, I drove up to the town where I'd met her."

"Let me guess," Flint said with the shake of his head.

"Yep, there had never been anyone by the name of Madeline Ross in Denton, Montana. No father, no brother that I could find." He shook his head. "She'd lied to me about her name and, it seemed, everything else. I went by the library, looked through the school annual for the year she said she'd graduated—a year ahead of me. Nothing. I thought I'd never hear from her again."

"You aren't the first man to be conned by a good-looking woman," Flint said.

He nodded. "Like you, I thought the whole thing had been a scam, especially when I got a message from her that she needed more money." He raked a hand through his hair, avoiding Flint's gaze. "She said she'd had to lie out of fear, but that she would tell me everything when we met and I gave her the money." He sighed. "I told her I couldn't raise any more, but that I would graduate soon and get a job and… She told me to forget it and hung up."

"I suspect she didn't let you off that easily."

Tucker shook his head. "I knew I'd been played, but a part of me wanted desperately to believe at least some of it was real. I held out hope that there really was an explanation. Later that night, she called to tell me to meet her at the bridge over the creek near our ranch and she would tell me everything."

Flint sat up a little in his chair. "I remember that night. When you came back to the house, your clothes were soaking wet. You were so upset. You said you were just angry with yourself because you'd fallen in the creek and to leave you alone. I wish now that I hadn't listened to you."

"I went in the creek, all right. When I reached the edge of the bridge she was waiting for me in the middle holding something in her arms. She told me not to come any closer or she would jump. Remember, I hadn't seen or heard from her in months." His voice broke. "She was holding our child. She said she'd had the baby prematurely, a little boy, and that he was sick and that's why she'd asked for the money. I promised I would get it, but she said it was too late, that I'd ruined her life. She said that her father and brother were demanding to know who the father of the baby was, but that she hadn't told, couldn't, because she loved me too much. I kept moving toward her. I had to. I thought if I could hold her... I tried to get to her, but before I could, she jumped."

Flint frowned. Tucker knew he had to be asking himself if all this had been just a scam, then why would she have jumped?

"There'd been a storm a few days before so the creek was running high," Tuck said. "I dived into the water but..." He bent over in his chair to stare down at his boots for a moment as he tried to blot out that night. The pain had stayed with him for all these years. Being back here just made it worse.

"She was gone," he said finally. "I found a torn piece of the blouse she'd been wearing and the baby blanket caught in some limbs." He wagged his head, unable to go on.

"That's why you came back now," Flint said with a curse. "The skeletal remains that were found in the creek. You think they belong to this Madeline Ross. You've been waiting all these years for her body to turn up?"

Tucker nodded slowly.

Flint shook his head. "I left earlier to go next door to the coroner's office. He estimates the woman was in her early twenties, but he doesn't believe that she drowned. Sonny says she died of a head wound from crashing into a log."

He stared at Flint. "So she must have hit a limb as she was being carried downstream by the current." Was that supposed to relieve his mind?

"The reason it took nineteen years for her remains to turn

up—if they are hers—is because she was found under dirt and driftwood yards from the creek. The coroner doubts she could have gotten that far with the head injury that killed her. This spring the creek got so high it overflowed into that old drainage and washed out the side of the bank along with the driftwood or the remains might never have been found that far from the creek."

Tucker sat back. His head was spinning. "I don't understand."

"It appears it was an accident. She must have hit her head while being swept down the creek."

"Still, it's my fault."

"Tuck, it was all a scam. She wasn't alone that night. She didn't hide her own body under the dirt and driftwood at the edge of the old creek bank. Someone was waiting for her downstream. They probably pulled her out, panicked since Sonny says the blow to her head would have killed her quickly. So that person buried her body and covered the grave with driftwood away from the creek."

"*What?* No, she came alone that night."

Flint sighed. "If she had come there alone, her vehicle would have been found when she didn't return to it."

Why hadn't he thought of that? Tucker felt sick to his stomach all over again. "Someone could have dropped her off."

"Right, with plans to pick her up. Tuck, she wouldn't have taken such a chance jumping in that creek with it running so high unless someone was waiting downstream to help her out. Whoever pulled her body from the creek that night was working with her. The person would have driven whatever vehicle they'd arrived in that night—after they hid her body."

He couldn't believe what he was hearing. Of course she wasn't working her scam alone. He was such a fool. All these years of believing he'd been responsible for her death and that of their son...

"I'm assuming the remains belong to the woman you knew given what you've told me," Flint said. "But until we get a positive ID…"

"I thought I killed her and the baby. Were her remains all that were found?"

"No sign of a baby. Did she ever show you any proof that she was pregnant?"

"No, but—"

"So you don't know that what she had in her arms that night was even an infant." Flint nudged the box on the floor with his boot. "It could have been a doll. It could have even been *that* doll. Do you have any idea who sent this to you?"

He shook his head. "Someone who wants me to still believe that I killed her. I'm surprised they didn't try to blackmail me."

"Tuck, I think whoever sent the box was trying to tell you that it had all been a scam—including the baby. But there is one way to find out." Flint picked up the phone and dialed.

"There was no note in the box?" the sheriff asked as he waited for an answer on the other end of the line.

Tucker shook his head.

"But they had to know that when the remains were found it would bring you home," Flint said. "You left town so soon after that night, they might not have known where you'd gone. Or they were so upset about what happened, the game was over—at least for a while."

"Well, they know where I am now, if that package is any indication."

Flint seemed to consider that. "The coroner, please," he said when someone answered on the other end of the line. "Did anyone else know about the two of you?"

"Madeline swore me to secrecy. I never told anyone." His head was spinning. Madeline hadn't survived the raging waters of the creek that night just as he'd feared. She'd apparently brought about her own death by misjudging the creek's current. "When will we know for certain that it's her?"

"The coroner is having DNA run on the hair follicles. If we knew where she was really from, we could check dental records. You met her in Denton? Then there is a good chance she's from somewhere around this area. Also, if she has family, they might come forward now."

"She said she had a father and brother. But she could have lied about that, too."

"Sonny?" Flint said into the phone. "I have a question for you."

Tucker hardly listened. He was staring at the box with the doll in it, trying to make sense of everything. It had been a scam. Even the baby, though? But if Flint was right and Madeline hadn't come alone that night…

His brother hung up. "Sonny says the remains of the woman he has at the morgue never had a child. He can tell from the pelvic bones."

"I shouldn't be surprised," Tucker said and rubbed a hand over his face, his brain fighting to reevaluate what he thought had happened that night. It had always been about money for Madeline. The plan must have been for her to disappear and whoever was working with her to blackmail him all these years. Only Madeline had hit something in the water and died. None of the rest had been real.

"You must think I'm a complete fool," he said.

"You were young and vulnerable. She targeted you. If the remains are hers, then she was a lot older than she told you, and I'm betting that you weren't her first—just her last. But her jumping into that creek…" Flint shook his head. "That was gutsy and dangerous. She must have known you were getting suspicious so she pulled out all the stops. But like I said, she couldn't have done it alone. Someone had to be waiting downstream to fish her out of the water. Except she hit her head and died. Between that and you leaving town, it threw a monkey wrench into their plan."

"They had me right where they wanted me."

Flint nodded. "They would have bled you dry with blackmail. There are a lot of limbs hanging over that creek. It's ironic, but it would appear she got cocky and wasn't able to pull off her last deception. All this assuming the remains are hers."

"Still, if the creek hadn't overflowed, she would have never turned up and I would have gone on waiting, believing I killed her and our son." Tucker glanced at the box on the floor with the doll inside. "Whoever sent that box knew I would come back to Gilt Edge now."

"Sure looks that way. If anyone contacts you, thinking they can still cash in, don't leave me out of the loop this time."

"I'm sorry I didn't come to you all those years ago. Before you saw me, I'd gone down to the pay phone at the edge of town and made an anonymous call. I said I'd seen a girl fall into the creek." Tucker gave his brother a sad smile. "I was scared, filled with guilt."

"You were just a kid. Nothing you could have done would have saved her. Sonny said she couldn't have survived her head injury." Flint frowned. "Now that you mention it, I remember Dad saying he'd seen sheriff's deputies down at the creek. When they didn't find a body, they would have assumed your call had been a hoax."

"Whoever she was working with had already hidden the body and cleared out by the time the sheriff's deputies got there."

"Tuck, you didn't kill her. She jumped in the river trying to get money out of you. Her death was an accident."

He rubbed the back of his neck for a moment. "Still, I've always felt I should have done more or at least done things differently. If I'd just raised the money and given it to her..."

Flint shook his head. "She would have come back for more. You have to realize that. She was a con artist."

He knew he'd been a damned fool from the moment he'd met Madeline. She'd been his first. She'd made him believe that she loved him as much as he did her. He thought he was going to save her from her horrible family.

And now, if those skeletal remains in the morgue were hers, she was dead—and had been for nineteen years. Not just dead. Caught up in her own scam. But who hid her under the driftwood that night downstream? Whomever she'd been in league with. The man she was *really* in love with? A man who had talked her into jumping off a bridge into raging water in the dark as part of a con? Or had that been all her idea?

He had felt responsible for her death and the baby's for so long it was hard for him to let go of the guilt. He'd been *played*. And not just by the woman he'd known as Madeline Ross. He'd been played by whomever she was working with.

"The worst part," he said with a bitter bark of a laugh. "Is that I really thought I loved her and would never love anyone else the way I had her."

But a completely different emotion was bubbling up inside him like a geyser in Yellowstone National Park. If whoever had been working with her thought they could blackmail him… He hoped they would try. He wasn't that teenager they'd tricked all those years ago. This cowboy was more than ready for them now.

CHAPTER FOUR

Billie Dee Rhodes stopped singing to smile as the back door of the Stagecoach Saloon opened early the next morning. A cool spring breeze rushed into the kitchen along with the freshly showered scent of the cowboy who entered.

The fiftysomething Texas-born-and-bred cook turned from her pot of chili she had going to smile at Henry Larson, the retired rancher she'd been seeing for months now. He'd started stopping by for a cup of coffee with her early in the morning months ago. Now it was an every-morning occurrence that had grown into something much more.

He looked around to make sure no one else was up and at work yet, then stepped to her and gave her a kiss. "Good morning, Tex," he said, smiling as he locked gazes with her. Neither of them could believe they'd found love at this age.

It was their little secret. Billie Dee had wanted it that way, but Henry was right about everyone who knew them getting suspicious. The retired rancher had already told his sons, who now worked his ranch.

But Billie Dee hadn't told the Cahills, the amazing family that she'd come to know since taking the cook position at the saloon. She felt as if she was part of the family and hated keeping it from them. *One of these days I'll tell them*, she kept assuring herself.

She poured Henry a cup of coffee and one for herself before joining him at the kitchen table. Henry was a big handsome cowboy with gray at his temples. The retired rancher had been a widower for over five years.

Billie Dee had come to realize that Henry was a man who could do just about anything and had. He was her hero in so many ways.

She'd joked when she'd moved to Montana that she was looking for a big handsome cowboy. She'd just never dreamed at her age that one would come along.

Henry had been so patient with her, making it clear that he wanted to marry her. So why was she dragging her feet? It wasn't like the man didn't know just about everything there was to know about her. Well, almost.

There was one thing she hadn't told him. That one huge regret of her life that she hadn't shared with him yet. So what was holding her back?

"Beautiful morning," she said, glancing out the window toward the mountains lush with pines and new green grass. She loved spring in Montana. Winter, though, was more a love-hate relationship. How could she not love the falling snow? Or being curled up in front of a warm fire with her cowboy? It was driving through it, scraping ice and snow off her windshield, fighting drifts to get out of her driveway, that she hated.

Henry kept telling her that once they were married, she would never have to do any of that again. She wouldn't have to cook at the saloon, either, if she didn't want to. Maybe that was another reason she was putting off the next step. She loved her job.

"No babies yet?" he asked after taking a sip of his coffee.

"Both Lillie and Mariah look like they could pop any second, but nope, not yet." Billie Dee was excited for them, but it would mean that Mariah and Darby Cahill would move out of the apartment upstairs over the saloon and into their house that was almost finished.

Darby had offered her the apartment upstairs rent-free. "You won't have to drive through the snow in the winter. All you have to do is come downstairs."

She'd been touched, but then again Darby and the rest of the Cahill clan didn't know about the romance brewing between her and Henry. "Thanks, I'll think about it," was all she'd said.

"You're going to have to tell them," Henry said now as if reading her thoughts.

"I was waiting until the babies were born."

Henry laughed and shook his head. "What are you so afraid of? That once you tell them, you will have to finally really consider marrying me?"

She smiled. "I do want to marry you. But…"

"I told you, you don't have to give up your job here, if that's what you want. And certainly not your wonderful independence."

Billie Dee reached across to put her hand on his. "I know. I promise, I'll do it soon."

He looked skeptical as they heard footfalls on the stairs and she quickly removed her hand.

Darby came into the kitchen, greeting them both. Billie Dee got up to get back to her cooking. Henry finished his coffee and said he'd see them later.

"I didn't mean to run him off," Darby said, coming over to join her at the stove.

She heard something in his voice and glanced at the young handsome cowboy turned bar owner. Darby was grinning.

"Okay, Henry and I are…more than friends."

He laughed. "Like I didn't already know that. So when is he going to make an honest woman out of you?"

She swatted at him with a pancake flipper.

"It's just an expression," he said quickly as if afraid he'd offended her.

"He's asked me to marry him."

"Billie Dee, that's wonderful. So?"

"So, I'm thinking about it. Now, don't go blabbing to the rest of the family just yet."

Darby shook his head. "Lillie has suspected for months. You can't keep something like this quiet, especially around my sister."

Driving toward the ranch, Tucker felt as if he could breathe for the first time in years. All he could think about was seeing his family. He'd start with his brothers Cyrus and Hawk, then he'd go down to the saloon that Lillie and Darby owned. He was excited to see them all, but there was still a weight holding him down.

Until he knew if the remains were Madeline… Until he knew whom she'd been working with…

The road to the ranch wound through towering pines adjacent to Miner's Creek. Everything was a beautiful lush green. He loved spring in Montana and had missed it. This time of year, the creek was still low. It was too early for the snow in the mountains to have melted and for spring runoff to begin. Turning into the ranch, he parked but didn't see his brothers anywhere around.

As anxious as he was to see them, he knew there was something he had to do first. He had to face the nightmare that had haunted him for nineteen years. Heading for the creek, he took the same path he'd taken that night. In the shade of the pines, the air felt cold. Montana in the spring was beautiful but still chilly. The weather could change from sunny and warm to snowing and threatening in a matter of hours this time of year.

He breathed in the scent of pines and was transported back to the summer before his senior year. It had been mind-blowing sneaking off to be with Madeline, keeping the amazing secret, captivated by her body and his new experience with sex. His emotions had been all over the place.

Even when she'd told him she was pregnant, he'd been ready to marry her and run away with her. He realized how foolish that had been. But he had been on a high like none other. He would have done *anything* for her. Still, a part of him wanted to have been the hero that night.

What if he had jumped into the creek in time to save her that night? Or talked her out of jumping... He reminded himself that she'd lied. She hadn't been scared of her father and brother that night. So why take the chance?

Money. And whoever was waiting for her downstream.

The path he'd taken broke out of the trees at the edge of the creek. He could hear the babble of the water over the smooth stones. The water would run clear and low for a few more weeks. He figured it would have been a fisherman who'd found her skeletal remains. He used to spend hours on this creek fishing with his father and siblings.

Ahead, he spotted the bridge and stopped for a moment, reliving that night. The moon had been full. Was that why she'd picked that particular night? He'd seen her in the moonlight standing in the middle of the bridge as he walked down the creek toward her—and she would have been able to see him.

Climbing up the steps to the raised footbridge, he stopped a few yards in—just as he had that night. The scene was so vivid. The moonlight filtering through the thick boughs of the trees. The smell of the creek and the lush brush filled the air. And the dark water, shadowed by the tree limbs hanging over it.

Madeline had stood on the bridge, clutching the bundle in her arms to her chest. He could almost hear her voice, raised in anger. Her telling him that he'd let her down. He'd ruined her life. Ruined not just her life, but their son's, as well.

He took a step forward and then another, just as he had that night. He'd been so sure that he could reach her, that he could change her mind, that their love for each other could overcome anything.

Fool. Hadn't she heard how his heart was breaking? How could she have gone ahead with her plan knowing how much he'd loved her?

As he reached the middle of the bridge, he stopped to look down. He still couldn't believe she'd jumped into the fast current that night. There hadn't been a railing on the footbridge back then. He could see her quickly stepping to the edge as he screamed for her to stop.

Tucker felt ice fill his belly at the memory. He could hear the roar of the water, the roar of his cry. He could see her hesitate for just an instant before she disappeared over the side.

He'd rushed forward in time to see her head go under in the swift current. It was the last time he saw her. He'd jumped in, but she was gone and so was whatever she'd been holding. The doll he'd gotten in the mail? If it was her remains that had been found, then she'd never had a child. Another lie. Another gut-wrenching lie.

Looking downstream he could see yellow crime scene tape caught on a tree limb out in the middle of the creek next to a deep hole where he used to fish. The tape flapped in the wind as if mocking him. This nightmare wasn't over. Whoever had sent him the package with the weatherworn doll knew something. What were they trying to tell him?

He'd been so lost in thought that he hadn't seen the figure come out of the trees until he heard the loud snap of a twig. He stared downstream as a young woman made her way to the edge of the creek. Dressed in jeans, sneakers and a jean jacket, she wore a baseball cap that hid her hair. She looked out at the flickering yellow crime scene tape for a moment, before making her way to a spot where it was obvious that the deputies had dug up what remains had still been buried. The woman stepped under the crime scene tape that hadn't blown away. She definitely didn't look like a cop.

But then what was she doing there? Morbid curiosity or... To his shock, she suddenly hugged herself, bending over as if in pain. He realized that she was crying. Huge sobbing wails carried on the breeze, making the hair on the back of his neck stand straight up.

What the hell? Had she known Madeline? He felt a chill run the length of his spine. A friend? Or the person who'd buried her there? Was it possible he was looking at the person Madeline had been working with?

She must have sensed him, because she turned toward the bridge. Seeing him standing there, she hurriedly wiped her tears and started to leave, but not before she did something that shocked him even more.

The woman spit on what had been Madeline's grave.

CHAPTER FIVE

Tucker was too stunned to move for a moment. What had he just seen? One thing was certain. The young woman who'd just spit on Madeline's grave knew her!

His mind whirled. Did that mean she knew who she really was? Because she had helped her con Tucker? Or because she had reason to hate her?

As the woman disappeared into the pines, he finally shook himself out of his shock and got his feet moving. He had to talk to this woman. If she knew something...

The footbridge was old, the boards uneven and slippery this morning with dew. Still, he ran after her, slipping and almost falling in his cowboy boots. He couldn't believe what he'd seen and heard. The sobbing. The pain he'd witnessed. And then...the hatred. It made no sense.

He'd only reached the pines when he heard a vehicle's engine start up farther away from the creek. Racing up the trail, he realized that the woman must have run back to her vehicle. Otherwise, he would have been able to catch her before she drove away.

By the time he cleared the pines, she had driven almost

to the road into town. He was too far away to get all of the
license plate numbers on the vehicle she was driving. But it
was definitely a Montana tag and the SUV was an expensive
pearl-white one. If he saw it again...

He turned and ran back toward the ranch, mind racing.
All those years ago, he hadn't been able to learn who Madeline really was. She'd lied about so much. This was the first
real lead he had on her. The irony of it was that her death
was his first lead.

He was finally going to learn the truth about all of it, including who had been waiting for her downstream that night.

All he had to do was find another mystery woman, this
one driving an expensive SUV.

The sheriff got the call just before heading home for lunch.
Maggie was making his favorite—barbecued short ribs. He
didn't want to be late. Also, he didn't like to spend any more
time than he had to away from his wife. As far as he was concerned, the honeymoon would never be over.

But it was also Tuck's first night home. He was thinking
he should get the family all together. Everyone would want
to see Tuck. And probably want to know everything. Poor
Tucker. His sister especially would demand answers and Lillie
could be relentless. It was one reason he hadn't told the rest
of the family. Given the circumstances, he could tell Tucker
needed time. His brother also needed to do this on his own—
at his own speed.

Flint saw that it was the coroner calling and picked up. "I
have a possible identification on your Jane Doe," Sonny said.
"Madeline Dunn, formerly of Clawson Creek, Montana."

Madeline Dunn? "Possible? How did you come up with a
name so quickly?"

"Dental records. I queried the dentists in the largest town
within about one hundred miles of Gilt Edge, faxed them

the X-rays and got a hit the first try. Great Falls, Montana, 106 miles away." He listened while the coroner thumbed through some paperwork. "An eighteen-year-old had an abscessed tooth pulled at the dentist there. But what made him remember the girl and her mouth was that she had four wisdom teeth on each side, something so strange that the dentist took her X-rays down the hall to show another dentist. Very rare apparently."

"That was lucky."

"It was twenty-three years ago. She had no insurance or identification, but she wrote him a check that bounced. The account had been closed. Madeline Dunn never returned and the dentist never got his money. He'd always wondered if she'd had trouble with all those wisdom teeth."

"Wait, twenty-three years ago?" Flint asked. He thought of the story Tucker had told him. It added up perfectly, including that Madeline Ross had been older than she'd told his brother. And obviously more experienced.

"That would make our deceased about twenty-two," Sonny was saying. "Am I good, or what?"

Flint laughed. "You're good, but like you said, it was all in the bones."

"So true, but someone has to read them. As good as I am, though, you might want to wait until we get the DNA back before you try to track down next of kin. Up to you."

"Thanks for letting me know, Sonny. Clawson Creek, huh? I think I'll hold off until we see what the DNA might bring up."

"As you wish," the coroner said.

Tucker reached his pickup. He still didn't see his brothers around. They must be out in one of the pastures. Well, he didn't have time to find them right now. He had to catch the woman before she could leave town.

Assuming that was her plan. He climbed behind the wheel of his truck, started up the engine and tore up the road. He knew his way around Gilt Edge. As he drove, he debated where she might be headed. There weren't that many ways out of town.

The one plate number that he'd been able to make out before she'd gotten too far away had been the first one. Five. Five was Helena, the state capital. The shortest way back to the state capital was the highway to the west. So that meant she would have to drive through downtown Gilt Edge to reach it.

He raced into town, all the time looking for the SUV. Like most rural Montana towns, there were more pickups than cars or SUVs. That pretty pearl-white one would stand out like a marquee. Also, she wasn't that far ahead of him.

A thought struck him, though. What if she knew the area as well as he did because she'd been here before with Madeline? There were at least six times when Madeline had come to see him to get more money or a favor out of him.

He was still confused by what he'd seen at the creek. The apparent grief, the crying and then the desecration on the primitive grave site. Very strange behavior. He had to wonder about the woman he was chasing.

Tucker thought about calling Flint but stopped himself. While he was sorry he hadn't gone to his brother for help all those years ago, he couldn't see any reason to involve the sheriff at this point. Not yet, anyway. But if the woman he was searching for knew Madeline...

If Tucker could get some answers on his own from this mysterious woman, he had to try. Madeline and whoever had been helping her owed him that, though it wouldn't make up for the past or the years he'd lost.

As he drove, looking for the pearl-white SUV, he told himself that if the woman he'd seen at the creek had been in on the scam with Madeline, then she could be dangerous. Maybe even more dangerous than Madeline.

When he found her, he would get answers. But one thought haunted him. Was he really ready to learn the truth? Even knowing it was a scam, he still wanted to believe that Madeline had cared. He remembered the look on her face that night on the bridge. There had been real pain in her eyes. He couldn't be wrong about that.

But what if he *was* wrong?

Even dead, she can break your heart again.

He told himself he wasn't that horny, green teen Madeline had seduced. Also, he'd already had his heart broken by her. No woman had gotten to him after Madeline. He wasn't sure any woman could. Not even Madeline herself could break his heart worse after the torment she'd put him through—let alone anything her coconspirator could tell him.

Kate Rothschild glanced in her rearview mirror. No sign of anyone after her. She'd been so sure the cowboy would try to chase her down after what he'd witnessed.

She swallowed the lump in her throat, determined not to cry again. She couldn't believe the way she'd broken down at the creek. But seeing that grave and knowing who'd lain in it all this time… She'd held back her pain for too many years and for all the wrong reasons. The grief had come out of nowhere and everywhere. She'd felt like a wounded animal and was sure she'd sounded like one, as well.

Seeing the cowboy on the bridge… She'd thought she'd been alone. She'd purposely waited for law enforcement to leave with their buckets of dirt. The last thing she'd wanted was for anyone to see her there, especially sobbing her heart out.

As she drove toward the small Western town of Gilt Edge, she assured herself that everything would be fine. She'd been right to come here. Not that anything could have stopped her. But she should have known she wasn't the only one interested in the spot where the woman had been found.

She glanced in her rearview mirror again and smiled. A pickup was tearing down the road behind her. Her pulse leaped at the sight. It was the cowboy; she'd bet on it.

Still smiling, she thought about speeding up and giving him a run for his money. But she was at the edge of town and there was a deputy sitting in his patrol car right by the city-limits sign. She had no choice but to slow down. The truck was gaining on her. If the cowboy wasn't careful, the deputy would pull him over.

The driver of the pickup slowed. He was right behind her now. She could see his collar-length dark hair under his Stetson. It was the same man. She glimpsed his dark expression and felt a shiver.

Her heart began to pound as she considered what he might do next. He definitely had come after her. Why else was he now riding her bumper? She couldn't help but wonder what he made of her…behavior at the creek. It appeared she would find out soon enough.

She doubted he was ready for her, Kate thought as she pulled her shoulder bag closer. She wouldn't need the hand-gun in it, she told herself, but she wasn't taking any chances.

Tucker couldn't believe it. He'd caught up to her before she'd reached town. There was no doubt it was the woman from the creek. And she'd seen him. Their eyes had met in her rearview mirror and he'd seen recognition.

He'd also seen the deputy sitting on the edge of town with his radar gun out. Tucker had had no choice but to slow down. Still, there was no way she was getting out of his sight. He would follow her until she pulled over even if it meant following her all the way to Helena.

To his surprise, she pulled over into the Yogo Inn, the local downtown hotel. He swung in behind her but waited for her to get out of her SUV before he exited his pickup. He didn't trust this woman after what he'd seen at the creek.

She climbed out after reaching into the back seat for her overnight bag. As she closed and locked her car door, she turned to look at him. There appeared to be amusement in her expression, before she headed for the front door of the hotel.

Jumping out of his pickup, he went after her. She had no chance against his long legs. Even at thirty-six he could still run like he had when he'd played football in high school.

"Hold up!" he called to her slim back. On the bridge he hadn't gotten a good look at her. She'd been wearing a jean jacket so he hadn't seen her figure. Now she wore only a T-shirt and jeans, and filled out both in an appealing way that momentarily distracted him.

Also, at the creek, her hair had been covered by a baseball cap. Now her long dark hair fell in a riot of loose curls down to the middle of her back. As she moved, it swayed in luxurious shiny ebony waves.

"Miss!"

She pretended not to hear him, he was sure of it. But she wasn't getting away. This woman was the closest he'd come to knowing who Madeline Ross really had been—and maybe what she'd been capable of.

He quickly caught up to her and, grabbing one slim arm, spun her around to face him. He was momentarily startled by her wide green eyes in a face that could have stopped traffic. Her cheekbones were high, her mouth bow-shaped.

He'd expected her to be alarmed. Or at least frightened by having a man accost her in a hotel parking lot. But as she stared back at him from the depths of all that emerald green, he only saw a curious regard. Her lips parted slightly as if waiting to be kissed before turning up at the corners in more pronounced amusement.

Taken aback, he had trouble finding his voice.

"I'm sorry, do I know you?" she asked as he quickly released her arm.

"Sorry," he said as he stared her. She was definitely the woman from the creek, but she wasn't at all what he'd been expecting. He'd assumed since she'd known Madeline that she would be more like her. This woman was much more refined, educated and apparently well-off. It seemed impossible that she could have been working with Madeline all those years ago.

So how did he explain what he'd seen at the creek?

He couldn't and for a moment he didn't know what was going to come out of his mouth. "I'm sorry. I thought you were…" He shook his head.

She hadn't moved, hadn't turned and run; she hadn't even tried to put a little distance between them. Instead, she was studying him with those wide-open green eyes. If anything, he saw interest in those eyes.

"Is there something I can help you with?" she asked, sounding genuinely concerned for him.

It made him angry. He should be concerned for her, given what he'd seen. What was worse was that he realized that this woman couldn't possibly be the person who'd been working with Madeline all those years ago. She wasn't old enough.

He felt like an even bigger fool. But still, he hadn't imagined what he'd seen at the creek. But what *had* he seen?

"I saw you at the creek earlier." He waited for her to explain. She didn't. "You seemed upset."

"Did I? Is that why you chased me down?"

"I got the feeling that you had some connection to the woman whose remains were found in the creek. I must have been wrong."

"No, you're not wrong."

That stopped him in his tracks. "I beg your pardon?"

"What did she call herself?"

He felt as if he'd fallen down a rabbit hole. "I'm sorry, who are we talking about?"

"The woman who broke your heart."

"Oh, her," he said with a laugh. "Are we still talking about the woman found in the creek?"

"Only if she's the one who broke your heart. Oh, I see. She *did*. I thought as much. Do I remind you of her?" she asked and tucked a lock of her dark hair behind one ear. A diamond earring winked in the sunlight.

"No, she couldn't hold a candle to you," he admitted truthfully. In retrospect, everything about Madeline had been disingenuous from her blond hair to her name. While everything about this woman was the real thing. Not that any of that had mattered when he was seventeen and in love for the very first time.

Tucker realized he was staring again—and having an even harder time following this conversation. He shook his head. "Sorry, I'm confused."

She chuckled. "I'm not surprised." She held out her hand. "Katherine Rothschild, but my friends call me Kate."

"Tucker Cahill." Her hand was small and warm, the skin silken, the manicured nails a sweet pale pink. "Rothschild," he repeated and held on to her hand a little too long. Anyone who had ever lived in Montana knew that name. "Your father—"

"Is the former senator and now a congressman in Washington, DC."

Clayton Rothschild was a mover and shaker in DC and one of the wealthiest men in the state. He owned almost as much land in Montana as Ted Turner.

"Cahill? Any relation to Sheriff Flint Cahill?"

"He's my brother." He frowned, suddenly wondering how a young woman like her—let alone a Rothschild—would know Flint. Not to mention what she'd been doing down by the creek earlier. She still hadn't explained what he'd seen. All she'd done was confuse him.

"You said you do have a connection to the dead woman?" He was having trouble believing that.

She smiled. "And so do you, I'm guessing. Do they have a positive identification on her yet?"

"Not that I've heard. How do you know all this?"

"About the skeletal remains being found? From the news. That's why I'm here. I'd planned to speak to your brother Flint. But it was nice to meet you instead. Well, I better get checked in before they give my room away."

"Wait," he said, realizing she'd sidestepped almost every question he'd asked her. "You haven't told me what you were doing at the creek earlier. I heard you crying. I also saw you spit on the woman's grave."

Kate Rothschild nodded, smiling. "Nor have *you* told me what she called herself, this woman who broke your heart."

"Madeline."

"Well, in that case, you should buy me dinner tonight," Kate said. "It appears we have some things in common."

"That's all you're going to say?"

"Of course not. Pick me up at seven." With that, she turned and headed into the hotel.

Tucker watched her go.

"It was nice meeting you, Tucker Cahill," she said over her shoulder an instant before the door closed behind her.

Kate had just stepped into the hotel when her cell phone rang. She checked the caller ID and saw that it was her mother calling again. She pocketed her phone and proceeded to get checked in. Her mind kept straying in the direction of

Tucker Cahill. She was still embarrassed that he'd witnessed her breakdown at the creek. But in a twist of fate, it had all worked out better than she'd planned. And now she was having dinner with him tonight.

Strike while the iron is hot, she thought and realized that she'd just used one of her mother's expressions. That was a sour thought.

Once in her room, she walked to the window and looked out on Gilt Edge. It was named after one of the gold mines back in the mountains that surrounded the town. Her phone rang again. She'd thought it was her mother again, but it was her father's personal assistant, Peter.

He was the last person she wanted to talk to considering their last discussion.

"Do you have any idea what you're doing?" Peter had asked before she'd flown home to Helena. She'd been in DC on an errand for her father when she'd heard about the young woman's remains being found in Miner's Creek—next to the Cahill Ranch. She'd been anxious to return to Montana as quickly as possible. Peter had insisted on dinner before her flight, and even before the entrées arrived, she'd regretted saying yes.

"I'm going home," she'd said, pretending she didn't know what Peter was referring to. While her father spent most of his time in Washington, DC, her mother preferred living outside Helena on the ranch. It was there that Kate and her brother had grown up.

"You're opening a Pandora's box," Peter had argued. "Think about what it could do to your father's career."

She had thrown down her napkin and pushed to her feet. "Her bones have been found. The box is already open."

"For God's sake, Katie, sit back down before you embarrass us both."

"I'm going to finish this—come hell or high water and no one, especially you, can stop me. And I'm not your Katie."

With that, she'd walked out, caught the flight home and then driven to Gilt Edge.

Her cell phone rang again. Her mother. She knew she couldn't keep avoiding her so she picked up. "Hello, Mother."

"Katherine." The word was filled with reproach.

Her mother was Helena's leading socialite. Kate knew that she liked being a big fish in a little pond, unlike getting lost in the crowd in DC where she was just another politician's wife.

But Mamie Rothschild would never admit that. Just as she would never admit there were any bad memories in that big old house outside Helena. Her mother didn't allow herself to acknowledge anything unpleasant. Her strong resilient mother was a survivor, she thought grudgingly, and she'd raised Kate to be one, as well.

"Did you get my message?" her mother demanded.

"No, what was it?"

"I've spoken with your father. He feels the same way I do. He said he would fly back from DC if he had to, but he'd prefer that you stop what you're doing."

She realized she could thank Peter for this. The next time she saw him… "I'm not doing anything more than what I always do, Mother." She pushed back the curtain at the hotel window and realized that from here she could see the cut in the trees where the Cahill ranch house must be—not that far at all from the creek. How convenient.

"We both know why you're in Gilt Edge and it isn't your interest in some story about bones found in a creek near there."

"You might be surprised by who or what I'm interested in."

Reproving silence filled the line. "I don't wish to talk about your personal life, if that's what you're referring to with that remark. Peter is just as upset as your father and I. You need to stop this."

"Actually, what I'm doing is getting ready to go on a date."

"Don't be ridiculous. How could you possibly be going on a date? You and Peter—"

"Are not serious. I've told you that numerous times."

"Well, maybe *you* aren't serious, but Peter is. You're making a mistake. Peter is perfect for you."

"No, he's perfect for what you and Father want for me. Tonight I'm going out with a cowboy. His name is Tucker Cahill."

"Cahill?" Her mother sounded breathless.

"Yes. He and I already share a special bond. We met today at the creek where the bones were found. I asked him to take me out to dinner."

Mamie would be horror-stricken if she'd known that Kate had lost control out at the creek—especially since there'd been a witness. And not just any witness. Tucker Cahill. With the Cahill Ranch so close, Kate shouldn't have been surprised to see the cowboy there, especially now that she had confirmed that they had something in common.

Tucker Cahill had known Madeline. From his expression earlier, he'd known her well. That thought turned her stomach. He'd chased her down to find out what she knew. And now she was having dinner with him tonight to find out what *he* knew. Talk about strange bed partners, so to speak.

Even stranger was who had brought them together.

"You need to come to your senses," her mother was saying.

"Oh, I have. I told you I would never let this go. Tucker doesn't know it, but he's going to help me."

Her mother sniffed angrily. "You have no idea what you're doing."

"On the contrary. I'm good at what I do, Mother, so I have a pretty good idea of what I'm doing."

The next words were delivered like a dagger of ice. "You know what I mean."

"I have to get ready for my date."

"I'm calling your father and Peter," her mother threatened.

"Daddy won't come home. Not for this. He will want to stay as far away as he can from anything...ugly. I'm afraid you're on your own since there is nothing you can say to stop me. As for Peter, you really are wasting your time. He has nothing to say that I want to hear." She disconnected, surprised how angry she was. Or how close she was to tears again.

Clearly she wasn't as strong as she'd thought. But she was as determined as she'd been every day for the past nineteen years. She wasn't going to let anyone stop her. Not even Tucker Cahill.

Tucker had just reached his pickup when his cell phone rang.

"Where are you?" Flint asked. "I just tried the ranch. Cyrus said they hadn't seen you."

He could hear the fear in his brother's voice. Flint had thought he might have left town again without a word. "Sorry, I got waylaid. I'm on my way there now."

"How about a change of plans? I just talked to Maggie. She's up for all of us going to the Stagecoach Saloon tonight and celebrating your return."

"Oh, that sounds great but I can't tonight. I have a date."

"*A date?* Tucker, you just got back to town."

"I know," he said with a laugh. "I'm as surprised as you are. If you saw her, you'd be even more surprised."

"Who is this woman?"

"Kate Rothschild."

"*Rothschild?* Of the Montana Rothschilds?"

"Apparently so."

"What is she doing in Gilt Edge?"

He couldn't tell his brother what he'd witnessed. Not until he knew more. "Just passing through, I think."

"And you just happened to cross her path?" Flint asked.

"Yep, must be fate." Even as he said it, he wondered if it wasn't true. They would never have met if he hadn't seen her at the creek today. He would have never known her connection to Madeline. Not that he did yet, but he would by tonight.

"Fate, huh?"

"You have such a suspicious mind."

Flint laughed. "I've been told that. It goes with the job. Look, I'm happy for you, but I was hoping we could get together your first night home. The rest of the family is anxious to see you."

"I know. They'll also want answers about where I've been, what I've been doing and why I left," Tucker said. "I'm not sure I'm up to an interrogation tonight. It's been kind of a rough day and a relief at the same time."

"I know. It was a lot to take in." His brother seemed to hesitate. "We might have an ID on the remains from the creek. They could belong to a woman named Madeline Dunn from Clawson Creek. She would have been twenty-two."

Tucker took in that information for a moment. "Madeline Dunn."

"I'm not going to try to find the next of kin until we get the DNA results."

"Dunn, huh," Tucker said. He finally had a name. After all these years of wondering who Madeline really was...

"Are you sure I can't talk you into changing your plans?" Flint asked.

Not a chance, Tucker thought. "Not tonight. But I'm anxious to see everyone, too. In fact, I'm headed for the saloon right now. Thought I'd swing by on my way back to the ranch. Any chance I can catch both Lillie and Darby there?"

"I just talked to them so I'd say there is a very good chance."

"Great, after that I'll go to the ranch and see Hawk and

Cyrus. I'm going to be staying out there in my old room if they'll have me."

"Are you sure you're all right?" Flint asked.

"It's going to take some getting used to. But I'm glad to be home—even under the circumstances. Don't worry about me, little brother."

Flint chuckled. "Sorry. I've worried about you for years. It's become a habit that is going to take time getting used to *not* worrying about you."

Tucker pulled up in front of the Stagecoach Saloon, which his sister and brother, fraternal twins, owned. "I'm at the saloon."

"If I don't talk to you later, have fun on your date."

"I'll try." But as he disconnected, he didn't think it was that kind of date. He was curious as hell about Kate Rothschild. But for the life of him he couldn't understand how Kate could have anything to do with Madeline, which made what he'd witnessed at the creek all that more intriguing. Add to that, she'd said they had something in common with the bones found in the creek.

His cell rang before he could exit his pickup. He saw it was Flint again and picked up.

"Tuck," his brother said without preamble. "Be careful on your date tonight. I just looked Kate Rothschild up on the internet. She's an award-winning investigative reporter for a big New York newspaper. I can't imagine what she's doing in Gilt Edge, unless she's interested in the remains found in the creek. In which case, she might also be interested in you. Is there any way she could have known about you and Madeline?"

CHAPTER SIX

Kate was still upset after the phone call. She'd known how her mother felt. She'd even accepted that her mother did her best to avoid anything unpleasant in life by changing the story. That meant telling the new, improved story until she actually believed it was true. Was it any wonder Mamie Rothschild's daughter had become an investigative reporter so there was at least a little truth in her life?

Moving away from the window, she thought about her date tonight. The elusive Tucker Cahill was certainly making this easier for her. She'd been suspicious when she'd learned that he'd left town nineteen years ago—right after graduating from high school. Right after Madeline seemed to have dropped off the face of the earth. Now, she didn't have to ask what had brought him back given what she already knew about him. She just hadn't expected it to be this easy.

Now that she'd met him, she had to admit, he wasn't what she'd expected. The cowboy was bigger, stronger looking, more solid—almost to the point of being intimidating. He reminded her of some of the romance-novel-cover models, with the rock-hard chest, smooth bronze skin and washboard stomach. No wonder women found that kind of man...appealing. She would love to get a load of Tucker's bare chest.

He looked only a little like his yearbook photos that she'd seen from before he'd left Gilt Edge. She wondered where he'd been, what exactly had kept him away as well as how he'd kept in such great shape and if she would have a chance to see him with his shirt off.

Speculating about his incredible physique kept her mind off how dangerous a game she was playing. Her parents had the right to be worried for her. Still, she had to laugh at where her mind had taken her. She wasn't immune to a handsome man, but she'd never dated one like Tucker Cahill. She'd always stayed clear of cowboys on the family ranch. The men she'd dated were clones of her father. Like Peter. Men her father would approve of.

She smiled to herself as she thought of what her father would make of Tucker Cahill with his too-long dark hair and those gray eyes fringed with long dark eyelashes, not to mention the chiseled jaw. Wouldn't her father have a fit if she'd ever brought home someone like him?

Katie opened her overnight bag and frowned. She'd packed what she needed for a short stay. No way had she planned on going on a date. Asking Tucker out had been impulsive, not that she regretted it on any level.

With a sigh, though, she picked up her shoulder bag, leaving the gun behind for this trip. She'd have to walk downtown and see if she could find something to wear tonight. Glancing in the mirror by the door, she took in the jeans, T-shirt and tennis shoes she was wearing. Not exactly date attire. She had planned on doing some exploring at the crime scene—before Tucker had seen her and she'd taken off.

He'd changed her plans. Tonight, though, she would find out just how much he knew before she decided how he was going to help her get what she wanted. Her mother had always encouraged her to dress for success. Tonight she was going to do just that.

Tucker's sister, Lillie, saw him first. She'd been standing at the bar rubbing her protruding stomach. When she spotted him, she dropped her hand, her eyes widening and quickly filling with tears, before she screamed his name.

"Tucker!"

He moved to her to take her in his arms. "Hey, little sis. What happened to you?" he asked with a laugh. "What ya got in there, my nephew or niece?"

Lillie was crying too hard to answer. Tucker looked to his brother Darby, who came around the bar. He stuck out his hand. "Darby, dang, you two are a sight for sore eyes. You're all grown-up." They'd been nine when he'd left.

A few regulars at the bar were craning their necks to see what was going on.

"Are you back?" Darby asked.

Tucker nodded. "Sorry it took me so long. I'll tell you all about it, but I can't right now. I have a date."

"A date?" Lillie demanded, finally finding her voice as she pulled back to look at him. "A date your first night home?"

"You sound like Flint."

"He knows you're back?"

Tucker laughed, hearing the jealousy in her voice. "I'm staying at the ranch and I haven't seen Hawk and Cyrus yet, but I had to stop by and see the two of you. We'll all get together soon and catch up, I promise."

Lillie wiped her eyes, her hand going to her stomach again. "You haven't even met my husband, Trask, or Darby's wife, Mariah, yet. Or Billie Dee."

"Billie Dee?"

"The best cook in Montana, probably the whole US," Lillie said adamantly.

He laughed. "I will meet them all. I'll catch up on everything, but right now I have to run." He kissed his sister on the cheek and waved to Darby. "It's so great to see the two of you again."

"Did Flint tell you a package arrived for you?" Lillie asked.

Tucker had forgotten about it for a while. "He did." He could see that Lillie was busting at the seams to know what was inside. "It was just somethin' I sent on ahead of me. No big deal." She looked disappointed. "No mystery. Sorry."

But as he left, he couldn't help but wonder who'd sent the doll and what exactly the message had been.

As he walked to his pickup, though, he saw that he'd gotten a different kind of message. Someone had stuck a folded piece of paper under his driver's-side windshield wiper.

He looked around before pulling it out. As he opened it, he saw the girlie lettering and felt a chill. He knew it was impossible, but he would have sworn it was Madeline's handwriting.

It read: *You shouldn't have come back.*

After a quick shopping trip downtown, Kate was ready when she got the call that her date was waiting for her downstairs.

Her *date*? This wasn't a date. This wasn't even work. This was about justice, plain and simple. So how did she explain the butterflies? She hadn't had butterflies the first time she went out with Peter or any other man that she could remember.

So why was she so nervous about going out with Tucker Cahill? She'd met her share of handsome cowboys. What made Tucker Cahill different?

It wasn't his crooked grin. Or that jolt of current she'd felt when he'd grabbed her arm in front of the hotel and she'd seen him up close for the first time. It was what she'd glimpsed in those gray eyes, a pain she'd recognized heart-deep.

Kate pushed the thought away, telling herself that Tucker Cahill was no different from any other man she'd interviewed for a story. He was merely a source. She would do the job she was damned good at. She'd get the information she needed from him, and if she couldn't get him to help her, she would have no reason to see him again.

But as the elevator door opened, she saw him and her heart took a roller-coaster-ride dip. In his dress Western attire, he was even more handsome. But it was the look on his face when he saw her that squeezed her heart like a fist. Had any man ever looked at her like that?

She looked away, not surprised to see that several women in the lobby were admiring the cowboy. As she stepped out of the elevator and started toward him, the women gave her an appreciative look—though a little green-eyed.

For a woman who didn't consider this a date, she'd put her hair up, leaving several dark tendrils to fall free around her face. Never one to wear much makeup, she'd kept it at a minimum, but at the last minute she had added just a touch of coral stain to her lips and two drops of her favorite perfume between her breasts.

The dress she wore was teal and fell over her curves like warm tropical waves. The hem hit just above her knees, calling attention to her long legs and the strappy new heels she'd purchased uptown.

From the widening of Tucker's gray eyes, it had been effective.

"You look amazing," he whispered as he leaned toward her. His lips brushed her ear, sending shivers rippling through her. She caught the scent of his cologne, something woodsy, masculine and surprisingly seductive.

She breathed him in, wanting more and feeling bereft when he stepped back, taking his scent with him.

"There's a restaurant within walking distance of the hotel,

if that's all right," he said, those gray eyes locking with hers. A woman without her grit could get lost in those eyes.

"Perfect." She figured she needed the fresh air to clear her head. This was starting to feel dangerously like a real date.

Tucker placed a large, warm hand at the center of her back. The heat burned through the sheer fabric of her dress as he steered her toward the front door. His touch sent a wave of knee-buckling need through her. She took his arm, feeling a little unsteady on her legs as she realized this wasn't going to be as easy as she thought.

Tucker had his breath taken away at the sight of Kate Rothschild as she came off the elevator. It hit him hard, as it had been a long time since a woman had done that to him.

He reminded himself of what he'd seen her do at the creek. Kate had some connection to Madeline. Add to that the fact this woman was an investigative reporter. He had no idea why she'd done it, but he didn't think for a moment that she'd suggested dinner because of his charm—or lack thereof.

"Why don't we cut straight to the chase?" he said once they were seated in the restaurant and had ordered wine. "What does a city slicker investigative reporter and daughter of a Montana congressman have in common with the skeletal remains of a woman found in a creek in Gilt Edge, Montana?"

Kate seemed taken aback by the question. He'd caught her off guard, something he doubted happened often. She smiled and leaned back as the waiter appeared with the bottle of wine and poured them each a glass.

After the waiter left, she said, "You do get right to the point."

"I've found it saves time. So why don't you tell me what I witnessed down at the creek?"

"I'm not sure what you think you saw," she began.

"You knew Madeline. And what I saw tells me that you had mixed feelings about her."

She laughed. "You sure that's what you saw?"

He met her gaze and held it. "We goin' to keep playin' word games? What's your connection to Madeline Dunn?"

"Dunn? You're sure that's her name?"

He saw that she hadn't known Madeline's last name any more than he had until earlier. "My brother thinks that might have been her last name. The DNA report hasn't come back for a positive ID yet."

She raised a brow and leaned toward him. That she looked beautiful tonight in the candlelight was definitely a distraction. But once you've been taken advantage of by one woman, you can't help but be gun-shy of all of them—especially one who smelled like sunshine after a rain.

"Since you know I work for a newspaper in New York City, maybe I'm doing a freelance story on the case."

He raised a brow.

"I admit I might have gotten a little emotional down at the creek earlier. It's a horrible thing for a young woman that age to drown and not be found for so many years."

"I don't believe you."

"What other possible reason could I have?" she asked with an innocent twinkle in those big green eyes.

"That's what I'm hoping to find out tonight."

"Strange," she said, her smile tempting him to do more than raise his wineglass to clink against hers. "I was hoping to find out more about you tonight, as well."

He fought the urge to dive into all that deep sea green and just swim around for a while. As leery as he was of this woman—and with good reason—he was also enjoying himself.

In the years he'd been gone, he hadn't dated. All his encounters had been in passing. But none of the women he'd met were like this one. That alone put him on guard.

Kate carefully touched her wineglass to his like a quick kiss. "To discovering all kinds of things about each other tonight."

There was daring in her gaze. He'd never been able to back down from a challenge. He suspected she had the same problem. "To unlocking all your secrets," he said, making her eyes widen a little before she laughed.

"Okay, cowboy. Why don't we start with Madeline and why you were on that bridge earlier? Remembering one special night, were you?"

His hand holding the glass jerked, almost spilling his wine. Kate's smile widened. "Am I moving too fast for you?"

Tucker felt his head swim. "*You* sent the package."

CHAPTER SEVEN

With Tucker on a date tonight, there was no reason Flint couldn't just enjoy an evening at home with Maggie. He still couldn't believe that Tucker was back. Back safe and sound. So why was he still worried about him?

Tuck was out with a reporter. That was worry enough. But it was more than that. He remembered what his brother had said about being in love with Madeline Ross aka Madeline Dunn. If that was her name.

The tentative ID the coroner had gotten was based on a dentist's memory of a woman's teeth from twenty-three years ago. The woman had paid with a check from Madeline Dunn's account, but that didn't mean she was Madeline Dunn.

He'd been in law enforcement long enough to know better than jumping to conclusions until he had the facts. Once they had the DNA, then he could track down the Dunns and see if it was a match. Tucker had said that Madeline had a brother. If they could find him or their father...

But what he didn't know was worrying him. Not that he believed for a minute that Tuck might have had something to do with the woman's death. He knew his brother. Well, he'd known the Tucker he'd grown up with, but there were nineteen years that hadn't been accounted for yet.

Flint shook his head, hating where his thoughts had gone. The woman had jumped, just as Tuck had said. The woman had been trying to con money out of his brother by pretending she was pregnant. Worse, she wanted him to believe that she was willing to kill herself and their baby if he didn't pay up.

Flint realized that he'd balled up his hands into fists at the thought of Madeline. How would his brother have reacted if he'd found out that night on the bridge that it had all been a huge lie?

"You're just tired," he told himself. His day had been filled with phone calls, problems with traffic and two DUIs that Harp had picked up. Most days, there were barking dog complaints, checks on elderly relatives, shoplifting kids and endless paperwork. Sometimes Flint wondered why he'd gotten into law enforcement.

Earlier, before he'd spoken with the coroner, he'd gone through missing-persons reports looking for a woman of about the age of the skeletal remains found in the creek, surprised there was none. He'd called around to the other towns. No missing-persons report on the woman during that time. That seemed strange unless she had no family in the state.

Now he hesitated. Why hadn't he considered earlier that his brother would be considered a suspect if anyone else was sheriff? It hadn't crossed his mind because he knew Tucker. Or at least thought he did.

He swore as he glanced over at the package with that damned doll in it. Someone knew Tucker would come back to Gilt Edge. The same person who'd been waiting for Madeline downstream? Or someone with an even darker ulterior motive?

He picked up his phone, dialed 411 and asked the operator for a family with the last name Dunn in Clawson Creek.

"I'm sorry, sir. I'm not showing any by that name. Could it be listed under another name or perhaps another town?"

He had no idea. Apparently the Dunns had left Clawson Creek. "That's all right. Thank you." Hanging up, he glanced at his watch. He was late and there were leftover barbecued short ribs from lunch that Maggie had promised to heat up for dinner. Mostly, he was anxious to see his wife.

Tracking down the family would have to wait until tomorrow. Another twelve hours wouldn't make that much of a difference after nineteen years.

Kate took a sip of her wine, giving herself a moment. She'd let Tucker get to her. This was not the way she'd planned for the night to go. But he'd given her no choice, she told herself. He wanted to cut to the chase? Fine.

She could tell that she'd caught him flat-footed with the package she'd sent, which had been her intention. Just as his had been when he'd called her on why she was interested in the remains from the creek.

"I wasn't sure the discovery in the creek was enough to bring you home. I thought the package might," she said.

Tucker blinked, clearly taken aback. "Where did you get...? Why would you send me something like that? How do you know me and that I've been gone, let alone know what Madeline put me through?"

"Isn't it obvious?" she said and picked up her menu. "Is the steak good here?"

He leaned over to take the menu from her hand. "If you tell me you were the one working with Madeline—"

"Don't be absurd," she said, taking back her menu.

"If all you wanted to do was get my attention, we could

have had this discussion on the bridge earlier. Why did you run?"

She lowered her menu. "Maybe I wanted to see if you would chase me, then I would know for sure that I had the right man."

"The right man? You could have made it easier for both of us by not running," he said, still eyeing her as if he thought if he looked deep enough, he'd see every truth she'd kept hidden for all these years.

She chuckled at his words, though it lacked the lightness she'd been shooting for. "Now, what fun would that have been if I hadn't let you chase me down?"

He growled under his breath. "How do you know about Madeline? No more games."

Kate took another sip of her wine, but from the look in the cowboy's eyes, he was no longer willing to play along. While she could be flexible when it came to her game plan, she didn't like it derailed so quickly. Worse, as she looked into Tucker's eyes… They were silver in the candlelight and beneath the growing anger and frustration, she could still see the pain. It was as raw as her own and yet his had been banked for nearly two decades while hers had grown with each passing year.

It made her more than determined to expose the woman. But in exposing Madeline, she would be exposing the men who'd fallen for her, as well. She hadn't cared before, but suddenly she didn't want to hurt this man.

"Madeline," Tucker repeated, making it clear he wasn't waiting much longer for an answer.

She could tell he was surprised that she knew about Madeline, knew enough to send the doll. Madeline had always been all about secrecy. It's how she did business. It's how she destroyed young men, chewing them up and spitting them out and moving on.

"My brother knew her." Kate hadn't planned to tell him that.

Suddenly the waiter appeared to take their orders.

Tucker waved the man away and leaned forward. "Your *brother?*"

She started to pour herself more wine, but he took the bottle from her, their fingers touching, a brush of warmth against her icy cold hand. He poured her more wine and put down the bottle.

But she didn't reach for her glass. She could see that he had already put the pieces together. "Clay," he said. "Clayton Rothschild III."

She felt her cheeks warm with the anger that was always just below the surface. Her gaze rose to meet Tucker's. "Madeline killed him just as surely as if she'd been the one to tie the noose around his neck." Her voice broke and she had to fight tears. No, this was not at all the way she'd planned this so-called date.

"He knew Madeline?" he asked, frowning. "That was about the same time as…" He broke off, shifted his gaze to hers again and held it. "He killed himself because of her?" He was shaking his head. "The package. The only way you could have known…" His gray eyes widened in alarm. "She pulled the same thing on him that she did me with the…baby?"

Kate nodded, unable to speak around the lump in her throat. She looked away. After all the interviews she'd done since she'd begun her career, she'd never let anyone get to her like this. But sitting across from a man who had known her nemesis…intimately, who knew how she operated, who had been hurt by her almost as deeply as her brother…

Staring into his gray eyes, she thought that maybe there was little difference between this man and her brother. That thought made her angry at both of them. How could they have fallen for such a woman? Tucker had left behind everything for nineteen years—his family, his ranch, his life to that point—because of Madeline. Clay had just taken a more drastic route to run away from what that woman had put him through.

"You want to know where I got the doll?" Her voice sounded strange to her own ears as she tried to rein in her fury without much luck. "It's the one Madeline sent my brother. At the time, I had no idea what it meant when it was found in the room where Clay…" Her voice broke again. "But I was determined to learn the truth about why my brother killed himself. I was thirteen. My brother was a senior in high school."

Tucker was staring at her with so much sympathy that she had to look away for fear of breaking down again.

"How did you find out about her?" he asked after a moment.

"My brother. I found a letter he had written her. His suicide note. Unfortunately, when I went searching for her, I realized that Madeline *Ross* never existed. She'd lied about who she was, no big surprise."

"Still, how could you know that the woman from the creek—"

"Clay said in the letter that he knew there was another man Madeline was seeing. A cowboy who lived in Gilt Edge with the last name Cahill. It didn't take much to put it together in the years since. At first I thought it might be your brother Flint. But when you took off suddenly, I figured you'd run away with her. That maybe the two of you had been in it together." She met his gaze. "Until I heard about the skeletal remains found in the creek near your ranch."

"So you sent the package to me."

"I'd hoped you were in contact with your family and that the package would get you home. I wasn't sure the remains were Madeline's let alone that you would return."

He looked shocked.

"I figured if you were the other man my brother had written about, then the doll might resonate with you."

Tucker let out a bark of laugh. "Oh, it resonated, all right. I've believed for nineteen years that I was the reason she killed herself and our son."

She shook her head. "How could you let her fool you like that?"

"I wish I knew. So you've known about me and Madeline for—"

"Years. That's how long I've been looking for you. You did a good job of hiding. Does your brother the sheriff know that you haven't been going by Tucker Cahill all this time?"

Tucker was staring at her again. "I see what you meant about the two of us having a lot in common. And what exactly were you going to do when you found me?"

She shook her head, unable to speak for a moment around the lump in her throat. "It was Madeline I wanted. If you were with her… But when the bones were found, I had a feeling you'd be coming back alone."

They both fell silent for a few minutes.

"I'm sorry about your brother," he said. "I had no idea there were…others."

"Yes, except with my brother Madeline obviously survived her leap into the river to be saved by whoever she was working with and continued to blackmail Clay until he couldn't take the guilt anymore."

"It wasn't just the guilt. I would imagine he thought he loved her."

Kate ground her teeth. "That makes it even worse." She'd never understood how her brother could have taken his own life. "She was that good?"

"When you're seventeen… But yes, she was good at making an inexperienced teenager fall for her."

She felt all the anger leak from her like a pinprick to a tire. It left her simply tired and, again, close to tears. Not even her parents knew everything about Madeline. It felt good to finally say what had been bottled up inside her to someone who'd known the woman.

"There's another reason I wanted to find you," Kate said. "I need to know everything about Madeline so I can find her accomplice."

The waiter tentatively came back to the table. "I don't want to rush you."

"No, it's fine. Are you ready to order?" Tucker asked her.

She nodded. For the first time since her brother had died, she didn't feel that hard knot in her chest. Finally, she would avenge his death. Tucker Cahill didn't know it yet, but he was going to help her.

CHAPTER EIGHT

Billie Dee couldn't quit thinking about Henry's proposal. She was deep in thought when Darby came into the kitchen the next morning.

"Can I make you some breakfast?" she asked, happy to see him. She was dreading the day when Mariah gave birth and the two of them moved out of the upstairs apartment. While she knew it was selfish, she liked knowing they were up there when she came in early in the morning to start the day's cooking.

"Thanks, but no breakfast today. I have some waitstaff interviews this morning. With summer and the busiest time of the year coming up, I need more help. Mariah is going to be busy *nesting*, same with Lillie. You thought any more about the apartment upstairs? No," he said with a laugh. "Of course you wouldn't want to move in up there, not with—"

Just then Mariah came down the stairs, her huge belly leading the way. Billie Dee put a finger to her lips. Mariah and Darby's twin sister, Lillie, were best friends and told each other *everything*.

He nodded and went to help his wife down the last few

steps before the two went to the front of the saloon to get ready to interview candidates before opening for the day.

Billie Dee turned back to her cooking. She liked to cook what she knew. And what she knew was Tex-Mex with a side of Cajun. Which in this part of the country seemed exotic— and often too spicy. Since she'd gone to work here, she'd introduced this part of Montana to her brand of cooking and this morning she was making up a batch of her famous chili.

When she heard more voices at the front of the old stage stop, she peered down the hall to see the candidates for the job.

Her breath caught. She had to grab the back of one of the chairs at the kitchen table for support. That face. She'd been looking for it in every young woman she passed for the past twenty-six years—terrified she'd see it and terrified she wouldn't.

The young woman looked up, her eyes a startling blue that rivaled even the Montana sky. And that face… But there was no recognition in the young woman's gaze.

The woman looked away and Billie Dee felt as if someone had just stomped on her heart.

Tucker was hauled out of his dream by his cell phone chime. Without opening his eyes, he reached over to shut off the phone, surprised it was morning. He didn't want to wake up. He could still feel the night on his bare skin as he clung to the erotic dream he'd been having.

Almost midnight, the Montana sky ablaze with stars. Hot water bubbled up from deep in the earth to pool in the middle of the large boulders as a small waterfall washed over the rocks like a lullaby.

He lay naked in the water waiting for her. He knew she could come to him in this isolated place. The natural hot spring was surrounded by mountain ranges, deep purple against the skyline. It was their special place. He could hear the faint tinkling of her silver anklet as it dangled from her ankle. Other than the anklet, the only other thing she wore was a large straw hat that hid her face. Strange, since there was only moonlight.

Her hair was tucked up under the hat as she padded barefoot toward him and the tantalizing pool. She had just reached the edge, stuck in one perfectly pedicured toe and reached to take off her hat...

His cell phone rang again. Cursing, he opened his eyes and picked up the phone to see who was calling at this hour. When he saw it was Flint, he answered, "What?"

"I guess I don't have to ask how your date was last night."

He could feel the dream slipping away. Worse, he'd glimpsed the face under the hat and... It hadn't been Madeline's. It was Kate's. The dream dissolved into a feeling of frustration. *Kate?*

"There a reason you called?"

"I forgot you've never been a morning person," Flint said. "If you get a chance, stop by my office."

He sat up a little. "Has something happened?"

"No, I just wanted to ask you more questions about Madeline."

"Madeline?" He swung his legs over the side of the bed as he tried to clear his head. "I told you everything I know about her."

"I talked to the sheriff up in Judith Basin County. He says the Dunns cleared out about twenty years ago and, as far as he knows, haven't been seen since. It was before his time, but he said they were an odd family. Said there were an older brother and some sisters. Stayed to themselves in some big old house outside town. As far as he knew, there wasn't anyone living there anymore. Could take time to track them down, if any of them are still around."

A dead end. Clawson Creek? It wasn't that far from Denton where he'd first met Madeline. He thought about what Kate had said about finding Madeline's accomplice.

"I don't mean to bring up bad memories," Flint said. "I just want to tie up what loose ends I can and put it all to rest. You have to quit blaming yourself for her death, though. It was an accident, one she brought on herself."

Tucker nodded. So why did he still feel guilty? Nor did it feel as if it was over. "What about the person who hid her body downstream?"

"Because the death was an accident, the person who hid the body would have been facing only misdemeanor charges for the improper disposal of a corpse. Since the statute of limitations has run out..."

"So you aren't going to pursue this? You aren't even going to look for whoever was helping Madeline?"

"I can't see using manpower when no charges could be filed, anyway."

He thought of Kate and that darned dream came back with her standing naked in the mist at the edge of the pool. He frowned as he remembered the tinkle of the ankle bracelet in his dream.

"Did your deputies find any jewelry at the scene?"

"No, why?"

"Maybe a little silver ankle bracelet with tiny bells on it. I believe Madeline was wearing it that night." He sounded lame even to himself. The woman in the dream who'd been Madeline up until that last minute had been wearing a silver ankle bracelet with little bells on it. Until this moment, he'd forgotten about the bracelet he'd bought her.

"I'll send Harp back out there. Will give him something to do."

"Who's Harp?" Tucker asked, still distracted.

"Harper Cole. Mayor's son and a deputy I inherited. While he's doing better at the job, he has a pregnant wife he calls every few hours to make sure she's all right."

"And that's a bad thing, him checking on his wife?"

Flint groaned. "You have to know Harp. He tends to overdo everything. So putting him on creek dirt duty will at least give all of us a break," his brother said with a laugh. "What do you have planned today?"

Tucker glanced at the clock, cringing at how early it was. "Going back to sleep."

"Sorry for waking you up."

"You don't know how sorry I am." He hung up but knew that the dream was gone. He sat on the edge of the bed, his head in his hands. Flint wasn't going to look for Madeline Dunn's accomplice.

But Kate Rothschild most definitely was.

Sleep was out of the question. All he could think about was how excited he'd been in the dream to see Madeline again and instead it had been… Kate?

He shook his head. What a crazy dream.

Kate would be even more disappointed by the news of the Dunn family disappearing, he realized. Let alone if he told her that Flint wasn't looking for the accomplice who'd no doubt hidden Madeline's body.

After dinner with her last night, he knew that the woman was out for blood. So maybe it was just as well that it had come to this end.

He picked up his cell phone thinking he should call her. She was probably a morning person. Mostly, he didn't want her finding out about this from anyone else. And yet, he hesitated as he tried to clear his head. That darned dream was still clinging to him like warm water from the pool he'd been waiting in.

Last night, she'd put her cell number into his phone—and taken his. She was determined that they "work together." Another reason he had to call her. He felt like Flint. He just wanted this behind him.

He searched for her number. It was going to feel strange

talking to her after the dream. Hell, he'd just seen her naked. The thought made him shake his head. It was nothing but a *dream*. And yet, it had been so real...

Before he could call her, his phone rang. Flint. Again.

He chuckled into the phone. "I remember you never letting me sleep in the mornings when we were kids."

"It wasn't my fault that you were a light sleeper or that we had to share a room or that I was a pesky little brother," Flint said, humor in his voice. "After I hung up, I realized you are probably going to drive to Clawson Creek to see what you can find out about Madeline. I'm not sure it's a good idea."

"Never crossed my mind," he said but realized it had because that was what Kate would do. "Someone up there knew her, might know where her family went after they left. Interesting they left about the time that she died. It's almost like they knew she'd died that night, huh."

Flint groaned. "See why I called you back? Are you looking for closure?"

He chuckled. "Maybe. Maybe I'm just curious."

"Even if you found some of her family, I'm not sure you can get the closure you seem to need. Worse, the person who buried her that night at the creek might not realize I can't take any legal action against them," Flint said. "It could be dangerous."

"Flint, stop worrying about me. I can take care of myself."

"That's what bothers me. I don't want to have to bail you out of jail."

"Don't worry, I'm thinking about taking Kate Rothschild with me. Her daddy will pay our bail." He disconnected.

The idea of taking Kate along had been an impulsive thought that now seemed like a good idea. She wanted answers. And he, he realized, wanted to see her again.

He found her number on his phone. She answered on the first ring. A morning person, he thought with a groan and realized he heard water running in the background. Just like that small waterfall coming into the pool in his dream.

"How do you feel about a road trip?" he asked without preamble as he tried to exorcise the dream once and for all. "Thought you might want to help me track down Madeline's kin. Dress casual. I'll pick you up in fifteen."

Kate put the phone back on the bathroom counter by the sink. Tucker had pulled her out of the shower where she'd been…daydreaming.

She considered getting back into the still-running warm shower. The water had felt so good, her skin slick with body wash. She'd been lost in the feel of it, lost in thoughts of Tucker Cahill, and hadn't realized where her hand had moved to until the phone rang. She had quickly opened the shower door and snatched up the phone as if getting caught doing something she shouldn't.

Now she reached in and turned the water off. That wonderful, sensual, dreamy feeling from earlier disappeared as she grabbed a towel to dry off. Madeline's kin?

She felt her heart race at the thought of getting this close to finding out who had helped Madeline, who was equally responsible for her brother's death. Madeline might be dead, but whoever was involved in the con with her wasn't.

Tucker had said he was picking her up in fifteen minutes. That meant she didn't have time to fix her hair. She pulled the wet mass of curls up into a ponytail. He'd said to dress casual. The best she could do were designer jeans, a sweater and calf-high boots rather than her sneakers, which were muddy from the creek yesterday. She grabbed her brother's baseball cap, pulled her ponytail through and looked in the mirror. Her green eyes appeared too bright and sharp enough to cut glass. Revenge is a dish best served cold, her mother always said.

On her way, she grabbed her sunglasses—and her gun, which she slipped into her purse.

She felt a shiver of excitement and apprehension move through her as Tucker pulled up in his pickup. She rushed outside as he reached over to shove open the passenger-side door for her to get in. She told herself this heady feeling had nothing to do with the handsome cowboy behind the wheel. She was merely high on adrenaline—and vengeance.

But one whiff of him fresh from the shower and she was reminded of earlier in her own shower and what had been going through her mind when he'd called.

CHAPTER NINE

"I'm surprised you called me," Kate said as she settled into the passenger seat of Tucker's pickup.

He shot her a look. "Why's that?" She smelled good. Too good. Her hair was still damp. He realized that must have been the shower he'd heard in the background this morning. After he'd called her, he'd taken a shower himself. Only his had been cold.

Turning in her seat to face him, she chuckled. "Given the way we left things last night, I didn't expect to hear from you again."

"Because I didn't ask you to sleep with me?" he joked as he headed north out of town. The drive to Clawson Creek would take just under an hour.

"Very funny. You didn't even try to kiss me."

He smiled over at her, unable not to think about his dream. "Maybe I'm not that kind of guy."

"Oh, and what kind of guy is that?"

"A complete fool. You were pretty clear about your feelings last night."

She sighed. "I said some things after dinner that I shouldn't have. I'm so angry with my brother for what he did, and unfortunately, I never got to say those things to him. I didn't mean to hurt your feelings."

He laughed. "I don't get my feelings hurt that easily."

"I'm angry at my brother and I might have taken it out on you last night."

"You think?" he asked, smiling, glad he'd called her. Not that he thought their search for the Dunn family would lead to anything. His brother had already told him that they'd cleared out nineteen years ago. Maybe they'd managed to disappear like he had.

"You were right about me and your brother being easily manipulated by the woman," he admitted after a few moments. "I know it's hard to understand, but you didn't know Madeline."

"Apparently neither did you or my brother. Sorry, but if you tell me she put a spell on you…" She sounded angry again. But he could also hear the pain in her voice. Her brother had killed himself because of Madeline.

"You must hate her."

She stared at him. He could feel her gaze boring into the side of his face like a laser. "Don't *you*? You lost nineteen years with your family because of her. She took your life— at least temporarily. She filled you with guilt. She screwed with your mind just like she did my brother. How can you possibly *not* hate her?"

He shook his head, making her swear.

"If you tell me that you still love her…"

"I *did* love her. Or at least the person I thought she was. Now I just feel sad for all of us. That she died in the creek that night… What a waste and for what?"

Kate shook her head. "I will never understand men. She *deceived* you and yet you still care about her."

"Haven't you ever had a man deceive you?"

"Not like that!" She whipped a hand through the air. But he saw the anger quickly ebb away as she leaned back in her seat and stared out at the passing scenery.

It was a beautiful Montana spring day, the sky robin's-egg blue with only a few fluffy white clouds bobbing along on the horizon. The air was crisp and everywhere he looked he saw new green grass and leaves. He loved this time of year. He wondered if Kate could appreciate this day or if her only thought was getting vengeance for her brother.

"If you don't want justice for what she did, then why are we looking for her family?" Kate finally asked.

"Truthfully, I have no idea what I hope to accomplish by driving up here. We can't undo anything that's been done. The statute of limitations has run out even if we could prove that one of them worked with her, let alone hid her body. My brother is dropping the investigation."

She sat up abruptly to face him. "He can't do that!"

"I'm afraid he is. Like he said, it's a waste of manpower since no charges can be filed even if he found the person responsible."

Kate shifted her purse on her lap. "Well, I'm going to find the people responsible and see that justice is done."

"Madeline paid with her life. Isn't that enough?"

Kate scoffed. "No. Yes, she got her just deserts. But there is still at least one of them out there who got away with it."

"So you want retribution? Anyone ever tell you that it's never as satisfying as you think it's going to be?"

"I'll be the judge of that. Whoever was working with her is just as guilty as she was. She might have done the…hard work, but her accomplice helped her perpetuate a lie that destroyed my brother. You might not acknowledge the damage the woman did, but I live with it every day and have for nineteen years."

"So have I," he said, lowering his voice as he heard the raw pain in hers as well as his own. "Don't think I got away unscathed. I've been where your brother was. I just chose a different way of checking out. I came back here filled with guilt and ready to have my brother lock me up."

"You were a *victim*."

Tucker laughed at that. "I was a testosterone-filled teenage boy who thought about sex every minute of the day. Yes, I was easy prey, but I can't put all the blame on Madeline. At any time I could have said no."

"But you did say no," Kate pointed out. "Isn't that when she pulled out all the stops and did her drowning-herself-and-the-baby stunt?"

He nodded. "And that is why I can't help but feel some guilt in her drowning. I let it go on too long. She might never have done that if I'd handled things differently."

Kate scoffed. "You think you and my brother were the only ones?" She shook her head. "She used that same drowning stunt on my brother. He thought she'd drowned and killed their baby. Who knows how many more teenage boys she'd pulled that stunt on? Doesn't feel quite so special anymore, does it?"

Tucker knew she was right. He felt a stab of anger mixed with a healthy dose of bitterness and regret when it came to Madeline. The horror he'd lived with after that night on the bridge was something he'd never forget. It had been beyond cruel. That she'd used it on others like him broke his heart. And that Kate's brother had killed himself... It was an un-speakable tragedy.

"But you still can't hate her," Kate said, shaking her head before turning to look out her side window again. "Well, I hate her enough for both of us. Madeline made a fool out of my brother. Whoever helped her is going to pay, one way or the other."

Ahead he saw the turnoff for Clawson Creek and slowed the pickup, suddenly worried that bringing Kate along might have been a mistake.

★ ★ ★

Madeline. The name alone set Kate off. Her anger had been like a red-hot poker in her belly for so long… Finding the man who Madeline tricked after her brother… She knew she had no right to take out her rage on Tucker. He was a victim like her brother.

Kate tried to rein in her anger, her regret, her bitterness against a woman she'd never met and now would never get the chance. But maybe with Tucker's help she would at least find out who had helped the woman deceive her brother.

She glanced over at him. She realized that she'd been sounding like a jealous girlfriend when she talked about Madeline with him. Taking deep breaths, she tried to calm down. But as she looked at him, she realized that it wasn't just about her brother.

She was furious with Tucker for falling for Madeline, too. What was wrong with these men? To make it worse, she found herself attracted to the handsome cowboy but at the same time wanting to smack him upside the head for being so stupid as to fall for Madeline. Add to that, she thought he was still captivated by a woman she hated—and resented. And envied?

The thought reminded her of this morning in the shower. She felt her cheeks flush and pretended to study the landscape as she tried to extinguish the thought.

After a few miles, she turned to him. "I'm sorry." But her attention was quickly pulled away as she looked out the windshield and realized they were slowing down. "This is where she lived?"

"Clawson Creek. Looks like there isn't much here. I would imagine someone knows what happened to the Dunns since it appears they left their mark here." He pointed to an old faded sign that read Dunn Lumberyard. "Could be a relative." He shot her a look, his gaze burning into her. "You sure you're up to this?"

She straightened. "Don't worry, I won't embarrass you."

"Seriously?" He laughed. "I'm more worried that you aren't going to get whatever it is you need from all this."

"No, you're not. You're worried that I'm going to lose it and get us both thrown into jail or worse."

"It has crossed my mind given your...strong feelings."

It was her turn to laugh. "We're just trying to find her kin and figure out if one of them was working with Madeline. For our own satisfaction since legally there is nothing your brother can do. Right?"

"Right." He sounded as if he didn't believe she was taking it as well as she pretended. Maybe he was smarter than he looked, she thought uncharitably.

"I can handle myself. I'm a damned good investigative reporter and I can take care of myself."

"I don't doubt that...at least when you aren't personally and emotionally involved."

"Give me some credit. I can be cool and calm. You'll see." She saw he was still having misgivings. The man was no fool. Except when it came to Madeline Dunn. "Thanks for bringing me."

He grunted. Ahead she could see what was left of Clawson Creek. Like so many Montana towns, it had shrunk to a minimum of businesses. Old abandoned buildings told of another more prosperous time for this small ranching community.

The lumberyard was a big barn of a building with a small office attached to one side. Behind it was a sawmill. Several loads of logs lay on the ground next to a huge pile of sawdust. Next to that was the apparatus that held the saw blade. The huge jagged-toothed blade gleamed dully in the sunlight as Tucker parked out front.

"Might as well start here. Looks like there isn't much going

on, though," he said. There was only one other vehicle parked
in front of the lumberyard, an old faded red pickup.

Kate let out a breath as she looked toward the office. The
windows were so dirty she couldn't see much of anything
inside. But there was a faded open sign in the corner of the
dusty window in the door.

The rest of the town appeared abandoned except for a couple of trucks in front of a café down the short main drag and
a few more in front of the bar across from it.

"If you want to wait here until—"

Kate was already out of his truck before he could finish.

He was shaking his head as he joined her on the sidewalk
out front. She stared at the warbled office windows, seeing
only her own dull reflection in them, and thought of her
brother.

Tucker was wrong. She'd waited years for this. She *would*
get satisfaction.

A bell tinkled as Tucker pulled the office door open and
let her lead the way inside. She was hit with a disagreeable
smell that didn't improve as they moved toward the counter.
The place reeked of burned coffee, years of cigarette smoke
and recent body odor.

"Hello?" Tucker called and glanced in the back.

From where she stood, Kate could see that there were few
supplies to be had behind the counter. She turned and headed
for the door, saying over her shoulder, "I'll go look in the
big building."

As she exited, she heard the sound of an engine running
somewhere deep in the back of the barnlike structure.

She'd only taken a few steps when Tucker fell in beside her.
Clearly he didn't think she could take care of herself. A small
part of her was touched at his protective behavior.

"You might want to let me do the talking," he said.

Kate smiled over at him. "Still worried about jail, huh?"

★ ★ ★

Tucker saw the smile and heard the words, but it was the determination he glimpsed in her gaze that worried him.

He followed the sound of what appeared to be lumber being unloaded with a forklift into the cavernous building. It was cool and dark inside the structure. The air smelled of fresh-cut pine. He breathed it in as they walked toward the sounds of life.

When he was a boy, he always loved going to the Gilt Edge Lumberyard with his father. It was usually summer when they were building something on the ranch, so the cool darkness of the big building filled with lumber was always a treat. But he loved the smell, as well. He still equated the scent of fresh-cut pine with his father and wondered when he would see him again. Ely had apparently gone back up into the mountains after he'd seen him in passing yesterday.

He'd barely seen Hawk and Cyrus. Both had already gone to bed when he came in last night after his date. He'd only gotten a chance to visit with them for a few minutes this morning on his way out.

Spotting him, Hawk had said, "I see you found your room again."

"Thanks for making it up for me," Tucker had said as he shook each of their hands and then on impulse pulled them into a hug. Lillie had told him yesterday at the saloon that they were both confirmed bachelors, but she was determined they weren't going to stay that way.

To him, they'd both looked like young ranchers, serious, hardworking and content in the lifestyle they loved. He probably understood that better than his sister did, he'd thought.

"Where have you been?" Cyrus had asked.

"Where haven't I been?"

Hawk had frowned at him. "We thought we'd never see you again. Why would you leave the way you did?"

"It's a long story, but suffice it to say a woman was involved," he'd told them. "In fact, there is another woman waiting for me so I need to run, but I'll see you later."

He still felt badly about running out on them like he had nineteen years ago—and again this morning. At some point, he would have to face them all with the whole story.

They were deep in the building when Tucker spotted the forklift operator hunched over the controls. As they neared, the forklift engine shut off. The operator jumped down off the rig, clad in canvas pants and jacket, heavy gloves and a baseball cap. It wasn't until the person looked up that he realized he was looking at a woman. Until that moment, he hadn't admitted that he'd come here looking for something of Madeline.

He'd known it was a long shot that they would find any of her relatives since who knew how many times Dunn Lumberyard could have changed hands over the years.

But all his illusions were dashed as the forklift operator turned. He wasn't going to find Madeline in this woman. Even from a distance, he could see that she was shorter, stockier and definitely not anywhere near as attractive.

When she looked up, he saw her eyes. They were dark as obsidian. Nothing like the startling blue of Madeline's.

Deputy Harper Cole knew shit duty only too well. When was the sheriff going to quit giving him busywork? He'd thought they were getting along so much better now that he was settled down, married and expecting his first child.

Apparently Flint still didn't trust him with anything important. But he knew that was only one reason he didn't like this assignment the sheriff had sent him on. He knew for a fact that the other deputies had brought back a load of dirt from the so-called grave site to the coroner's office and had sifted through it. So why would Flint ask for more?

It made no sense. To simply find a few finger bones?

He looked across the creek to the dark, dense pines and felt a shiver. Most crime scenes didn't bother him. He'd seen his share of dead people. But he'd never been a fan of cemeteries. His grandmother used to say that she could see and feel the dead. It was why, she said, she never went to the cemetery to visit her dead husband. "It's all those other dead people I don't want to see." His father, though, was fond of saying that the old woman was nuttier than Christmas fruitcake.

Harp remembered the feel of her bony fingers digging into his arm as she leaned toward him and whispered, "Your father doesn't know his head from his butt. I was cursed with the gift. Dead people never really die. Some of their spirit always hangs around the spot where they died. I've seen your grandfather sitting in that chair over there, snoring, since that's what he did most of the time."

He'd glanced over at his grandfather's recliner and had been relieved not to see any old man snoring there. "Don't believe me?" she'd prodded. "You ever feel the hair rise on the back of your neck? That's when they brush against you to let you know they're still here."

Now, standing at the edge of the creek, Harp rubbed a hand over the back of his neck. The bucket with the spade he'd brought tapped against his leg, making him jump. Shadows had settled in the pines and he could hear the wind in the tops letting out a low moan.

Pulling out his cell phone, he called his wife. Vicki answered on the fourth ring, right before he was starting to get worried. "Why didn't you answer sooner?" he demanded.

"I was in the bathroom. You know I have to pee a lot. What's wrong?"

"Nothing." He looked toward the pines and grave site where he needed to dig a bucketful of dirt for the coroner. "Just working. I wanted to make sure you were doing okay."

"Harp, you don't have to worry so much. I'm fine. The baby is fine. Are you sure you're fine, though?"

"Don't worry about me. The doctor said you could have that baby any day. You're keeping your phone on you, right?"

"Yes, Harp," she said with a chuckle. "I go into labor, I call you. I promise."

"Okay, I should get back to work. Glad I have cell service out here. In case I need to check on you." He disconnected, not wanting to waste his battery, and started across the creek.

The water was so low this time of year the creek appeared to be dry because of all the boulders. Soon all those rocks would be under a rushing roar of spring runoff water. But right now he was able to step from one to the next without getting his feet wet.

Cold clear creek water ran between the rocks. He looked from it to the pines and back down, his apprehension growing. Why hadn't he just filled the bucket on the other side? The coroner wouldn't be any the wiser.

He misstepped, his boot sliding off a rock and into the water. He dropped the bucket and spade to catch himself and almost lost both. One boot already wet, he said what the hell and waded after the bucket, catching up with it when it caught in the slow current downstream.

Icy cold water filled both boots. He waded across to shore, cursing under his breath. He would make this quick. *Shouldn't take any time to scoop up a bucketful of dirt and get out of here.*

But first he had to move deeper into the pines. He stepped into the shadowy darkness, his boots making squishy sounds with each step. The body had been found in an old creek channel buried under some driftwood. Now, though, the wood had been moved to the side, leaving a gaping hole where the woman had rotted to nothing but bones.

Harp felt the hair rise on the back of his neck. He let out a curse as he pulled the spade from the bucket. He was a few yards away from where the other digging had taken place, but he didn't care. He began to fill the bucket as fast as he could. The pines continued to moan over his head. He shuddered as something seemed to brush against him. He shoveled faster and faster, so fast he almost missed it.

He stared down at the object that had caught the dim light and blinked. His heart began to race. For a moment, he didn't believe what he was seeing.

Flint had been uneasy all morning. At noon, he went home. Maggie was making them sandwiches in the kitchen when he walked in. They'd had a home built for them on the ranch after their marriage last year. Maggie had designed the kitchen so it faced the southeast and caught the morning sun and stayed bright and airy the rest of the day.

"It won't be hot in the summer," she'd said. "That's why we have the deck off the kitchen, so we can eat out there on nice days."

He'd kissed her, thankful that he still had her. Last year, he'd thought for sure that they would never be together again. But here they were, happily married, and his ex-wife, Celeste, was happily long gone. He always felt like knocking on wood when he thought of his ex. Gone but not forgotten.

Maggie looked up as he came into the kitchen. "Something wrong?"

"I feel like I shouldn't have told Tucker where to find Madeline's family." He'd told her why Tucker had left right after high school and she'd been so sympathetic. Having had a bad relationship before she'd met him, Maggie could relate.

"Why would you keep it from him? The investigation is over, right?"

He nodded. "It looks like whatever happened to the woman was an unfortunate accident that she brought on herself. Whoever hid her body… Well, the statute of limitations has run out so there is no reason to pursue it."

"You think he's looking for some kind of payback?" Maggie asked.

"I suspect he's just trying to make some sense out of all of it. If anything, I think he needs closure. He's lived with guilt for so many years." Flint shook his head. "It makes me so angry with myself. If I had pressed him for what was going on all those years ago…"

"Flint, don't do that to yourself. You know you tried to talk to him."

He took the plate she offered him and followed her out to the deck that overlooked Gilt Edge in the distance. They'd built on the side of a mountain on the ranch where they had a view of all four mountain ranges that surrounded the lush valley.

"I know you're right. Tucker has always done things on his own."

"Like every other man in your family," she said with a laugh as she sat down across from him.

His cell phone rang. "It's Sonny." The bad feeling was there before he accepted the call.

"I finished my heart attack corpse and was looking again at young woman from the creek. I found something you need to see," the coroner said.

"I'm just about to have lunch with my wife. Can it wait?"

"It isn't like Madeline Dunn is going anywhere."

He disconnected and looked at his sandwich. Sonny had just ruined his appetite.

"Trouble?"

"Always."

Maggie sighed. "I can wrap up your sandwich so you can eat it later," she said with a laugh since this happened more often than not.

"I'm sorry."

"Don't be. I have this book I started reading last night. I'm dying to get back to it." Maggie owned a hair salon in town but she'd taken time off to oversee the construction of the house and furnishing it. Now that she was pregnant, she was talking about not going back. She had two stylists working at the shop, so there was no need to do more than stop in and see how things were going.

Flint was glad to see her taking it easy. This was the first break from work that she'd had since she was a teenager, he thought as he followed her back into the kitchen. "How are you feeling?"

"Wonderful," she said, smiling, her hand going to her slight baby bump.

"If you're worried about your brother…" she said as she wrapped up his sandwich and put it in a small brown bag.

"I'm always worried about one of them," he said with a nervous laugh. "It's just me being silly. I'm sure everything is fine." But he wasn't sure at all as he kissed his wife, holding her tightly for a moment before he headed for the coroner's office.

CHAPTER TEN

Billie Dee tried to assure herself that she'd been wrong about the young woman Darby had hired. She didn't know the woman and the woman obviously hadn't recognized her. But it was something about that face… It felt like a memory that she couldn't quite access.

When she looked at Ashley Jo Somerfield, she felt a jolt. Her heart would race. Goose bumps would ripple across her skin. She had almost had to bite her tongue to keep from saying something to her.

But then Ashley Jo would look up and see her and there would be no recognition in her gaze. The young woman would smile and Billie Dee would tell herself what an old fool she was.

The back door of the saloon opened, making her jump. She'd been so lost in her thoughts that she'd lost track of time.

Henry stepped in. The moment he saw her, he cried, "Billie Dee? You are as white as a sheet. What is it?"

She stepped into his arms. "Just hold me," she said. "Just hold me tight."

"Sweetheart, what is it?" he finally asked after a few minutes of wrapping her tightly in his arms. "When I come in here and you aren't singing..."

She smiled up at him, realizing she was crying. She pulled away and went to the cupboard to get cups. But as she started to pour the coffee from the big pot she kept on the stove, he took it from her.

"Sit. Please. Let me do this."

Normally, she would have put up an argument. She hated not being able to do things for herself. But this time, she went to the kitchen table and sat.

It was still early in the morning. But soon Darby and Mariah would be coming down the stairs. Outside the window, the Montana spring day was spectacular. The sky was so blue it hurt to look at it. The cottonwoods next to the old stagecoach stop had leafed out and now fluttered in the breeze. Rays of sunshine burst through the window, making dust particles dance in the air.

On a day like this, Billie Dee should have been rejoicing. She'd been so happy. So excited about life. Until the moment she'd looked down the hallway and seen Ashley Jo Somerfield.

Henry put a cup of coffee in front of her before taking a chair across from her. As he wrapped his big hands around his cup as if for warmth, he asked, "Is it me?"

She shook her head, fighting tears. "There's something I need to tell you."

He put down his coffee cup and reached across the table to take her hand.

How did she get so lucky with this man? But what if she told him and—

"Billie Dee, there is nothing you can tell me that will change my mind about you."

She couldn't help giving him a skeptical look.

"Trust me. I have suspected there was something else you needed to tell me before you married me. I've been waiting.

But lately, I've noticed that something has you upset—even as hard as you've tried to hide it."

She couldn't believe this man. He knew her better than she knew herself sometimes. She swallowed the lump in her throat.

"It's Ashley Jo."

He frowned. "Who?"

"The new young woman Darby and Mariah hired. The moment I saw her…" Her voice broke. "I thought she was my daughter, the daughter I gave up for adoption twenty-six years ago."

He squeezed her hand. "Oh, Billie Dee, that must have been very difficult for you."

Tears flooded her eyes. She pulled her hand away to reach for a napkin on the table to dab at her tears. "It was the hardest thing I've ever done and the one thing I have regretted every day since."

"You wouldn't have done it if you'd had a choice."

She smiled through her tears at him. How had she thought he wouldn't understand? "Don't you want to know why I had no choice?"

"You'll tell me when you're ready. Do you still believe she is your daughter?" he asked.

"She looks just like me at that age. It's like looking in a mirror. I thought she must have come here because of me. But when our eyes met… There was no recognition at all."

"We must find out for sure," Henry said, always the practical one. "It will be simple enough."

"I should have known you would help me."

"Of course," he said as he took her hand again.

"But what if she really is my daughter? If she came here not knowing… That would be too much of a coincidence. But if she does know and she is the child I gave up and she doesn't want—"

"Let's not cross that bridge until we come to it. We start with proof and go from there, okay?"

She nodded, feeling as if a load of concrete had been lifted off not just her shoulders but her heart.

"How will you find out?" she asked.

"Leave that to me."

The woman working in the lumberyard took them in with a cold dark-eyed stare. "You need somethin'?" Her voice was gravelly and disinterested as she moved to pick up one of the two-by-fours that had fallen off the stack.

"Do you happen to be one of Madeline Dunn's relatives by any chance?" Tucker asked.

The woman, who he realized was much younger than he'd originally thought, pulled off her gloves and stopped to actually look at him. "No. Who's asking?"

"I'm Tucker Cahill," he said, holding out a hand. The woman didn't take it. "And this is—"

"Katherine Rothschild, reporter with the *Times*. And you are..."

The woman's smile was condescending. "I sell lumber. So if you don't need any..." She started to turn away and head in the direction of the office.

"Madeline Dunn murdered my brother," Kate said, going after her before Tucker could stop her.

As Kate grabbed her arm, the woman stopped in her tracks and slowly turned around. "I have no idea what you're talking about," she said, shaking off Kate's hold on her. "I never even met Madeline."

The woman shifted her gaze slowly to Kate. Kate stepped closer until there were only inches between them. "Madeline Dunn is responsible for my brother's death, and I want to know where I can find her brother and sisters."

"I was ten when they left town. I have no idea where they

went and I couldn't care less. My father bought this lumber-yard from them years ago. We haven't heard from them since they left town."

"I still want to know your name," Kate said. "You can either tell me or I can—"

"Carly Brookshire. Happy?"

"Not really. Did you know what Madeline did for a living?"

The woman locked gazes with Kate. "Waitressed." The way she said it, she was daring Kate to argue differently.

"We're not looking for trouble," Tucker said.

"You come here threatening me, I'd say you've already found trouble." The woman pulled off her baseball cap, scratched at her drab short brown hair for a moment and slapped it back on as she scowled at Kate. "If your dead brother was anything like you—"

"He wasn't. That's why I'm here. And I'm not going anywhere until I find Madeline Dunn's siblings."

"I told you. I don't know where they went."

"You don't know anyone who might have heard from them?" Kate asked, calling the woman a liar.

Tucker stepped between them. "Look, we just need to talk to someone who might know where they went."

Carly scowled at Kate. "Maybe someone knows over at the café where Madeline worked. Or you can try the bar where their brother worked as a swamper."

"A swamper?" Kate asked.

The woman rolled her eyes. "The guy who swamps out the bar in the mornings. You know, mops it, cleans it up? But that's all I know. So if you aren't in the market for lumber, don't come back here." With that, she stepped around Tucker and headed toward the daylight.

He stared after her silhouette for moment, before he turned to Kate.

"You call that cool and calm?" he demanded into the cold quiet of the massive building.

Kate let out a breath. "There wasn't any hair pulling or punching."

"Came damned close, though."

"I could have taken her."

He laughed and shook his head.

"I could have. Anyway, she knows more than she's telling us."

"Maybe." He studied her. "Ever heard the expression you can get more with a little sugar than gasoline?"

"I don't believe that's the expression but being direct works better with some people." She looked at her watch. "I could use something cold to drink right now. How about you? Café or bar first?"

"Might as well rile up everyone in town since you're on a roll."

"Won't have to. By now she's already on the phone warning everyone to keep their mouths shut."

He scoffed. "You think everyone in town has some reason to protect the Dunns?" He couldn't help being amused by that. "I doubt the entire family were criminals let alone that the town was in on it."

Kate raised a brow. "You should know how small towns work. They protect their own—even twenty years later." She started out of the building. He caught up to her, anxious to get back out in the sunshine and out of this cavernous cold darkness. More and more, he wondered about Madeline's family. Did the townspeople have reason to protect them all?

As they exited the mouth of the building, he felt eyes drilling into his back and turned. He couldn't see Carly, but he could feel her watching them.

The coroner was holding the skeleton's head in his gloved hands when Flint walked into the morgue.

"Is there a problem?" the sheriff asked.

"Not for this woman anymore," Sonny said. "Can't say the same for you."

"I'm not in the mood for riddles today."

"Sorry. Check this out." The coroner waved him closer. "I x-rayed the bones and found something I didn't expect. It was under the splintered wood that covered the wound I thought killed her."

"That you thought killed her? What are you saying?"

Sonny shook his head as if disappointed with himself. "Seemed pretty clear-cut. She fell into the creek, hit her head, died and ended up in a pile of driftwood downstream with some help."

"Sonny—"

"The X-ray revealed a .22 slug burrowed in the skull."

Flint stared at him. "What?"

"This woman was shot. Apparently the killer didn't think a bullet was sufficient. The blow to the head was *after* she was shot in the head."

"Are you telling me—"

"She was murdered. I should have seen it sooner, but the splintered wood that crushed her skull covered the spot where the bullet lodged in the bone. I would imagine a firearm that small just didn't do the job."

Flint couldn't believe what he was hearing—let alone seeing. *Madeline Dunn was murdered?* He'd wanted to believe that it had been an accident. That the woman had made a mistake jumping in the creek with the water running that high. That after she'd collided with a limb, her accomplice had dragged her from the water and then panicked and buried her under that driftwood in the old channel yards from the creek.

"So she was alive when she got out of the water?" he said, feeling as if he was lagging behind even though his mind was spinning.

"Seems more likely she was shot and then nailed with a tree limb. She must have gotten into an altercation with someone and bit the bullet, so to speak."

Flint groaned and Sonny apologized. "It's not you," the sheriff said. "When I thought it was an accident..." He couldn't tell the coroner how deep his brother Tucker was in all this.

"No statute of limitations on murder. But nineteen years. How will you ever find who did it?"

Flint shook his head. "This opens a whole can of worms." He stared at the skull in Sonny's hands and thought about the woman who'd done a number on his brother. Even dead, she could still ruin his life.

Behind them the door to the morgue opened. Flint looked over to see Deputy Harper Cole standing there, holding a bucketful of dirt.

Harp was grinning, never a good sign. "What is it?" Flint demanded.

"I found something," Harp said. "I was digging near the grave site like you said and..." He looked absolutely giddy. "Might not be anything but..."

"What is it?" Flint snapped.

"Two shell casings for a .22 caliber pistol and this." He held up a tarnished silver ankle bracelet with tiny bells on it, the clasp on it broken.

CHAPTER ELEVEN

The bar was just up the street, so Tucker and Kate decided to walk. Tucker stole a look at her as they walked and found himself smiling. She was gutsy; he'd give her that.

The Lucky Horse was one of those old-fashioned bars with a weathered metal sign of a rearing horse out front. There were four vehicles parked at the door, all at odd angles. As they neared, Tucker could hear the blast of the jukebox.

"I wonder what made the horse lucky?" Kate said as he reached for the door. An earsplitting, boot-stomping song blared out, accompanied by the smell of stale beer.

The lumberyard's cavernous building had been dark but nothing like this bar. What windows there were at the front were covered with a fusion of plants that had grown thick against the glass. Tucker suspected the plants had been alive longer than he had and had grown over the window in their search for sunlight.

A handful of men were draped over the bar, all seeming to be talking at once. Tucker wondered if they'd heard about Madeline's death. In a small town like this, he figured it would be the biggest news to come down the pike for some time.

But they seemed to be arguing over a ball game. All conversation died instantly as the door opened and they walked in. They all turned in unison to stare at them. As the door closed behind him, his eyes finally adjusted to the dim light. The song on the jukebox ended, pitching the bar into a heavy silence before another one came on just as loudly.

Kate moved to the end of the bar farthest away from the men. Tucker joined her. The bartender studied them for a long moment before he walked with a noticeable limp down the bar.

"Whadda ya need?" From the greeting, Tucker figured Kate was right. Carly Brookshire had called to tell him they were coming.

In his fifties, the man's buzz-cut dark hair was peppered with gray. He scowled at them from a prematurely haggard face. A pair of hard eyes took them in with a modicum of contempt.

"I'll take a Bud," Tucker said and looked to Kate.

"Make mine light with a shot of tequila chaser."

At the word *light*, the bartender sneered, but that look vanished quickly after he heard the word *tequila*.

"Hope you don't want a lime with that?" he asked, clearly amused.

"Not necessary," Kate said.

He studied her for a moment, then let out a bark of a laugh and headed back down the bar.

Kate climbed up onto a stool. "And I'll roll you for the jukebox. Unless there isn't anything better than that on there."

He half turned to look at her. Clearly he'd been warned about Kate, but he didn't seem to mind her mouthiness.

Coming back down the bar, he scooped up some quarters from his tip jar and tossed them on the bar. "My treat. Enjoy yourself."

"Thanks. I will." She spun off the stool and went to the jukebox.

Tucker listened to her drop in quarters. A few moments later some soft rock began to play to replace the country boot-stomping. The men down the bar all looked disgusted, but Kate had definitely managed to get their attention.

"You like trouble, don't you?" Tucker asked when she joined him on the bar stool next to him.

She just smiled.

The bartender brought their drinks, dropped two bar napkins and put a can of beer on each, then poured a shot of tequila from a dusty bottle and put it beside Kate's. "You need a glass for your beer?" he inquired of her.

She gave him a disbelieving look, downed the tequila and chased it with a long pull from the beer can.

Tucker almost expected her to let out a loud belch. The man seemed to enjoy the show, though. He was smiling and chuckling to himself.

"Now, if you would turn down the jukebox so we can talk," she said as she leaned her elbows on the bar.

"We have nothing to talk about," he said, suddenly looking wary again.

"Let's talk about Madeline Dunn and her family." She glanced down the bar. "Unless you want me to yell what I have to say over the jukebox."

"You can't just come in here—"

Kate spun off her bar stool again, walked over to the jukebox, reached behind it and pulled the plug. The music died off, leaving the bar deathly quiet.

"Hey! You can't—"

"If it was me," Tucker said to the bartender, "I'd just tell her where we can find the rest of Madeline Dunn's immediate family before she starts tearing up this place."

"What was left of them struck out of here years ago for parts unknown. Now, get out of here before I call the sheriff."

Tucker tossed down the money for their drinks and motioned to Kate that they were leaving.

"You have to admit that went well," she said, the moment the bar door closed behind her.

"It's not over yet. Keep walking," he said under his breath. They hadn't gone far when he heard the bar door open and slam shut. "Don't look—"

But of course she did. "There're three of them, but they're just posturing on the front stoop."

"You are going to be the death of me," he said but couldn't help grinning as they headed toward his pickup.

"What about the café?" Kate asked.

"Now doesn't seem like the time."

"Well, that was fun," she said.

"*Fun?* Only if we get out of here without me getting my butt kicked by those three back there."

Kate laughed. "You could take all three of them."

"I'd rather not today, if you don't mind."

"Hey!" a male voice called from behind them.

"Keep going to the truck," Tucker said, handing her the keys.

"*Hey—*"

Tucker turned to see one of the men from the bar headed toward him. The other two had apparently gone back inside. Still, the last thing he wanted was a confrontation. The years he'd been gone were often filled with a rage he hated. It had taken a long time to get that under control. He didn't want to go back to using his fists to solve his problems.

The man kept coming toward him and was three yards away when Tucker asked, "Can I do something for you?"

"Probably not, but I can do somethin' for you." The man

stopped, looked behind him and still seemed to hesitate. "You was asking about the Dunns."

He nodded, waiting.

"I can tell you where at least three of 'em is." He motioned with his head toward the west. "Old town cemetery. The others? Who knows."

"Why is everyone so closed lipped about answering questions about them?" Tucker said.

The man looked away. "This is a small town. A lot of people like to keep their skeletons in the closet, if you know what I mean. Them Dunns? They was a peculiar bunch. Kell, the old man, was one of those lunatic Bible-thumpers. Strange family. Stayed to themselves. People 'round here don't like talking about 'em, just glad they up and left. Best not to keep askin' around."

"Thanks."

The man shrugged. The bar door opened in the distance behind them. "I should get back. Tell that woman reporter…" He seemed to think better of whatever he was going to say. "The townspeople don't want to see no article about the Dunns, you understand?"

Billie Dee was cooking up a batch of her chicken and dumplings when the back door opened. She'd been expecting Henry so she was surprised to see that it was Ashley Jo Somerfield.

"Hello?" the young woman called as she stuck her head in the doorway. "I was told I could come by early any morning I wanted to."

"Come in," Billie Dee said as she quickly wiped her hands on her apron and grabbed the door.

"I brought a few things. Mr. Cahill said I had a locker back here in the kitchen?"

She waved the woman in, telling herself she wasn't hearing a Southern accent under what was obviously educated diction. "I'm Billie Dee Rhodes, the cook," she said and held out her hand. "I don't think we've properly met."

"Ashley Jo Somerfield. You're from Texas?" Up close, Ashley Jo was even more striking than she'd been at a distance. But it was her blue eyes that sent Billie Dee's heart soaring. Eyes so like her own.

She realized that she was staring. Worse, Ashley Jo had asked her a question. "Texas? Yes."

"Where?"

"Houston," Billie Dee said. "What about you?"

"I was a military brat, never lived in one place long. Never have been able to." The young woman had a beautiful smile. It, too, was familiar.

"Well, welcome to Montana and the Stagecoach Saloon," she said. "I have to ask. What brought you to this part of the world?"

Ashley Jo drew in a long breath and let it out slowly. "I'd never been this far west. Or north for that matter." She shrugged. "I've found that sometimes life just takes you to the most unique and interesting places if you let it. Ever feel that way?" Billie Dee could only nod as the young woman continued. "My parents are convinced that I'm looking for something that doesn't exist." She laughed. It had a musical sound to it. "Maybe so, but I feel as if there is some part of me I need to find before I can settle down." She laughed again. "Sorry, I tend to talk too much when I'm nervous."

"You have no reason to be nervous here," Billie Dee said. "The Cahills are wonderful to work for."

"And you're quite the cook. Something smells wonderful," Ashley Jo said, stepping past her to the stove. "Let me guess. Chicken and dumplings? I haven't had that since I left home. My mother uses an old family recipe. I'd swear yours looks and smells just like hers."

"Your locker's over here," Billie Dee said around the knot in her throat. "You can bring a padlock—"

"That's what Mr. Cahill told me, but I have nothing worth stealing—not that I expect it's a problem here. I already feel at home." She met Billie Dee's gaze and held it. "I felt welcome the moment I walked in and smelled your chili cooking."

"You must have spent time in Texas," Billie Dee said.

Just then Darby came downstairs and he and Ashley Jo headed into the bar. A few moments later Henry walked in the back door.

Billie Dee threw herself into his arms. "I have to know if she's my daughter. I can't take this not knowing."

The sun was low in the sky by the time Tucker and Kate found the old cemetery miles from town. The landscape was stark. A fierce wind blew a tumbleweed across the road in front of the pickup. In the distance, a hawk circled against a blinding blue sky before catching a thermal and rising to disappear from sight.

The cemetery had the same dismal look as the landscape out here. A half-dozen old dead cottonwoods had grown along a nearby ditch bank. Their stark dark limbs cast eerie shadows over the weathered headstones. Spring hadn't come yet to this place, adding to the overall gloom.

Tucker parked at the end of the road since there was a chain across the path into the deserted cemetery. He looked over at Kate. She was staring out with a look of revulsion. He thought of her brother and wondered where he was buried and how many times she'd visited his grave over the past nineteen years.

"You're welcome to wait here," he said.

She quickly shook her head. "I wouldn't think of letting you go alone. But I should tell you. I'm deathly afraid of snakes. They don't even have to be poisonous."

"What are the chances there are snakes in all those tall weeds?" he joked. "Seriously, stay here. Unless there is something else you're even more afraid of."

"Now that you mention it," she said as if bracing herself to face her worst fear as she opened her door. "I'm also terrified of water."

"Well, we're in luck. There isn't any out here."

She smiled over at him and stepped out.

Tucker broke a trail through the tall weeds, hoping that if they came upon a snake Kate at least wouldn't have to deal with it. The air smelled of dust and last fall's dried vegetation. The wind had laid over huge patches of weeds long ago. Now the gusts that scoured the ridge only managed to kick up dust and howl between the barren dead limbs of the cottonwoods.

"This is like looking for a needle in a haystack, but at least the cemetery is small," Kate said as they moved through the gravestones. "I wonder why they stopped burying people here?"

Tucker looked around for a moment. He could think of a number of reasons. "I saw a newer cemetery as we left town that was closer and probably had better access to water since it was kept up."

She nodded as they moved through the weeds and headstones. A dust devil started a few yards away but quickly died off in a shower of grit.

Kate brushed a lock of hair back from her face as she bent to read one of the stones. The breeze felt colder. Or maybe it was just the bleakness of this place and these forgotten deceased.

Tucker was ready to give this up. What was the point, anyway? "I think we should—" The rest of his words died in his throat as he spotted a name that gave him chills. He pulled up short. Madeline Dunn.

"Find it?" Kate asked as she joined him. She let out a breath.

"The grandmother." The stone next to it read Ingrid Dunn. "And that would be the mother, Ingrid the Evil."

He looked over at her in surprise, realizing that she knew more about this family than he'd thought.

She looked shamefaced for a moment. "Clay. In his journal, he mentioned that Madeline was named after her grandmother. Also, that Madeline had once told him about her crazy mother."

"His journal?" Tucker's voice sounded strangled.

"I might not have been completely honest with you," Kate said, avoiding his gaze. "My brother didn't just leave a letter. He kept a journal while he was involved with Madeline. He had this idea of becoming a writer someday." Her voice broke. "So he wrote down everything he knew and felt about her." As she finally met his eyes, she said, "And what he'd found out about the man Madeline was cheating on him with… *You.*"

"You just decided to tell me that now?" Tucker demanded.

Kate could feel the anger coming off Tucker in waves. "I was going to tell you, but…" She looked into his steely gray gaze, hating that she'd kept this from him.

"But what?"

"The time just didn't seem right. So I'm telling you now."

He shook his head and took a few steps away from her. She watched him ball his hands into fists, then release them and ball them again. Finally, he turned toward her. The wind ruffled his dark hair sticking out from under his Stetson as he settled his cold eyes on her again.

She tried not to flinch. "I should have told you."

"You think?" He narrowed his gaze. "So you knew who I was when you came to Gilt Edge."

"No. I told you that I thought it was either you or Flint. I thought it was probably Flint, until I found out that you'd left right after high school. I told you. I assumed you left with Madeline."

"I still don't understand why you would assume that."

"Because I couldn't find her any more than I could find you," Kate said.

"You really have been looking for me for nineteen years?"

"Not all of that time. I didn't have the resources when I started my quest at thirteen. Also, you did a very good job of dropping off the grid. I assume that was on purpose, which also led me to believe that you and Madeline were on the run."

He dragged off his Stetson and raked his fingers through his hair in obvious frustration. Slapping the hat back onto his errant long hair, he took a few deep breaths before he said, "So when a woman's body was found in the creek next to our ranch…"

"I figured that you killed her."

He jerked back in shock. "Why would you think that?"

"I didn't know you yet so it was a reasonable assumption given the way you left town."

"That's why you asked me to dinner. Because you thought I was a murderer?"

"That was one of the reasons."

He shook his head before eyeing her openly. "And the other reason?"

Kate had to look away. "You probably aren't going to like this, either, but I saw a vulnerability in you. Probably the same one Madeline saw in you."

"Glad you noticed. Thanks. So then you decided to take advantage of me."

"No, I…*liked* you. Maybe I felt a little sorry for you."

He swore under his breath but softened it with a smile. "And yet at dinner you read me the riot act."

She laughed. "I was caught between sympathizing since

you'd lost the love of your life—at least according to you—and wanting to pick up a chair and hit you with it for being so…"

"Stupid?" he suggested.

"Susceptible," she said diplomatically.

Tucker chuckled at that. "And by the way, Madeline wasn't the love of my life."

She shrugged and felt that ache in the pit of her stomach as jealousy reared its ugly head again. That Tucker still felt something for Madeline after what she'd done to him drove her to distraction. She told herself it was because of her brother, but she knew that was a lie. This man, stupid or vulnerable or susceptible, had gotten to her.

"I'm going to want to see his journal," Tucker said.

"I know. Maybe that's another reason I didn't tell you until now. It's—"

He nodded as if she didn't need to tell him and squatted down in front of one of the gravestones. "Private."

Misty Dunn. 10-12-1977–6-5-1999.

What had Tucker hoped to find out here in this godforsaken place? Flint was right. He was looking for closure, but every door he opened seemed to slam shut in his face and leave him even more frustrated.

"You planning to dig up the grave?" Kate asked as she squatted down next to him.

He noticed something moving in the wind. It was the only color on the ground. A deep red petal caught in the base of the weeds. He reached for it, surprised to realize what it was. A rose petal.

"Someone recently left flowers here." He handed Kate the petal he'd found. She pressed it between her thumb and forefinger, then released it to the wind to watch it fly away.

"It could have blown over from someone else's grave," she said and looked around. "Or not."

Not only did it appear that no one had been out here in years, but also there were no vases on the graves, not even plastic flowers next to any of the headstones. This place was forgotten.

"So did your brother write anything about Misty Dunn?" he asked, still peeved over her keeping the journal a secret from him.

"No. Just Madeline. I don't think he knew anything about them. So who was she?" She moved closer to stare down at the stone. "Uh, Tucker?" Kate said as she knelt next to him. "Notice anything interesting about those dates?"

His thoughts had been far away. Now he focused in on the date Misty had died and felt his heart lurch in his chest. "That was the year I graduated and left."

"Misty died not just the year Madeline died—but days after, right? You graduated just before Memorial Day week-end in May?"

"Yes."

"But that isn't the only thing." Her voice sounded strange. "My brother had discovered Madeline's real birth date. According to this gravestone, Madeline was born on the same day as her sister Misty."

He stared at the crude numbers cut into the stone. "That can't be right."

"Unless they were twins." Kate stood and let out a sigh of disgust. "Don't even tell me there was more than one of them."

His stomach seemed to drop. "Madeline had a twin?"

CHAPTER TWELVE

As they drove back toward Clawson Creek, Tucker seemed lost in his own thoughts. Kate didn't feel much like talking, either. She regretted not telling him right away about her brother's journal. She could make all kinds of excuses why she hadn't. In truth, she hadn't wanted to share it with anyone. Nor had she. Not even her parents knew about it.

So why had she told Tucker?

Her phone rang, startling her since it had been quiet for so long. Earlier she'd wanted to check something online as they were leaving the cemetery only to find there was no cell phone coverage that far from town.

She saw it was her mother and declined the call. If it was anything important, she'd call her when she got back to the hotel. Knowing her mother, though, she would keep calling. Turning off her phone, she pocketed it and leaned back in the seat to watch the landscape blur past.

Madeline had been a twin? An identical twin? She couldn't imagine anything worse. Had Misty still been alive, Tucker might have come face-to-face with the woman, thinking she was Madeline.

She glanced over at him. Would he have fallen for the sister in Madeline's place? No matter what he said, he would always be hung up on the woman. It riled her to no end but she wasn't about to dredge through her feelings to understand why.

As he started through town, she said impulsively, "Stop at the café."

Tucker shot her a look.

"Please. I promise to be on my best behavior."

"I don't know what that is," he said but slowed and pulled into the parking lot next to the Busy Bumblebee Café. It was anything but busy.

"I think it would be better if I went in alone," Kate said and opened her door. She saw Tucker's worried look but ignored it as she closed the door and hurried toward the ancient-looking diner.

The inside was a lot like most small-town cafés she'd been in. There were four worn booths on one side and three tables on the other with a short counter across the back that looked into the kitchen. An old-grease smell hung in the air.

A male cook looked up from the pass-through but lost interest quickly. A woman who'd been sitting at one of the counter chairs swiveled around but didn't get up.

Kate headed toward her, but the woman motioned for her to take one of the booths. She started to tell her that she wasn't going to order anything when the waitress got up, hurried to her and whispered, "You'll want to order something."

Taking a few steps back at the woman's intent expression, Kate slid into the farthest booth from the kitchen. Carly Brookshire would have called and warned this woman that someone was in town asking about Madeline Dunn. She watched the waitress glance nervously toward the cook in the back before she pulled out her order pad and waited.

"So what would you like to order?" the woman asked.

Since she hadn't even been given a menu, let alone wanted to order anything, she said, "What would you suggest?"

"Maybe something to go like a grilled ham and cheese."

Kate smiled. "Perfect. I'll have two to go."

"Good choice." The woman took her time writing something on the pad she'd pulled from her apron pocket. With a flurry, she ripped the piece of paper off and placed it face-down on the table. Then she began to write on the next sheet.

Confused, Kate watched the woman go back to the kitchen and in a loud voice order, "Two grilled ham and cheeses to go."

The cook mumbled something Kate didn't catch. She waited, thinking the waitress would come back. She'd gotten the impression the order was just to keep the cook busy while they could talk.

But the waitress stayed in the kitchen talking to the cook until she returned with a greasy brown bag and announced that it would be twelve dollars.

Kate handed her a twenty and started to ask a question, but the woman cut her off. "Here." Picking up the paper from her pad that she'd left on the table earlier, the waitress said, "You'll want this," and stuffed it in the sack with the sandwiches. "You have a good day." Then she turned and went back to the kitchen.

Realizing that the waitress wouldn't be back with her change, Kate rose, grabbed the sack and walked out.

"What happened?" Tucker asked as she slid in.

"I'm not sure. It was…strange."

"What did you get?"

She opened the bag as Tucker pulled back out onto the street. The paper from the order pad was already starting to soak up grease. She looked at the writing and realized that the woman had written her a note.

"Maybe not so strange."

"Do I get one of those sandwiches?" Tucker asked.

She shot him a look. "Seriously?"

"It smells good."

Shaking her head, she pocketed the note from the woman until she had time to think about it without Tucker's input, handed him a sandwich and watched him eat every last bite. She knew what Tucker would say. Pure and simple extortion.

The note had read: *Want to know about Madeline Dunn? $500.* Under that was a phone number.

Kate's stomach growled, making Tucker grin over at her. She ate half her sandwich and gave the rest to him. After that, she must have fallen asleep because she woke to find the pickup no longer moving. She sat up, feeling disoriented. For a moment, she'd forgotten where she was, who she was with, until she saw that she was sitting in front of the hotel in his pickup.

"Nice nap?" Tucker asked, not unkindly. "You must be exhausted."

She nodded, realizing it was true.

"I want to see Clay's journal."

"I know. I don't have it with me. It's under safekeeping back in Helena." Did he believe her?

"If you say so."

"It's true." She desperately wanted him to believe her, but she had kept the journal from him and now he was questioning her honesty. "I can't send for it. No one but you and I know about it. But I promise you can see it." She thought of him reading it. "Unless you change your mind. I'm afraid a lot of it will upset you."

He smiled at that. "I won't change my mind."

She unhooked her seat belt. "Well, thank you for taking me with you."

"Yes, it made for an...interesting day."

Having nothing more to say about that, she opened her

door and got out. And now she was keeping the note from the waitress in the café from him. "Talk to you soon?"

"Soon," he said, making it sound like a promise. Or a threat.

Tucker watched Kate until she disappeared into the hotel lobby. All the time, he was wondering if he would ever see Clay's journal. Maybe Kate was right. Maybe it was better that way. Not that he wouldn't fight tooth and nail to read it, anyway.

He drove back to the ranch only to find that his ranching brothers were out working. Soon he would have to return to the workforce, too. He'd done all types of work and had become handy at a lot of manual labor. So what did he want to do for the rest of his life?

Tucker knew he couldn't think about that now. He felt lost. *Madeline had been a twin.* If Clay had her birth date correct. He thought about calling Flint and seeing what he'd been able to find out about the Dunn family. As he pulled out his phone, he saw that his brother had called him and left a message. He hesitated, remembering that Flint had asked him to come by the sheriff's department. He wasn't sure if he was up to it right now.

Tucker knew he was putting off facing whatever Flint had called about. But he also knew it was only a matter of time before his friends heard he was back in town. He'd left so abruptly without even saying goodbye and then he hadn't kept in touch over the past nineteen years for obvious reasons. He wasn't even sure any of his old friends would want to see him. But he didn't want them hearing about his return through the Gilt Edge grapevine, so he put in a call to the friend he'd been the closest to, Jayce Burton.

Jayce had become a lawyer with his own shingle located on the main street in town. There was no home number listed online, so he called the business number hoping to catch him before he left for the day. He expected he'd have to go through a secretary or receptionist but was put right through to his old friend.

"Jayce Burton, attorney at law."

"Jayce… It's Tucker." Silence. "Tucker Cahill."

"Tucker?"

"I'm back in town and I thought maybe—"

"Hell, yes. You're buying the first drink at Stacy's tonight. Forget that. I'll buy if you can make it in ten minutes. I'll call the boys."

Tucker had to laugh. Nineteen years had passed but with Jayce it was as if he'd only seen him yesterday. "Ten minutes and I'm buying." He hung up, glad he'd called.

Looking around the ranch house where he'd grown up, he felt as if he'd never left. Nothing had changed and yet he knew it had. *He'd* changed. But it sure felt as if time had stood still in Gilt Edge. The small Western town had grown some, mostly spread out more into the valley.

He couldn't help but wonder how staying here all these years had changed his once best friends. He was actually excited to see them all again. It felt as if a weight had come off his shoulders, learning the truth about Madeline.

He immediately felt guilty for the thought. Madeline was dead. She'd died that night in an attempt to con him out of money. Not that it made her any less dead. Or him feel any less guilty.

Even though Kate wanted him to, he couldn't hate Madeline. All he wanted to do now was put her and the past behind him. Seeing his old friends seemed like a good place to start.

"Tucker!" Jayce came rushing across the bar, a beer bottle already in hand, to give him a high five. "Damn, I can't believe it. We heard you were dead. Or in prison." He grinned to show that he was kidding and then pulled Tucker into a bear hug.

"It's great to see you. You haven't changed at all," he said, meaning it. Jayce was a tall, slim former cowboy turned lawyer. He still wore Western shirts and jeans but he'd traded his white Stetson for a Cubs baseball cap.

"Let's get you a beer. The others should be here soon," Jayce was saying as he steered him toward the bar. "When I called them, they thought I was kiddin'." His friend studied him for a long moment. "The way you left… Well, I was worried."

Fortunately, just then the front door opened and Cal Bertram and Lonny Pence came through the door. Cal had always been big when they'd played football together, but now he was even larger. He let out a whoop when he saw Tucker.

Tucker couldn't help but smile as Cal lumbered toward him. While they were the same height, Cal outweighed him by a good hundred pounds. Cal grabbed him around the waist and picked him up off the ground, laughing.

"I can't believe it," he kept saying as he set him down and cuffed his shoulder. "Where have you been?"

"Let's not get into that until we've all had a beer," Jayce cut in, turning to Lonny. "What are *you* having?"

Lonny said he'd take a beer. While the other two had seemed glad to see him, Lonny held back. Tucker got the feeling Lonny didn't want to be here and wouldn't have been unless Jayce had insisted.

"Lonny," Tucker said and held out his hand. "It's good to see you." While Jayce had been the star quarterback and the team captain, Tucker and Lonny had been backup quarterbacks, with Lonny spending much of his time on the bench. Lonny had never seemed to mind. He seemed to idolize Jayce, and since Tucker and Jayce were good friends, they all got along.

"Tuck." Lonny finally met his gaze. "I thought we'd heard the last of you."

Lonny was a little shorter than Tucker, slimmer built. At thirty-six, he'd grayed at the temples. While Jayce hadn't seemed to change at all, Lonny seemed...tired.

"So what are you doing now?" Tucker asked him.

"Just working the ranch and helping out at the body shop with Cal and Rip." Rip was Lonny's cousin. "You going to ranch with your brothers? Or are you leaving again?"

"Right now I'm just enjoying my family. I suppose you know Lillie is pregnant." He shook his head. "It's still hard to believe. She was only nine when I left. And Darby... He and his wife, Mariah, are also expecting. You have kids?"

"Two girls, but they live with their mother in Spokane, Washington."

The bitterness in his tone brought Tucker up short. "I'm sorry."

"It's not like it's your fault. You have any kids?"

Tucker shook his head. Fortunately, Jayce interrupted to say they should take a booth so they could all visit. Lonny accepted the beer Jayce handed him and took a long drink as the others stepped to the booth.

"You all right?" Jayce whispered to Tucker.

"Lonny seems...down."

"Been that way for years," his friend said, keeping his voice down so Lonny couldn't hear. "He married Annalise, you remember her? Cheerleader, tiny, top-heavy?"

Tucker got a sudden picture of her. "She had a really wide mouth, right?"

"That was her. Lonny was nuts about her. I think he still is," Jayce whispered as they slid into the booth where Cal was drumming his thick fingers on the table to a beat only he could hear.

But he smiled as Tucker slid in next to him and stopped

drumming to ask, "So what happened? You left so quick. You take that girl with you?"

Tucker blinked.

"Cal," Jayce said. "Give him a chance to enjoy his beer before you begin the inquisition."

"No, it's okay," Tucker said. "What girl?"

Cal shot Jayce a look and began drumming again as Lonny sat down.

Tucker saw Lonny look from Cal to Jayce. A silent message passed between them and his stomach dropped. The girl. These guys were with him that day in Denton when he'd met Madeline. He'd thought they hadn't seen her, hadn't known why he'd stayed behind. He'd thought they'd bought his story about running into an old friend. He'd told them he'd catch a ride back to Gilt Edge and that they should go on without him. Of course they'd seen through his ruse.

"You saw her that day," Tucker said.

"So we're finally going to be honest?" Lonny asked.

"Knock it off, Cal," Jayce snapped. Cal quit drumming and mugged a face.

"I didn't think it was still a secret," Cal said and picked up his beer. Clearly he was nervous and upset.

Jayce groaned and shook his head. "Tucker just got back."

Like that made a difference. "Okay," Tucker said, feeling like a fool. They all knew about Madeline. "So you all saw her. You all knew she was why I was staying behind that day. Why didn't you say something?"

Cal looked to Jayce, who was taking a drink of his beer.

"We all figured she was why you skipped town when you did," Cal said. "Ya knock her up?"

Jayce swore and put down his beer a little too hard on the table.

"Hey, we used to be best friends," Cal pointed out. "I can't ask him that?" he said to Jayce.

Tucker could feel the tension around the table. He felt as if he'd been left out of a private joke. "What's going on? Jayce?"

Another look went around the table. Lonny chuckled and took a long draw on his beer. He appeared to be enjoying this.

Tucker swore. "Tell me what the hell is going on."

Jayce glanced away for a moment. "Look, we knew you hadn't ever...so we—"

It was all he could do not to smack himself in the forehead. *"You set me up?"* He couldn't believe this.

"We'd heard about Madeline and figured..." Cal shrugged. "You were our friend. We were just trying to help you out."

"Thanks a lot." Tucker rubbed a hand over his face before picking up his beer and draining half of it. "How did you hear about her?"

Jayce looked to Lonny. "Didn't you say you knew someone who'd met her?"

"It was almost twenty years ago," Lonny said. "I can't remember. I thought Cal suggested her."

"No, I thought you said you got the name from your cousin," Jayce said to Lonny.

"Rip?" Tucker thought this couldn't get any worse. "It would have been nice if you'd given me a heads-up."

Cal picked at the label on his bottle of beer. "We figured you'd be embarrassed. What we didn't expect was that you'd fall for her. We wanted to warn you but then we'd have to admit what we did. So what happened to her?"

"She died in the creek next to the ranch nineteen years ago," he said.

All three men stared at him, openmouthed.

"The skeleton that was found? That was her?" Cal said. He huffed out a humorless laugh. "I heard she liked to swim naked. You think she was naked?"

Jayce swore. "Damn it, Cal. Could you be any more inappropriate?"

"We didn't all become uptight lawyers," Cal said and took a drink of his beer.

"I'm sorry, Tuck." Jayce shook his head. "We had no idea."

"But right by your house," Lonny said. "If that's why you left like you did, why did it take them so long to find her bones?"

Tucker finished his beer and got to his feet.

"Come on, don't go away mad," Lonny said, looking much happier than he'd been earlier when he'd come into the bar.

"I'm not mad," Tucker said.

Jayce got up and walked him to the door. "I don't know what to say. When you pulled away from all of us and someone said they saw you and her together…"

"You should have told me."

"I wanted to, but I was afraid it would ruin our friendship. As it was, I guess it did. When you came to me, asking if I would buy some of your stuff…"

"She was a con woman, Jayce. She turned me every way but loose and ultimately made me believe that it was my fault that she died that night."

"I had no idea. I just thought she was…you know, easy. I should never have gone along with it that day. I've regretted it for years."

"It's all water under the bridge, so to speak," Tucker said. "Thanks for the beer." He pushed open the door, just needing fresh air. All these years he'd believed he and Madeline had been fated as well as a secret lovers. He let out a bark of a laugh as he started toward his pickup. Could he have been any more a fool?

He'd only had one beer, but he decided a walk would do him good. He needed to clear his head. Everything he'd believed nineteen years ago had been wrong. Being young was one thing, but being trusting and blind…

The town was so quiet. He used to joke that Gilt Edge

sidewalks rolled up at eight o'clock every night. It wasn't far past eight and the streets were deserted. Right now, though, he couldn't get over what he'd learned. It had been a setup. His friends just helping the virgin among them.

He felt his face heat, and yet, at the same time, he couldn't be angry with them. He knew their hearts had been in the right place. It was their heads he wanted to slam together.

If Rip had told them about Madeline… It surprised him that Lonny would be the one who had heard about her. That didn't seem likely, but who knew how his friends had come up with Madeline. He was the fool who'd fallen for the woman, who apparently anyone could have had for the right price.

As he walked, he thought about what Kate had said last night at the restaurant as they were leaving. "Maybe she *did* love you." He'd known she'd said it to take the edge off some of the other things she'd said after dinner. But at the time, he'd thought maybe it was true.

He scoffed at that now. With Madeline it was just one lie after another. As a car pulled up next to him and slowed, he didn't look over, figuring it was probably Jayce or Cal or maybe even Lonny, wanting to rub more salt into the wound.

"Tucker!"

He stopped and turned to see Kate behind the wheel of her pearl-white SUV. She had the passenger-side window down and was leaning toward him.

"I need to walk," he said, not up to talking any more about Madeline tonight.

"Mind if I walk with you?"

He counted to ten. "I'm not really up for talking."

"Fine with me." She pulled over and parked. When she got out he saw that she was dressed as she'd been earlier. She seemed like a woman who changed clothes at least a couple of times a day. Maybe not. He wondered if she'd had as bad a day as he had.

She fell in beside him as they continued down the empty main street. A few cars passed in the darkness, but no one stopped. After a couple of blocks of not a word out of her, he pointed to a park just off the street.

The grass was damp already as they walked through it. He headed for the swings, remembering being a kid in this town and playing late into the night, so long that his father would have to drive around and find him and chastise him all the way home for worrying his mother.

He sat down on the first swing. Kate took the one next to him and pushed off with her feet as she began to swing back and forth. She smiled as she went higher and higher.

He pulled his swing back out of the way so he could watch her. Her smile broadened each time she managed to pump to a great elevation. He heard a giggle escape her, her head falling back, her long hair like a dark cloak behind her.

He couldn't help but smile, too, as he watched her lose herself in the simplest of childhood pleasures.

"My friends set me up with Madeline," he said when Kate returned to the present and, having quit pumping, slowed.

"What?" She dragged her feet to come to an abrupt stop to stare at him.

"They wanted to get me laid. Apparently I was the only virgin of our little group." It was hard to admit, but the darkness and the park helped. He breathed in the cold night air. "They didn't expect me to fall for her."

He was glad that Kate said nothing for a few minutes. She was sitting on the swing, making designs in the dust at her feet with the toe of her boot, when she said, "I didn't tell you what happened in the café. The waitress wants to meet with me. It seems she has information about the Dunn family."

When he said nothing, she looked over at him. "I called her. She knew Madeline. She'll tell me everything she knows as long as I'm willing to pay for the information and not use her name if I write about this."

"You're going to write about this?"

She shrugged.

He stood, letting go of the swing. "Do what you want, but I'm done. I don't want to know any more about Madeline or any of it."

"You don't want to go with me to meet the woman?" Kate asked as she caught up with him.

"No." He kept walking.

She grabbed his arm and spun him around to face her. "What do you want, then, Tucker Cahill? If not revenge, justice, closure? Tell me."

His gaze locked with hers in the starlight canopy over their heads. Her eyes widened as if she saw what he was feeling. "What I want?" He grabbed her shoulders and dragged her to him. He could see that she'd thought he was going to kiss her.

Instead, he pushed her long hair aside and pressed his lips to a warm, sweet spot just below her ear, then began to work his way down her slim throat.

"If you're trying to change my mind about going north to meet this woman tomorrow..."

He continued down slowly, planting kisses with small licks of his tongue. He deftly slipped loose the top button of her blouse with his fingers to trace the swell of her breasts above the lacy bra.

She shivered, but she didn't try to stop him. Was she waiting to see how far he would go? The idea intrigued him. If she wanted to see who blinked first, she was about to end up naked and—

"Tucker." Her voice sounded choked with emotion. When she stopped his hand from releasing the second button on her blouse, he felt her trembling.

His own heart was pounding. He knew exactly what he

wanted. His lips and tongue on her warm smooth skin. His face buried in the generous swell of her breasts. The hard pink nub of her nipple in his mouth. Just the thought of what he wanted to do to her drove him insane.

She pulled back and cast her gaze down as she rebuttoned her blouse. "I'm going north in the morning with or without you."

As if he hadn't known that. He said as much.

"Whatever this was…" She waved her hand through the air. She sounded as shaken as he felt. "You can't use your… charm to change my mind."

"That wasn't my charm," he said, aware of the ache low in his belly. "Anyway, I thought you could tell the difference between a man trying to seduce you and one who is trying to manipulate you."

She raised her gaze. Their eyes locked. "You think there is a difference?"

"Damn straight."

He saw her shiver before she said, "We might have to investigate that at some point."

"Promise?" he asked, only half teasing.

She tried to look away but he caught her chin and kept her gaze on his.

"There is a whole lot I want to investigate when it comes to you," he said. "I was only getting started a few minutes ago. Being around you—"

"I thought Madeline made you gun-shy?"

He let go of her chin. He knew she'd only brought up Madeline as a way of keeping him at arm's length. Apparently she was more afraid of whatever this was between them than even he was. Because of Madeline? Or had some man done a number on her?

"I'm still a man, Kate. Never doubt that." He turned and

started down the street, the growing, aching need almost painful.

"I know you say you're done with all this, but don't you want to know the truth?" she asked when she caught up to him.

"I already know the truth." He slowed some, making it easier for her to keep up, hoping she'd just drop this but knowing she wouldn't.

"I'm meeting her at some rest area between here and Clawson Creek."

He shook his head as he looked over at her. "You can't be serious."

"Five hundred dollars' worth of serious."

Tucker sighed. "You're just throwing your money away."

"Probably." She walked without looking at him. "But I will find Madeline's accomplice. If you don't care about justice—"

He let out an oath. "I'll go." He'd stopped walking so abruptly that she had to turn to look back at him.

"You're sure?"

"I can't let you go alone to some rest area in the middle of nowhere to meet some…more than likely flake who will just take your money, if not your life."

"Well, when you put it like that, I'm glad you've changed your mind and want to go with me." She smiled at him and got a sad smile from him. He could tell that she felt at least a little guilty for dragging him back into this.

He didn't know why he'd put up a fight against going with her. Had he really thought he could just walk away? As if he could walk away from this woman and not regret it.

Still, he cursed himself for getting in deeper with her. He didn't give a damn about Madeline or her accomplice. But Kate…

"I should get back to my hotel," she said. "I'll pick you up in the morning. Nine?"

"I'm walking you back to your car." She mugged a face at him and started to argue, but he quickly cut her off. "My pickup's back that way."

"Well, in that case..."

They walked a few yards. He could tell something was bothering her even before she came to a stop and turned in front of him to confront him.

"Tucker, I feel as if I've forced you to go with me tomorrow."

He let out a laugh. "You're good, Kate. But I'm a big boy. I don't do anything I don't want to." Their gazes held for a moment before she turned and started walking again. "And we've already established what *I* want."

She swallowed and continued to walk.

Tucker fell in beside her, the night feeling too intimate as they moved through the quiet town. This woman would be the death of him.

CHAPTER THIRTEEN

Kate was still trembling inside after what had happened in the park. The man evoked feelings in her…needs in her. She'd stopped him, knowing exactly where he'd had been headed. And right there in the park!

Worse, she'd wanted it. Why else had she conned him into going with her in the morning? She was furious with herself. Why had she told him about her meeting with Tammy Holden, anyway? Hadn't she known that he wouldn't let her go alone? Of course she had. Wasn't that why she'd told him, because she wanted him to go with her?

She shook her head. She'd always prided herself on her independence. She certainly didn't need Tucker to go with her tomorrow. But this had nothing to do with independence or that kind of need. This was a whole different matter and one that terrified her.

Going out with men like Peter had always been…safe. With those kinds of men there was no chance of losing her heart—let alone losing her mind. With Tucker, she feared it would mean total surrender—mind, body and soul.

The worst part was that now, back in her hotel room, she

ached for Tucker's touch again, afraid no other man would evoke such need in her. The realization made her even more angry with herself. Kate pulled out her phone, telling herself she would call him and tell him she was going alone.

The thought of hearing his voice...

Pocketing her phone without making the call, she told herself she'd just get up earlier and go without him. Putting that matter behind her, she got ready for bed. Once between the cool silken sheets, though, she knew the oblivion of sleep eluded her.

She kept feeling his warm fingers slowly unbuttoning her blouse. Only, when she closed her eyes, this time she didn't stop him. He both frightened and captivated her; she could admit it lying here alone in the dark. She desperately wanted to see not just how far he would go, but where she would let him take her.

Tucker was still too worked up to sleep. He stopped by the Stagecoach Saloon. He hadn't seen much of his family since he'd been back. He found Darby behind the bar. A country song played on the sound system, and he could smell burgers grilling in the back.

"Those burgers for that table over there?" he asked his brother, motioning to a table of six by the window. He could see that the place had been busy not long before this but it was late enough that most everyone had called it a night.

Darby grinned. "Go back to the kitchen and ask Billie Dee to throw another burger on for you. Just tell her what you'd like with it. How is it that you haven't met our authentic Texas cook?" his brother asked. "I guess it's because we haven't hardly seen you since you've been back." He quickly held up his hand. "No judgment. Honestly."

Tucker chuckled. "You sound like Flint." But he said it good-naturedly. "It's been kind of crazy since I returned."

"I would imagine it's an adjustment. Go order your burger and say hello to Billie Dee, then come back. What can I get you to drink?"

"Just a cola." As he approached the kitchen, he heard singing. He recognized the song as an old gospel hymn he'd heard when he spent some time down South. He waited until she finished. But before he could speak, she started in on another song. "Excuse me," he said, hating to interrupt her.

She spun around and her face instantly lit up. "Bless your heart. You must be Tucker." She hurriedly wiped her hands on her apron and rushed to give him a hug. He blinked in surprise and then had to smile. "I've heard so much about you. I was starting to think you were a figment of everyone's imagination. I'm so glad you're not." She pulled back to survey him. "You are just as handsome as Lillie said you were." She let out a wolf whistle and rushed back to the burgers on the grill.

"I'd love a burger, if it isn't too much trouble."

"Ah, honey, nothing is too much trouble for a Cahill." She opened the refrigerator, took out a patty and slapped it on the grill. "I'll holler when it's ready. What would you like with it?"

He told her to surprise him and Billie Dee laughed. She went back to her singing and Tucker returned to the bar smiling.

"You met Billie Dee," Darby said, his affection for the woman obvious. "Isn't she something? And, boy, can she cook. Wait until you taste her shrimp gumbo."

Tucker sat down at the bar. "You working all by yourself?"

"Mariah helped earlier, but she and Lillie are both about to go into labor any minute so we've picked up more help before the summer season. Ashley Jo Somerfield is one of our new ones. You'll meet her. I sent her home once it slowed down." A bell dinged down the hall in the kitchen. "I'll be right back."

Darby took off, returning with plates of burgers for the table of six.

Tucker took the time to look around the place, his heart swelling with pride in how well Lillie and Darby had done. That they were both married, expecting and obviously happy made him more glad than he could say. They'd done better than he had.

Darby stepped behind the bar again. "I just want to give you a heads-up. Lillie is planning a welcome-home party for you."

Tucker groaned.

"I know. But maybe you don't remember how she was at nine."

"Bossy, mouthy, stubborn to a fault?" he asked and laughed.

"Well, she is much worse now."

"When is this party?"

"Next Saturday, here. It's supposed to be a surprise, but I thought you'd appreciate knowing."

"Thanks." He studied his little brother for a long moment. "I remember you as a kid. You were always thoughtful and never caused any trouble."

"I left that to the rest of you."

"Flint told me about what happened—you and Mariah almost getting killed." Tucker shook his head. "Sounds like it was a close call."

Darby nodded. "But it's over and look how it's turned out. I'm about to be a father and Mariah..." His smile broadened.

"Sounds like you hit the jackpot in all kinds of ways." He turned on his bar stool. "This place is great."

"Lillie fell in love with this old stagecoach stop and was determined to save it. The saloon and café seemed like the perfect way to protect the building and make a living."

"You didn't want to ranch the family place?"

"Naw, I leave that to Cyrus and Hawk and maybe you?"

Tucker shrugged. He hadn't thought that far ahead.

"You know there is a place for you here, whatever you decide."

"Thanks, Darby."

Billie Dee brought out his burger. "I put a little something special on yours," she whispered with a wink and then was gone.

"Do I dare ask?" Tucker said to his brother, who quickly poured him a cola. He took a bite and laughed. "Unless I'm mistaken, that's a green chili and Mexican cheese in there." It was delicious.

After he finished his burger, Tucker went back to the kitchen while Darby closed up the saloon. "That was the best hamburger I've ever had in my life," he told Billie Dee, who was busy singing and cleaning up the kitchen. "I don't know what all you put on it, but it was amazing."

The heavyset Texan woman laughed heartily. "I thought you might like it. You've made your sister so happy to have you back. You know, she's so excited to have this baby. She wanted you here when that happened."

"I'm pretty excited about being an uncle myself."

"You have a good night, then," Billie Dee said. "Welcome home."

It wasn't until he went outside that he found the note tucked under the windshield wiper on his pickup. He looked around but saw no one.

The earlier group who'd had burgers had left a long time ago. He doubted any of them had left him a note.

Kate? He hoped it would be from her, but she wouldn't do anything so covert as leave a note under his wiper blade. She was more of an in-your-face kind of gal.

He knew he was just kidding himself. It was from the same

person who'd left the first one. He hesitated, then lifted the wiper blade and pulled out the note. He opened it in the glowing neon of the Stagecoach Saloon sign behind him and read. *Leave while you still have the chance.*

The handwriting was the same. Girlie. Did the writer want him to believe it was from Madeline? He shook his head. Maybe her ghost? Well, too bad. He didn't believe in ghosts and he was back, like it or not, and he wasn't leaving. As he slid behind the wheel, he crumpled the note and tossed it away. Only then did he catch the sweet once too familiar scent.

His heart began to pound. It had been nineteen years since he'd smelled that scent and the memory of it struck at gut level. The note had been scented with Madeline's perfume.

"Thought you'd leave me behind?" Tucker asked when Kate found him waiting outside her hotel the next morning earlier than their agreed-on time.

"I said I'd pick you up."

He grinned. "So you did. But I just had a feeling I should meet you here."

She'd been caught. Still, she lifted her chin in the air. "I got an earlier start than I thought."

"Uh-huh."

He had suspected exactly what she'd had planned. That he knew her that well gave her a strange feeling. It felt both intimate and dangerous. She gave up trying to convince him of her motives as she unlocked the SUV.

"Couldn't sleep?" he asked, amusement in his tone.

"I slept like a baby, I'll have you know." Another lie.

He merely grinned as she climbed behind the wheel and tossed her purse on the space between them. "I was hoping you'd changed your mind," he said as he pulled his door shut.

"I thought you knew me better than that."

"Oh, I know you," he said softly. Their gazes met and held.

She felt that stirring in her belly like something was waking up inside her again. She thought of last night, his mouth on her bare flesh… After a sleepless night she didn't want to go down that road.

He looked away as if he'd felt something, as well. "I guess if you're determined to throw away your money…"

"If she tells me where I can find Madeline's siblings, then it's worth every dime." When he said nothing, she turned the key and started the engine. "You don't have to come along."

"Yes, I do." That look again, the one that left her unsettled, that left her wanting.

"If it's to protect me—"

He laughed again. "I suspect if this woman tries to bamboozle you, you won't be the one who needs protecting."

She smiled and glanced down at her purse. "I can take care of myself." When she looked up, she saw her mistake reflected in Tucker's gray eyes.

Before she could stop him, he picked up her purse. His gaze widened as he felt its heft. She had started to pull out but now hit the brakes. But it was too late. He'd already pulled the pistol out, pointing it at the floorboard as he stared at her.

"What?" she asked as she took her foot off the brake and continued to pull out onto the street. She waited for the lecture she was sure was coming.

"Madeline's accomplice. You're planning to *kill* them."

"I wouldn't say planning."

Tucker shook his head. "Whoever helped Madeline isn't worth going to prison over for the rest of your life."

"What makes you think I would go to prison?"

"Even your father's high-paid lawyer—"

"Do we have to talk about this? Just put the gun back in my purse. Please."

He hesitated for so long she feared he might do something

crazy like throw it out the window. But after a moment, he checked to make sure the safety was on before he placed it carefully back into her purse. He set the purse down behind the seat, out of her reach.

"Did you have that with you yesterday?" he asked after a few miles of rolling foothills and mountains, dark green with towering pines.

"Yes, but you might have noticed, I didn't use it."

He shook his head and turned to look out at the passing landscape.

"Sorry you came along?" she asked after a few more miles.

"I'm sorry about a lot of things. Being with you isn't one of them."

That answer warmed her more than it should have.

"Where is this rest area where we're meeting this woman?" Tucker asked after they'd driven north for twenty minutes.

"It should be coming up soon. She apparently didn't want anyone in Clawson Creek to know that she was talking to me."

"Or she chose an isolated rest area in this part of the state because she figured it would be empty this time of year."

She seemed to ignore his sarcasm. "Her name is Tammy Holden, forty-one. She was born and raised in Clawson Creek, so she should know about the Dunn family. All she told me is that if I wanted to know about Madeline, then I should talk to her. She and Madeline would have been the same age."

He looked out the window, wondering what Madeline would have looked like now at forty-one if she had lived. That they could have had a son who was almost twenty blew his mind.

But there never had been a son, he reminded himself. No baby. All a lie. He ground his teeth just thinking about it and the perfumed note someone had left for him last night. And now he was on this road north again when he should be putting this whole thing behind him. He no longer needed closure, he told himself. He just needed peace.

He looked over at Kate and realized he'd never get it with her until she found the person who'd helped Madeline with her deception. But then what? Worse, why was he doing this? Did he really want to find Madeline's accomplice? Didn't he just want to put it behind him?

Kate reached over and turned on some music as if she could see him agonizingly playing it all over in his head—just as he'd done the past nineteen years. All the what-ifs. What if he'd done this or that? What if he'd done it all differently?

"Stop blaming yourself," she said as she drove.

He laughed. "How do I do that?"

"My brother loved her, too. Even when he found out that there had been others." She glanced over at him. "Even when he found out about you."

Tucker felt himself flinch at her words. This woman had known about him for nineteen years and yet he hadn't known she or her brother had existed. A part of him wished he'd left it that way.

It was that other part of him he was struggling with. Kate. He'd never met anyone like her.

"You really didn't know I was the one?"

She seemed startled by the question for a moment.

"Your brother's journal. He didn't know my first name?"

"No. All I had was Cahill. Like I said, I figured it had to be either Flint or you."

"The package was a nice touch, though." He wasn't about to admit how he'd reacted at the sight of that doll.

"I'm sorry about that. I had to know if you were the one. I thought you must be since you took off nineteen years ago.

Add to that Madeline disappearing, as well. Then I saw you on the bridge at the creek."

"And made me chase you down."

She nodded without looking at him. "I wanted more time to think about how to approach you. But you solved that problem quickly enough."

He stared at her profile. She was a striking woman, strong, determined. Her bow-shaped lips were turned up in a slight smile. He couldn't help but smile himself. What was he going to do with this woman? The thought stirred all kinds of erotic thoughts.

Tucker banished them as he recalled the gun in her purse. The fact that this could get dangerous hadn't escaped him— or her—for that matter. "Someone left me a message under my wiper blade on my pickup last night at the Stagecoach Saloon, which my brother and sister own. It wasn't the first one I've gotten. Someone wishes I hadn't come back. They want me to leave. They also want me to believe that Madeline is still alive." He didn't mention that extra touch—Madeline's favorite perfume.

Kate shot him a worried look. "That's ridiculous. They aren't trying to blackmail you, are they? Bastards," she said under her breath. "It wasn't enough to break men's hearts, take their money, deceive them. They want to drive you crazy? There is an inherent meanness in these people."

"We don't know that the whole family was involved," he pointed out. "What if Madeline had been forced to do what she had?"

"By whom?"

"Her father or brother."

Kate made an angry sound under her breath. "You just keep looking for excuses for her, don't you?"

"I'm trying to understand." He turned in his seat to look at her. "You loved your brother, respected him at some point, thought he wasn't stupid, am I right?" She nodded, though grudgingly, and he continued. "So how is it that your brother and I both fell for this woman? Isn't it possible that we saw some good in her? Yes, we were horny teens but why isn't it possible that there was something worth redeeming in her and that Clay and I recognized it?"

Kate shook her head. "If Madeline had cared about either of you, she wouldn't have done what she did. She broke my brother's heart, then she killed him as if she was the one who helped string him up."

Turning the radio up louder, she drove with that angry, determined look on her face. When her cell phone rang, she picked it up from where she'd laid it on the SUV's center console. He saw the name Peter flash as she checked it, then declined to take the call.

Until that moment, he hadn't realized that she had a man in her life. Of course she did. The thought was like a punch to the face. Who the hell was Peter?

The rest area was just where Tammy had said it would be. And it was just as deserted and empty as Tucker had said it would be. This one was nothing more than a men's and women's outhouse beside a paved parking area off the highway.

It was no surprise to her, since she'd already checked it out on the internet. Tucker seemed to think she was reckless. Not when it came to her job or her well-being or her heart for that matter.

She didn't leave things to chance. Nor did she take anyone's word for anything. Becoming an investigative journalist had been a no-brainer. She came by a healthy dose of skepticism naturally as well as a lack of trust in people.

Kate had also been able to confirm what Tammy Holden had told her. The woman's life was online and easily acces-

sible even if her Facebook account hadn't been open to everyone—which it had been.

Tammy was an open, though boring, book. From what
Kate had gathered online, the woman had married at least
once, had given birth to three offspring when she was still
quite young given their ages. Divorced at least once, she lived
with her mother in Clawson Creek and had at least two grand-
children she was raising. At forty-one, she worked at the café
and seemed to be the sole support of her household.

"You'll be lucky if she shows," Tucker commented.

"She'll show. I have five hundred dollars that say she will."

He chuckled at that. "Good point."

She pulled into the empty rest area and glanced at the clock
on the dash. They were early. Still, she worried that this trip
wouldn't be worth even close to five hundred dollars. Worse,
she'd invited Tucker along only to get into an argument with
him again.

As she turned the SUV so she could see the highway from
Clawson Creek, she glanced over at him, feeling guilty. "I'm
sorry."

"You can quit saying that since there is no reason to be
sorry about the way you feel."

"I'm not sorry about that. I'm sorry I make this harder for
you."

He smiled over at her. "Actually, it is just the opposite."

Parked, she turned the key. The only sound was the *tick,
tick, tick* of the cooling engine.

"Was I the only one your brother knew about?" he asked
after a moment.

"Yes, but she told Clay there were others and there would
be more. She made it sound like she had no choice. So of
course he thought he could save her from this life." She shook
her head, surprised that after all this time she still felt tears
burn her eyes.

"How do your mother and father feel about what you're doing?" he asked, his gaze on the empty highway.

"They disapprove." That was putting it mildly. "They want to put it behind them. They're good at that. They seem to be able to pretend that Clay is away at university or off working in Africa. I'm…not so good at pretending. It's one of my many flaws."

"I'd love to hear more about your many flaws," Tucker said.

But from up the road, she saw an older-model large brown car headed their way. Her pulse quickened as she realized she was closer to finding out the truth than she'd ever been in the past nineteen years.

CHAPTER FOURTEEN

The large car seemed to float on the horizon, followed by a dark cloud of smoke. The sound of its engine reaching them before Tucker could see the figure behind the wheel.

As the woman braked and pulled into the rest area, the sun gleamed dully off the weatherworn brown paint of her older-model car.

"Ready?" Kate asked before opening her door.

He grunted in answer, dreading what this woman was going to tell them. Kate was right. He wanted to believe that Madeline had been forced into doing what she had. Being a liar was one thing. Being a coldhearted, conniving bitch was another. But he feared that the only person who knew the truth was dead. Then again, Kate was right. Someone had helped Madeline with her con. That person would be just as guilty as Madeline.

Waves of heat rose from the rest area's dark pavement. Spring had come to Montana with a vengeance.

Tammy Holden sat behind the wheel of her car as they approached. Was she going to change her mind and take off without a word? Not if she wanted the five hundred dollars Kate had brought her.

The woman seemed to hesitate before she finally opened her car door and slowly climbed out. She looked around as if she thought she might have been followed—or that *they* had. But from this wide spot along the highway, they could see for miles. The road both ways was empty. It wasn't like this stretch of pavement ever got much traffic.

More to the point, what did the woman have to fear? Were people that afraid of the Dunns?

"Thank you for coming," Kate said. Tammy nodded and looked at Tucker. "This is Tucker Cahill."

Like him, he figured Kate was looking for a reaction to his name. How much did this woman know about Madeline and her…business?

But Tammy's face remained expressionless as she gave him a nod. "You bring the money?"

Kate reached into her pocket and brought out five one-hundred-dollar bills. She thumbed them, pocketed them again and said, "Why don't we talk in my car?"

Tammy licked her lips, looked toward the large SUV and said, "I can't stay long. I have to work an early shift today."

The three of them walked to the rig. Kate opened the side door. "I think we'll be comfortable in here so we can see each other." She climbed into the third-row bench seat, leaving the other two second-row seats for them.

Tammy seemed again to hesitate, then got in, taking the far seat. Tucker left the door open as he took the other seat, and Kate showed them how to swivel their chairs so the seats faced each other.

Cozy as it was, Tammy looked uncomfortable and anxious to get this over with—take her money—and leave. "What do you want to know?" she asked the moment they were settled in.

"You said you knew Madeline and her family," Kate began. "What was she like?"

The woman shrugged. "Strange like the rest of her family."

Tucker groaned inwardly. "In what way?"

"Odd," the woman said.

"Tammy, I need more than that for five hundred dollars," Kate said.

"I don't know what you want me to say. They moved to town when I was sixteen. Bought the lumberyard. Built that huge place outside town. It was like a castle with a moat."

"A moat?" Tucker asked suspiciously.

"Well, not a real moat, but a rock wall around it and two vicious dogs that kept people out. You should have heard the stories she told me about what went on in that house." The woman's painted-on eyebrows shot up.

"What *did* go on in that house?" Kate asked.

"Her father was some sort of religious nut who woke them up in the middle of the night to pray. Her parents fought all the time. Her father was so cheap they barely had enough to eat. He held late-night séances with the devil. It was enough to make my hair stand up on end."

"Late-night séances with the devil?" Tucker asked sarcastically.

"At least that's what Madeline told me."

Tucker shot Kate a look. "And you believed her."

"Her father wouldn't let the girls go to public school. Not good enough for them. Fine for the son, but the girls were homeschooled. At least that's what everyone was told. Of course that was before the crazy awful mother died."

"Wait, so if Madeline didn't go to school, when did you ever see her if the house was such a fortress?" Tucker asked.

"She'd escape and come to my house," Tammy said. "She liked to borrow my clothes because hers were so awful. Long skirts, dresses, nothing cute, let alone low cut. Later she got a job at the café part-time. Her father would drop her off and pick her up." She shuddered. "He had these weird eyes. Possessed is what everyone said. He was always watching her, she said. He told Madeline that if he ever caught her with a boy, he'd lock her in that house and never let her out."

"So he was protective," Kate cut in.

"And with good reason. Madeline was always flipping her long blond hair and making cow eyes at the men who came into the café so she got bigger tips."

Kate smiled. "She have a lot of boyfriends?"

"Never in town. Her father wouldn't allow it. That's why she was always sneaking off when her father was away on business to meet boys, then coming back to the café and bragging about what they gave her."

"You ever see her wearing a diamond pendant?" Kate asked.

"Pendant?"

Kate described it to her and the woman nodded.

"A family heirloom?" Tucker asked quietly, and Kate nodded without looking at him. He guessed Clay had given it to her.

"She wore it one day at the café. But I didn't believe it was really a diamond and it made her mad. She didn't wear it after that because nobody believed her. When I asked her about it, she said her brother stole it and pawned it in Great Falls."

"So they were poor?" Tucker asked, hating the picture Tammy was painting of the Dunn family, let alone Madeline. He still wanted to believe that someone else might have been behind the con and that Madeline had been a victim as much as he had.

"Poor?" The woman let out an unpleasant sound. "Rich as sultans."

Kate wondered how many sultans this woman had known. "How do you know they were rich?" She'd found *rich* meant a lot of different things to a lot of different people. She couldn't help sounding skeptical. *Rich* to this woman could mean just about anything.

"That huge house. Madeline said her father was a businessman, but some people in town thought he was some kind of criminal."

Kate just bet they did.

"No one but family was allowed inside."

"So you were never invited out there?" Tucker asked.

Tammy shook her head. "Like I would go." She shuddered. "It was worse for her sisters."

"Sisters?" Tucker asked and looked at Kate as if she'd forgotten that it appeared Madeline had a twin.

"You knew them, too?" Kate asked.

"They were too afraid of their father to sneak out, Madeline said. I would see them at the upstairs window sometimes when I'd go over there and hide in the bushes until Madeline came out. My mama would have licked me good if she'd known I did that. I wasn't supposed to go near that place."

"But you saw her sisters," Kate prodded.

Tammy nodded enthusiastically. "One of them would wave, then quickly get away from the window so she didn't get in trouble." Looking at her watch, she said, "I really have to go pretty soon."

"Did she have any other friends?" Kate asked.

"Not that I know of. Just her sisters and me."

"How many sisters did she have?" Kate asked.

"Two. Misty and Melody."

"Misty?" Tucker said. "We went out to her grave."

Tammy looked away. Suddenly she appeared nervous. "Don't like speaking of the dead. They say she killed herself, but I wouldn't know anything about that."

"But you just said you saw the sisters occasionally," Kate

pointed out. "Surely you would have heard if one of the sisters died."

"Yes," she said, glancing again at her watch. "We heard stories. Heard her father pushed her down the stairs. Also heard she was found hanging in her room."

Kate tried not to shudder. "People thought he'd killed his own daughter?"

Tammy shrugged.

"So where is Madeline's father now?" Tucker asked.

The woman shook her head. "No one knows what happened to any of them. One day they all disappeared. The house was empty and they were gone as if they'd never existed. Heard the father got a job back East." She shrugged again. "Most everyone just thought good riddance and were glad to see them go."

"Back to the sisters," Tucker said. "Madeline and Misty were twins?"

"Identical twins?" Kate asked.

Tammy looked confused.

"Did Madeline look exactly like her sister Misty?" Kate asked.

"They all looked alike."

"What do you mean they all looked alike?" he asked.

"The sisters. They were triplets. I really have to go." Tammy pushed out of her seat. Tucker moved to let her exit the SUV and Kate quickly followed. As she passed him, she mouthed, "There are *three* identical Madelines?"

"So you have no idea where we can find her brother?" Kate asked once they were all outside the SUV.

Tucker could see that Tammy was ready to roll. She shifted on her feet and kept looking at her watch. "K.O.? Last I heard, someone said they saw him working in a bar in The Gap. But that was a while back."

"What about her sister Melody?" he asked.

"Probably with him wherever he is. They were close, you know?" He didn't know and asked what she meant. "All cut from the same cloth, as my mother used to say." Tammy shrugged. "Listen, I need the money now. I have to get to work. If I'm late, they'll suspect somethin'. You don't know how people talk in small towns."

Tucker had a pretty good idea after growing up in Gilt Edge. "Why wouldn't people talk to us about the Dunns?"

"Everyone's afraid of them. And that house out there?" Tammy rolled her eyes. "People say they've seen lights on at night, but the electricity is off. They say it's haunted by Misty Dunn." She shivered.

Kate took the bills from her pocket and handed them to her. The money disappeared into Tammy's pocket in a blur.

"You didn't know Madeline was a triplet, huh," Tammy said. "It was so eerie seeing all three of them together since their father forced them to dress alike, even wear their hair the same. I saw them once in their yard. I couldn't tell them apart. It gave me a funny feeling, you know what I mean?"

"I think I do," Tucker said.

With that, she headed for her car, leaving the two of them staring after her dumbfounded. A few moments later the engine coughed a few times, finally caught and, the muffler dragging, Tammy Holden drove away in a cloud of exhaust.

Tucker watched her until the vehicle went from a speck against the open landscape to nothing. Even the gray exhaust blowing out the back dissipated into the Montana spring day before he looked over at Kate.

Billie Dee felt antsy. Henry had said he would help her. But she was used to helping herself. She knew she wouldn't rest until she knew the truth about Ashley Jo.

How many times had she looked into the faces of young

women on the street—always searching for that one face? A familiar face that could be her daughter's? And then Ashley Jo had walked in.

Billie Dee had to know. She'd come into work early, feeling like a thief as she made her way to the file cabinet. Darby kept the employment information on his employees locked, but she knew where he kept the key.

Moving through the near dark of early morning, she walked toward the front of the building. Normally, she loved this time of the morning when the place was deathly quiet.

But now it gave her the heebie-jeebies. Moving behind the bar, she found the shelf. The small metal box was at the very back. She doubted anyone other than Lillie and Mariah even knew it was there. Darby never took it out except when he thought no one was watching.

That made Billie Dee feel even more guilty. She was always watching. It was a bad habit, one she'd picked up when she'd had a killer after her.

Reaching into the back of the shelf behind packages of bar napkins, she pulled out the metal box. For a moment she feared it would be locked, that Darby had taken an extra precaution since hiring an employee he didn't know.

But the box opened without any problems. The key lay in the bottom along with other extra keys to the place. This key was small and silver.

She picked it up, surprised how icy cold it felt. As icy cold as her heart right now. Why hadn't she asked Darby about Ashley Jo? But she knew the answer to that.

Billie Dee didn't want him questioning why she wanted to know. Or making anyone suspicious of her motives.

Feeling as if time was running out, she hurried down the hall to the file cabinet. Her fingers shook so hard that at first she couldn't get the key in the lock. Good thing she hadn't gone for a life of crime since she was so bad at this.

Finally the key slipped into the lock; she turned it, took a breath and pulled out the drawer she knew held the employment applications.

Ashley Jo's was at the front. Her heart pounding, she withdrew it. For a moment, she couldn't bring herself to open it. What if the birth date was wrong? What if it was right?

Regretting what she'd done, Billie Dee still couldn't stop now. She opened the folder. Her gaze quickly took in the basic information until it lit on age.

Twenty-six.

Her heart threatened to beat out of her chest. Twenty-six.

She hurriedly looked for a birth date. Her head swam and she had to reach for the back of a nearby kitchen chair to steady herself.

But then she saw that the date was wrong. It should have been March 13, 1992. But the date read March 15, 1992.

She stared at it, heart dropping. Ashley Jo couldn't be her daughter unless…unless the wrong birth date had been put on the birth certificate.

At the sound of a vehicle, she quickly put the folder back, slammed the file cabinet and hurried to the bar to return the key. She'd just pulled out the small metal box when she heard the sound of the garbage truck as it lifted the huge containers next to the building.

The key safely in the box, the box back where she'd found it, Billie Dee began to breathe normally again. All the way back to the kitchen, though, she felt guilty. Her religious upbringing, she thought, knowing it was much more than that.

She'd been guilt-ridden for twenty-six years.

"Triplets?" Kate said the word like a curse. "Just when I thought it couldn't get any worse. There were *two* more of them?" Standing in the middle of the rest area parking lot,

she looked over at Tucker as if in shell shock. "I know what you're thinking."

"I don't even know what I'm thinking," he said truthfully. His phone rang. He hadn't realized that he'd turned it back on since this morning. He pulled it from his pocket, saw it was Flint and declined the call. His gaze settled again on Kate. She was shaking her head, looking sick.

"Three Madelines?"

"Not anymore," he said. "Sounds like it's down to one."

"One is too many," she said under her breath.

He looked toward the horizon, trying to get his balance. It was as if the earth had tilted on him again. Since the day he'd met Madeline, he'd been off-kilter. He wondered if the ground under him would ever feel stable again, because after getting the note on his pickup, it was clear that they weren't through with him.

"You think they were all in on it and that this last Madeline might be the one," she said as if capable of reading his mind.

He turned his gaze away from the horizon to look at her. "There were times when Madeline seemed so distant, as if..."

"As if she wasn't the same person." Kate nodded, her jaw tight.

"Did your brother—"

"He said he never knew which Madeline he would see, the one who loved him, or the one who just wanted money from him."

He stared at her. "Was it possible he knew they were triplets?"

Kate shook her head. "He didn't even know she had a sister from what I've read in his journal. He thought it was just her, her brother, father and mother." She sighed. "So you think all three of them could have been working together. Then Madeline drowns, Misty kills herself and Melody... What does Melody do?"

Tucker shook his head.

"She leaves Clawson Creek in the middle of the night with her father and brother, never to be seen again."

"It looks that way," he had to agree.

Neither of them said anything for a few long moments.

"Are you going to be all right?" Kate finally asked, breaking the silence between them.

He nodded and met her gaze. "What about you?"

She shrugged.

"It's possibly sadder than even I thought." He'd told Kate the truth. More than anything, he simply felt sad for all of them because of Madeline, no matter how many there had been of them. But to think that one of them was still out there that looked exactly like the woman who'd… Who'd what? Turned him every way but loose? Sent him running from his home and family for nineteen years? Filled him with guilt that he still hadn't been able to throw off?

Or worse? What had Madeline done to him? Maybe more than he wanted to admit, because for all those years, he'd protected his heart as if wrapping it in cast iron.

But Kate had split that iron shell wide-open and left him vulnerable again.

"So we find the last Madeline," she said as if still tapping into his thoughts. "You aren't going to pretend that you don't want to, are you?"

"I don't want to. Like I told you before, I want to put all of this behind me. I only came up here with you today for backup."

She stared at him as if she didn't believe him. "You aren't curious about the last Madeline?"

"You ever hear the expression about curiosity and cats?"

Kate laughed and shook her head. "You're only kidding yourself. There is no way you can let this go."

"You might be surprised." He started for her SUV. When

he reached it, she was still standing where he'd left her. Only she didn't look like the confident, determined woman he'd come to know. She looked as if all this was wearing her down. He knew the feeling.

"Come on, I'm buying lunch at the Stagecoach Saloon," he called to her.

She walked slowly, the shock of what they'd learned no doubt like another weight she had to carry. Melody could be the Madeline who'd pushed her brother over the edge. She could also be the one he'd fallen for. She was the last person Tucker wanted to find.

Now more than ever he just wanted to forget the whole thing. No good would come of finding Melody Dunn. But he feared Kate wasn't giving up. As she reached the SUV, he could see the determined set of her shoulders and that need for vengeance burning in her gaze again.

He couldn't do this anymore. But if he stopped, that would mean letting Kate go on alone. He wasn't sure he could do that, either.

CHAPTER FIFTEEN

Kate wanted to lick the bowl. She hadn't realized how hungry she was until Tucker's brother set the chili in front of her. The aroma alone made her stomach growl loudly. She'd looked up to find Tucker smiling at her. He had a great smile. When he turned it on her like that, her stomach fluttered and she found herself wanting to bask in that smile always.

"So you liked the chili?" he asked now, humor in his tone.

She finished scraping up the last of it and licked her spoon. "I've never had chili like that."

"It's because you've never had Billie Dee's Texas chili," Darby said with a laugh from where he was behind the bar. She'd liked Tucker's brother immediately.

"How many handsome cowboys are there in your family?" she asked, embarrassing both men.

"Just me and Tucker," Darby joked. "Flint, Cyrus and Hawk…" He shook his head. "Can't hold a candle to us. But I wouldn't mention that to them."

Kate loved the easy banter between the brothers as well as the atmosphere of the saloon. It helped her relax after the day she'd had. When Darby's very pregnant wife, Mariah, came into the bar, Kate was taken with the love she saw between husband and wife.

"When is your baby due?" she asked.

"Any minute." Mariah smiled at her husband. "And it can't come soon enough."

"She can't have the baby until Lillie has hers," Darby explained before seeing Mariah upstairs so she could lie down to rest. "My sister is determined that they will go into labor at the same time. If you knew my sister..."

"You need another bowl of chili?" Tucker asked as Kate watched Darby leave.

"They are so in love," she said and then realized he'd asked her a question. "More chili? Don't tempt me." She pushed her bowl away so she wouldn't weaken. "You are so lucky to have such a large loving family."

He reached over and took her hand, squeezing it gently. "I wish you'd give up this quest of yours."

She smiled. "But you know I can't."

"Can't or won't?"

Kate shrugged. "Does it matter? I have to do this, but I won't drag you into it again, though. I'm sorry. I saw how hard today was on you. But I have to ask. Aren't you even a little curious about Melody Dunn, 'the last Madeline'?"

He withdrew his hand, making her sorry she'd asked. "The woman on the bridge that night is dead. Given the date of Misty's suicide, I suspect she was the one who was there to drag her near-dead sister from the creek that night. She must have been horrified to see her sister's head wound and realize she was about to die.

"Since we all know how that ended, it was probably why she killed herself. So much tragedy. Finding Melody won't bring your brother back or change anything that happened. As far as I'm concerned, it's over."

"What if Melody is your Madeline?" She hated the catch she heard in her voice. Tucker heard it, too.

He gave her a pitying look. "I'm not chasing a ghost. Not anymore. Madeline is dead. That part of my life is behind me."

"I hear the words," she said as she looked into his gray eyes. "But I wonder if Madeline will ever be truly gone. And now that you know there is another one out there…" She shook her head. "You are going to be looking for her in every woman you pass on the street. She isn't through haunting you." As she said it, she realized that made her heart ache.

She'd gotten too close to this man. Madeline would always be his first love. He would always measure every woman against that distorted "Madeline" image. "A woman would be a fool to fall for you," she heard herself say. "How could she ever measure up?"

With that, she stood abruptly and headed for the ladies' room before she began to cry.

"Where's Kate?" Darby asked when he returned from going upstairs to check Mariah.

"Ladies' room." Tucker was still shocked by not just Kate's words but the emotion as well as the truth in them. He'd held every woman he'd met in the nineteen years he was gone up to some standard that was pure fantasy. Madeline had been a con woman. She hadn't loved him. She'd only been after his money. And it wasn't as if she was some siren who had amazing seduction skills. That's why she only hit on teenage boys.

It didn't matter if there were three of them or a half dozen. None of the so-called Madelines had been in it for the love. For the thrill? Maybe. For the money? Absolutely.

He reminded himself he didn't even know that was the case. Madeline could have acted alone. They had no proof that even her sisters had been involved. And yet…

He swore under his breath as he moved from the table where he and Kate had been sitting to the bar.

"Rough day?" Darby asked after waiting on one of the regulars at the other end of the bar. This time of the afternoon, the bar was relatively quiet, but his brother said it would be picking up soon.

"Interesting, confusing day."

"Well, this news will probably make it better. Trask called. Lillie's in labor. I don't think Mariah is far behind. Which means Lillie might have to cancel your surprise party Saturday here at the saloon. Surprise!"

He laughed. "I can only hope."

"But it will only be postponed. Remember that determined little sister you used to have? She was nothing like the grown-up version when it comes to stubbornness and determination."

"I know someone like that," Tucker said, thinking of Kate and her reaction minutes ago.

"So the party will happen at some point. You should bring Kate."

"Not a good idea."

His brother studied him openly. "So what's with you and the reporter?"

He thought about that for a moment and chuckled. "I have no idea. Half the time, she drives me crazy. The other half..." He laughed and shook his head.

"I see."

"You don't see anything," Tucker snapped good-naturedly. "It isn't like that."

"Right."

He watched his brother wash glasses for a moment. "I like her, that's all. Well, most of the time. She certainly speaks her mind enough. You don't have to ask her for her opinion."

Darby was laughing. "You're preaching to the choir. So

what you're saying is that she intrigues you, infuriates you, entices you, captivates you, tempts you."

"I wouldn't put it that way exactly."

His brother grinned at him. "Any way you want to put it, you're falling for her. I know the symptoms well."

"No," Tucker said, shaking his head while at the same time remembering the dream he'd had. "Most of the time, she doesn't even like me." At the sound of Kate's footfalls, he slid off the stool and reached for his wallet.

"Put that away," Darby said. "My treat."

Tucker started to argue, but his brother insisted.

"Trust me, I enjoyed your lunch as much as the two of you apparently did," Darby said, still grinning.

Kate said her goodbyes as Tucker waited. He could see that his brother liked her. Most people did, he suspected. Except maybe people she was browbeating information out of, like Carly Brookshire and that bartender in Clawson Creek.

"I got to meet Billie Dee," Kate said as she slid behind the wheel of her SUV. "I had to compliment her on her chili. What fun she is." She shot him a look as she started the engine. "Look, if I stepped over the line earlier with what I said—"

"No, but you're wrong," Tucker said. "I'm over Madeline. It's why I don't want to pursue this anymore."

She nodded, but he could see that she wasn't buying it. They didn't talk the rest of the way to her hotel where he'd left his pickup.

"Good luck," he said after she'd parked and he'd gotten out in front of the hotel. "Since there is nothing I can say to stop you, just be careful."

Her smile was sad. "It was nice knowing you."

Suddenly he couldn't stand the thought of never seeing her again. "We could have chili at the Stagecoach again sometime. If you're still around."

Her smile made his heart ache. "I don't think so," she said as she turned and started to head toward the hotel.

"My sister was throwing me a surprise welcome-home party Saturday. But now she's in labor. Whenever the party is…go with me."

She turned to look back at him and laughed. "Not much of a surprise."

"Seriously," he said as he closed the distance between them. "I want you to go with me."

"All right. Family can be…too much sometimes, huh? You need me to run interference."

"That would be nice. I've managed to dodge a lot of the questions, and if I know my sister, she'll corner me unless I have protection."

"Shall I bring my gun?"

"Definitely not," he said. "I don't want you to come for that reason alone."

"No?"

"No. I can't stand the thought of not seeing you again."

She brightened. "Then I guess I'll see you Saturday. Or whenever your sister is back on her feet." She was smiling as she turned and walked away and he realized he was, too.

Back in her hotel room, Kate felt like a balloon buoyed by the wind. One minute she was up and soaring, like when Tucker had asked her to his surprise party. The next, she was plunging toward earth, like when he'd told her he was through looking for the Dunns, through working with her. The day had been long and disturbing to say the least. She would go on but without Tucker. She didn't need his help. But she couldn't deny that she would miss his company.

At times like this, she needed a hot shower, she told herself. She was surprised how close she was to tears again. As she started to head for the shower, she realized that her phone had been off most of the day after she'd gotten that call this morning from Peter, and she hadn't bothered to check it since. She pulled out her cell.

If she was hoping that Tucker might have called to say he'd changed his mind about helping in her search for K.O. and Melody, she was even more disappointed. The only calls were from Peter, three of them. And her mother. *Six* of them in the last half hour? That was a lot even for Mamie Rothschild. She listened to the last message.

"You need to call me. It's urgent." Her mother sounded breathless, maybe a little more than usual.

Urgent with her mother could mean just about anything, though. Maybe she didn't have anything to wear to some political bash. Or maybe she needed the name of the caterer they'd once used. Or maybe it really was an urgent matter that did require Kate to return her call.

She punched in the number and waited for the phone to ring. Usually her mother picked up quickly. Especially if it really was urgent.

Kate was starting to worry when after five rings her mother finally answered. "Katherine, thank God you called. It's your father. He's had a heart attack."

"Where is he?" All she could think was DC and how she was going to get there quickly.

"Here in Helena. He flew in last night. I told you he was coming home because… Well, you know why. He was upset…" Her mother burst into tears. "What are we going to do?"

"I'll leave now. I should be there in a few hours. Are you at the hospital?"

"No, I wanted to wait for you. You know I'm not good at things like this."

Her mother could plan a dinner for over a hundred, put together a fund-raiser for thousands, but even when Clay and

Kate were little, she couldn't handle putting a Band-Aid on them if they were bleeding.

"Sit tight, I'm on my way." She disconnected and called the hospital but could find out nothing about her father's condition. As she threw a few things in a bag and headed for the door, she texted Tucker.

Family crisis. Headed home. Thanks again for lunch and everything. She hit Send before she could change her mind.

In the car, she used the Bluetooth system to call her father's personal assistant. Peter's phone went straight to voice mail. She swore and left a message. "Call me. It's Kate."

As Tucker drove away from the hotel toward the ranch, he knew he couldn't keep dodging Flint's calls. But there was something he needed to do first.

Jayce looked up in surprise as Tucker walked into his office. The front door was open and no receptionist was at her desk. He was beginning to wonder if Jayce had a receptionist at all.

"Tuck." Jayce was on his feet, but after a few steps he stopped. "Look, if you want to punch me, let's step out back. Hate to get my blood on the carpet in the office. We just had it redone." He smiled to show that he was joking.

"I don't want to punch you."

"Whew, I'm glad to hear that. You look like you've been working out the past twenty years—unlike me, who's been sitting behind a desk."

"I wanted to talk to you," Tucker said. "You have a minute?"

"Sure." He motioned him in, offering him a chair, before he said, "I'm sorry about the other night. I was so glad to see you. I wish Cal hadn't brought all that stuff up. But at least now it's out in the open."

Tucker nodded as he took a chair. "Were you aware that Madeline Dunn had sisters?"

"That was her name?" He shook his head. "I didn't know her at all. It was Lonny. He said Rip knew of a girl who hung around Denton after games—blonde, pretty, available for a price. So we all chipped in." He shrugged. "Remember? Your birthday was coming up."

"I know you didn't do it maliciously," Tucker said. "But you still should have told me."

"Truthfully, I didn't know you were still seeing her until it was too late."

"Is Rip still around?"

"Took over his father's auto shop. Cal works down there. Lonny helps out there, too."

"Maybe I'll stop by and talk to him," Tucker said, getting to his feet.

"I guess I don't understand what it is that you're looking for," his friend said. "Isn't it over?"

Tucker sighed. "The problem is, it doesn't feel over." He thought about the notes he'd found under his windshield wiper. "Not everyone is glad I'm back. As for what I'm looking for?" He shook his head. "I guess I'll know when I find it."

Tucker found Rip working at the body shop, just as Jayce had told him. Rip was a jovial large rounded man who looked as if he belonged in a fraternity-house-party movie. In his early forties, he still had a boyish, florid face and an infectious laugh. He was the guy you paid to buy you beer when you were underage. So it wasn't much of a surprise that he would have known about young women of ill repute back in the day.

"Tucker, my man!" he said when he saw him. Wiping the grease from his hands on a rag, he strode to him, gave him a high five and a complicated handshake that involved a hip bump, which ended in Rip laughing heartily at how inept Tucker was at it.

"Never thought I'd see you again. So you're back? You need a place to stay, I know a guy…"

Tucker had to smile. Rip always knew a guy who could provide you with whatever you needed. "Actually, I wanted to ask you about Madeline."

Rip frowned for a moment. Tucker saw him glance toward where Lonny was leaning under the hood of a car with a crushed fender. He didn't see Cal anywhere around.

"The woman you suggested for me my senior year."

"Did I?" Rip said with a laugh and another look at Lonny.

"I believe Lonny was the one who asked you about her," Tucker said, even more convinced that Lonny had already told Rip about Cal letting the cat out of the bag at the bar the other night. "Madeline?"

"Madeline," Rip said. "Doesn't ring any bells but I'm sure the boys were just looking out for you."

Tucker nodded, wishing they had been looking out for him and never set him up with a con woman, but he kept that thought to himself. They were little more than kids who never thought much about consequences.

"You don't happen to know her last name, do you?" He was fishing, pure and simple, as he tried to make sense out of who knew what.

Rip looked startled by the question. "*You* don't know it? Didn't you leave town with her?"

"No. That body that was found in the creek?"

"The woman who drowned?"

He didn't correct him. "It looks like it was her."

"No kidding?" Rip sounded surprised. Tucker didn't think any of this had come as a surprise, though, given the way Rip kept looking in Lonny's direction.

"I thought maybe you might remember her last name since you were the one who apparently suggested her to Lonny," Tucker prodded.

Rip frowned. "I've suggested a lot of girls to Lonny," he said with a laugh. "But I thought it was Cal who asked me about a girl for you." He shrugged. "It's been too many years. Madeline. Now that you mention it, I think I do remember her."

Lonny appeared even more intent with whatever he was doing under the hood of the car in the next bay.

"Her last name was short, funny." Rip leaned his head back and looked at the ceiling.

"She told me her name was Ross."

Rip shook his head. "She called herself a lot of different names. No, it was… Dunn. That was it. Dunn. I only remember because it was so close to the word *dung*." He shrugged as if apologizing. "You two sure hit it off."

Tucker said nothing.

"Madeline Dunn." Rip chuckled. "I do remember her. I always wondered what happened to her."

"You have any idea where she was from?"

"North of Denton, though that's where she spent most of her time. Some town up there… Clark Creek. No, Clawson Creek, that's it. Wow, I haven't thought about her in years. You say she's dead? Too bad. But then a girl like her…" He shook his head.

Tucker's cell phone rang. He saw that it was Flint—and it wasn't his first call today.

"I should let you get that. I need to get back to work, anyway," Rip said. "Good to see you, Tuck. If you ever need any bodywork…" He raised his arms to take in the shop. "Hell, if you ever need anything, I'm your man."

Kate didn't know that Peter had flown home with her father until the two came through the front door of the Helena ranch house. She went straight to her father.

"Don't fuss over me," Clayton Rothschild insisted. "It was nothing. I'm as strong as a horse. Isn't that right, Peter?"

Peter had been standing off to one side. As she turned her gaze on him, she saw that he'd been staring at her.

"I'm going up to see your mother," her father said. "Give you two a moment to talk."

Kate could have told him that she and Peter had nothing to talk about, but she saved her breath. Her father had such high hopes that she and Peter would hit it off. After a few dates, it had been clear to her that was never going to happen.

"Glad to see you're home," Peter said.

"Only temporarily."

He looked surprised—and clearly disappointed. "I thought with your father ill—"

"He just said it was nothing. Strong as a horse, remember?"

Peter stepped to the bar and poured himself a drink. He'd taken a gulp of it before he turned to offer her one.

She declined, annoyed that he treated this home as if it was already his. "My father was right about one thing. We need to talk. You might want to pour yourself another one of those because you aren't going to like what I'm going to say."

"If this is about the lamebrain idea of yours to investigate the woman your brother was seeing…"

She gritted her teeth, knowing without a doubt that her father and Peter had discussed this. Discussed *her*.

"I won't be going out with you again. Even though I was honest with you, you've let my father believe that the two of us are—"

"Stop!"

His sudden outburst startled her. Before she could speak or move, he strode to her, grabbed her arms and gave her a shake. "You listen to me," he said, his voice strained. "I didn't come back all this way to argue with you. I came back to ask you to marry me." He let go of her to fish a small velvet box from Tiffany's out of his coat pocket.

"Stop," she said. "I'm not going to marry you."

His eyes narrowed. "You haven't even seen the ring yet."

"I don't need to see the ring."

He looked down. She could see him clenching his jaw in anger. "Is this about that cowboy?" He raised his gaze to hers, his eyes glittering with malice. "The one who shared a woman with your brother?"

She slapped him so hard that her hand stung. The sound echoed through the high ceilings of the room. Then she turned and rushed up the stairs toward her room. Behind her, she heard Peter pour himself another drink.

Billie Dee couldn't help being anxious after Henry told her his plan.

"Didn't you say that Darby and Mariah go over to their new house most afternoons to see how things are coming along?"

She'd nodded. "He leaves me and Ashley Jo in charge."

"All you have to do is text me right before he leaves."

So she had. Five minutes later, Darby and Mariah left as Henry was coming in the back door with a carton of strawberries.

"Billie Dee making her shortcake?" Darby said with a grin. "Make sure she saves me some."

As Darby drove away, Henry put down the strawberries and said, "Join me in the bar. I've never asked you if you drink."

"Alcohol?" she asked as they walked down the hall and into the bar part of the building. There were only a couple of regulars at the bar visiting with Ashley Jo.

Billie Dee knew that Darby was happy with his hire. The young woman was personable, was always on time and did whatever she was asked.

"She has experience at both bartending and waitressing,"

Darby had said the one time she'd inquired about Ashley Jo. "Mariah gave her a thumbs-up, as well."

Billie Dee had smiled at that. "The Mariah seal of approval."

Darby had looked hard at her then. "Why do you ask? Have you seen something I should be worried about?"

"No, no, not at all," she'd said hurriedly. "She seems delightful. I haven't had much chance to be around her so I was curious how she was working out."

Darby had seemed to breathe a sigh of relief. "I have to admit, I don't trust myself. I thought Kendall was a great hire and look how that turned out."

"Kendall was very good at what she did," Billie Dee had agreed. "She'd pulled the wool over all of our eyes while having her hand in the till." Was that why she was worried that Ashley Jo was hiding something?

"Well, if you see or hear anything, you'll let me know, right?" Darby had asked. "I depend on you, Billie Dee. You're family."

Family. The word had cut her to the quick.

As she joined Henry at the bar, she tried not to stare at Ashley Jo. The young woman laughed at something one of the regulars said. It was a musical laugh but one that chilled her because it seemed so familiar. Henry didn't seem to notice her reaction to it.

Seeing Billie Dee and Henry, Ashley Jo excused herself and hurried down the bar. "My two favorite people," the young woman said. "What can I get you?"

Henry looked to her and Billie Dee realized that she hadn't answered his question.

"I'll take a margarita, if you don't mind making me a blended one?" she said.

"I'd be delighted." Ashley Jo turned to Henry. "And what can I get you?"

"The same, please," he said, smiling over at Billie Dee.

Ashley Jo went to work making their margaritas. She seemed quite adept at it; Billie Dee couldn't help but notice. She herself had worked her way through college as a bartender. Not that something like that was hereditary.

"Are you all right?" Henry whispered.

She nodded but knew he could tell it was a lie. Until she knew for sure...

Henry was watching Ashley Jo carefully but managing not to stare. She had no idea what he was up to until she saw Ashley Jo take a sip of the cola she'd poured herself. It wasn't until their margaritas were served and they'd each had a sip and assured Ashley Jo that they were amazing that the young woman started to take her cola back down to the other end of the bar.

Henry knocked his margarita off and into his lap, the glass breaking as it made contact with the floor.

Billie Dee jumped back in surprise. Ashley Jo turned and headed back. As she put down her cola glass, she grabbed a bar rag.

"Don't touch that," the young woman said to Henry. "Darby will have my head if there is any bloodshed before he comes back."

Henry moved out of her way as she began to clear up what had slipped onto his bar stool. "I'll get the broom and dustpan," Billie Dee announced.

When she returned, Henry was behind the bar. He stealthily slipped Ashley Jo's glass into the plastic bag in his pocket. He replaced it with an empty dirty glass.

Billie Dee met his gaze. He was betting that Ashley Jo wouldn't remember that she'd finished her cola in all the confusion.

But what if she did? What if she knew they were onto her and left?

She knew that made no sense. But if Ashley Jo was who she thought she was… Then she'd come here for a reason. She wouldn't leave until she got what she wanted.

Once outside the body shop and in the sunlight and fresh air, Tucker took the call from Flint as he walked to his pickup.

"Tucker? Did you get my messages?"

He realized that he hadn't checked his voice mail. "No, I just saw that you'd called a few times."

"Are you in town? Can you stop by the office?"

Before, his brother's request had been offhand, nothing to worry about. His heart began to pound. A note in Flint's voice warned him that something had come up and it wasn't good news. "Is this about Dad?"

"No, Ely's fine, as far as I know. He's up in the mountains. It's about Madeline Dunn."

Tucker held his breath for a moment before letting it out. "I'll be right there."

Five minutes later, he pushed open the door to the sheriff's office. The dispatcher waved him toward Flint's office. He found him sitting behind his desk, a frown on his face.

He stepped in, wondering if he shouldn't be sitting for whatever news the sheriff was about to give him. He sat heavily in one of the chairs, bracing himself for the worst and yet unable to imagine what that might be.

"I've got some disturbing news. Madeline's death wasn't an accident," his brother said. "The coroner found a .22 slug embedded in her skull. I'm now investigating this as a homicide."

Tucker blinked. "She was *murdered*? Someone shot her?" He'd pictured her smacking into a tree limb hanging over the water as she was swept downstream. Hurt and dying, he'd seen her helped out of the water by whoever she was working with, stumbling up onto the bank, making it the few yards to the old creek bed before collapsing. And there was where she had been put to rest for almost twenty years.

That was how Flint had said the coroner suspected it could have happened. "Now you're saying it wasn't a head injury. Someone *shot* her?"

"The .22 slug was *under* the splintered wood. She was shot, then apparently struck with a limb, Sonny says. The one shot wasn't probably enough to kill her so…"

"So someone finished the job with a tree limb." Tucker couldn't believe what he was hearing.

"That isn't all. You asked about a silver ankle bracelet?"

All he could do was nod.

"Harp found it along with shell casings for a .22." Flint opened his drawer and brought out two plastic bags. One had the .22 slug in it and two shell casings. The other the bracelet. "Do you recognize the bracelet?"

He tried to swallow. He did. He'd given it to Madeline. His phone signaled that he'd just received a text. He reached into his pocket, saw that it was from Kate. His heart swelled just seeing it until he read what it said.

"I'm sorry, Tuck," his brother was saying. "But you understand now why you can't continue looking for Madeline's family. This is now a murder investigation."

CHAPTER SIXTEEN

Tucker called Kate once he was back at the ranch and in his room alone. He was still shaken from what his brother had told him. Madeline had been murdered? Whoever was waiting for her downstream had apparently killed her. But why?

Kate answered on the second ring.

"Tucker." She put so much into that one word it made him realize how much he'd missed her. He swore silently under his breath as he remembered what Darby had said.

"I got your text. Is everything all right?" he asked.

"It is now. When my mother called, she said my father had a heart attack." She groaned. "It turned out to be nothing more than indigestion. My mother probably gave it to him."

"I'm so glad that's all it was."

"Is everything all right there?" she asked as if hearing something in his voice.

He had to tell her. Worse, this would only make her more determined to find the rest of Madeline's family. Now Kate would be looking for a murderer—as if it hadn't been dangerous enough before when they were merely looking for a con man or woman.

"You haven't heard anything from any of the Dunns, have you?" he asked.

"No, why?" She sounded suspicious.

He could understand how she'd made a career as a reporter. "Just wondering. The thing about stirring up hornets is that they often come back to sting you when you least expect it."

"Have you been stung?" More suspicion. He really needed to get off the line.

"Not yet, but I'll tell you if I am. Do the same for me, okay?"

"Why not? You're sure everything is all right there?"

"We can talk when you get back. You must be tired after driving all the way to Helena."

"I am. But while I'm here, I thought I'd do some digging into the Dunn family, then I'll be headed back there. You'll still be around, won't you? The party Saturday and all? Or whenever."

"Don't worry. I'm not going without you."

"Good. Thanks for calling."

"Have a good night."

"You, too."

He waited until she disconnected first, then held the phone for a few moments longer. She sounded okay. If she'd heard from one of the Dunns she would have told him. He tried to assure himself of that but, knowing Kate, he doubted it. She was too much like him. She liked proving she could take care of herself and that worried the hell out of him because now she was dealing with a murderer.

Instantly he regretted keeping that information from her. She had to know what she was dealing with. He called her right back, but the phone went to voice mail. He hesitated. "Kate." He was aware of the pleasant feel of her name on his tongue. "Kate," he said and swallowed. "Madeline's death wasn't an accident. She was murdered. Call me."

He'd barely hung up when his cell rang. Thinking it was Kate, he picked right up. "I'm glad you called me back."

"Tucker, it's me, Darby. Lillie is definitely in labor and going to have the baby sometime tonight. Now Mariah seems to be in labor, as well. I have to take her to the hospital. Can you close up the bar for me?"

"I'll be right there." He pocketed his phone and headed for the door.

Kate had been so excited to see that she had a message from Tucker. But when she listened to it, she felt as if the ground had buckled under her.

Madeline had been murdered?

That wasn't possible. Tucker had told her that the coroner said she'd hit her head on a tree limb and died because she'd underestimated the power of the river. That she'd paid the price for her arrogance.

Murdered? She hated the woman but for a moment she was overwhelmed by the waste of it. How many lives had been wasted because of this woman and whoever she was working with? Madeline had lost her life over money and so had Kate's brother.

She fought the urge to scream, to cry, to feel worse than she had for nineteen years. So now she was looking for a murderer. Did Tucker really think that was going to make her stop? If anything, she was more determined than ever. She wanted to find this nest of vipers and expose them all.

Too bad, though. For years, she'd dreamed of confronting Madeline. But confronting one of her identical sisters would have to do.

"Karma is a bitch," she said to herself as she thought of Madeline. And then wondered what Tucker's reaction to the news had been.

Tucker was in such a hurry to get to the saloon as he'd promised Darby that he almost didn't see the note tucked under this wiper blade. He swore and glanced around before he plucked it off.

Whoever had left it had the gall to come onto the ranch? He closed his fist around the note, smelled Madeline's perfume and swore again as he started to throw the note to the truck floor.

As angry as he was, he knew he had to read it. He unfolded it and quickly read the words. This time, there was no doubt about it. Whoever had written this note wanted him to believe it was Madeline's girlish flourish. *You should run—before things get really rough. Take your girlfriend with you or she'll be sorry, too.*

He tossed the note aside and started his pickup, spraying gravel with the spinning tires as he tore out of the yard. He drove faster than he usually did, anxious to get to the saloon so Darby could get Mariah to the hospital—if they hadn't already left.

Glancing over at the note, he realized it was time to tell Flint about the threats. This one was definitely that. And it didn't just threaten him. This time, the writer had mentioned Kate. He thought about calling Flint, but as he came around a curve, he saw red and blue lights flash to his right and swore. A few moments later the sound of a siren filled the spring air as the sheriff's deputy's car came after him.

Unable to do anything else, Tucker hit the brakes, pulled over and jumped out, leaving his pickup door open.

"Stay right there!" a deputy ordered as he exited his patrol SUV. "I said stay there."

Tucker stopped walking toward the officer. "My brother's wife is in labor. I have to get to—"

"Return to your vehicle," the deputy ordered.

"You don't understand. My brother—"

"Sir, back up. Now!" The deputy's hand went to the gun at his hip.

Tucker did as he was told, even though it was wasting

valuable time. He climbed back into the pickup, the deputy on his heels.

"License and registration," the officer ordered as Tucker put down his window. The name on his uniform read Deputy Harper Cole. Harp? The one his brother had told him about?

Over the years, he'd crossed paths with cops like Harper Cole. They looked for trouble everywhere, believing that most people lied, cheated, stole and broke the law. He suspected Harp was one of them.

Sighing, he pulled out his wallet and handed the deputy his license, then started to reach in the glove box for the registration. He just wanted to get this over with so he could get to the saloon and relieve his brother before the baby was born right there in the bar.

"Don't move!"

Startled he turned to find the deputy had drawn his gun and was now pointing the barrel end at him.

"Slowly get back out of the truck. *Now!*"

Tucker felt a shiver of fear snake up his back, but he did as he was told. If this deputy was as incompetent as Flint had insinuated… "Deputy, I'm not sure what's going on, but my brother is the sheriff and—"

"What's that?" the deputy demanded as Tucker stood next to his truck, the driver's-side door standing open, the interior light on.

"What's that?" He saw the deputy look past him to something in the pickup. Turning, he peered into the truck. His heart dropped like a body off a bridge. Lying on the passenger-side floorboard in clear view was a pistol.

"Step away from your vehicle and keep your hands where I can see them," the deputy said as he got on his radio for backup.

"What is this about, Officer?" he asked slowly, carefully, as his mind whirled. What was that gun doing on his floorboard? It must have been under the seat and come out when he'd stopped so abruptly. But what was it doing under his seat to begin with?

"That your gun?"

Tucker swore silently. Even from a glance, he knew it was his .22 pistol, the one he'd sold, along with his saddle, all those years ago to give Madeline money.

"I don't know how it could be since I sold the gun before I left town," he said.

The deputy's radio squawked. "Harp?" He recognized his brother's voice.

"Sheriff, going to need you to meet me on the road from your ranch. I think I just found the murder weapon."

Tucker swore under his breath but said nothing because he suspected that the deputy was right. Which meant that who-ever had killed Madeline had put the gun under his pickup seat to frame him.

He and Kate had stirred up the hornet's nest and now Tucker had been stung good.

Flint couldn't believe what was happening. When it rained, it poured. He'd been thinking that just before Harp's call. Darby had called to say that Mariah was in labor. Lillie was already in labor. They were all headed for the hospital.

Now Flint turned on the siren as he raced out to the ranch road looking for his deputy. Harp had found the shell casings from the gun that had allegedly killed Madeline. Tests would be done on the slug found lodged in Madeline Dunn's skull, but the chances that the casings and the slug were from the same gun were more than good.

And now Harp had discovered what he believed to be the murder weapon and was about to make an arrest?

Flint swore. He just hoped the deputy had enough sense to leave whatever he'd discovered where it was. Sometimes Harp could be way too impulsive. Undeniably, he'd been a better deputy over the past months. But he went off half-cocked more times than not in his attempt to be the best deputy ever.

Still, Flint couldn't help being impressed. Harp had said he wanted to have another look down at the creek and had headed out that way earlier. Maybe there was a lawman in the overgrown kid, after all.

Ahead, he was surprised to see Harp's patrol SUV—and Tucker's pickup—parked beside the road. Harp's lights were flashing. As he drew closer, he saw that Harp appeared to be holding a weapon on his brother. Flint let out a curse, quickly parked and got out.

"What the hell?" he said as he headed for Harp. "Put that gun away. Right now, before you shoot someone."

Harp looked unfazed. "Sorry, Sheriff, but I picked him up for speeding. He was acting strangely and the next thing I saw was a gun on the floorboard of his pickup. A .22 pistol."

Flint shook his head. "Holster your weapon right now or—"

With a groan, Harp did as he was ordered.

"Darby called me," Tucker said. "He needs someone to close up the saloon. I was headed there when…" His voice dropped off.

"You need to see this, Sheriff," Harp said. At his insistence, Flint stepped to look into his brother's pickup. A .22 pistol lay on the passenger-side floorboard.

"That's the gun in question," Harp said. "The woman was killed with a .22 caliber, right? She was your brother's girlfriend, who just happened to be blackmailing him at the time…"

Flint regretted having the report typed up for Tucker to sign. Of course Harp would have found out about Tucker's involvement. He'd wanted all his ducks in a row should anything ever come up about Madeline Dunn's death. Little did he know at the time that it would turn out to be murder.

"Looks like a slam *dunk* to me," Harp was saying. "I know he's your brother but let's not forget that he ran nineteen years ago and only came back thinking she was nothing but bones."

Flint looked from the gun to his brother hoping for some kind of logical explanation. What he saw chilled him to his soul. "Tuck?"

"I think it's best if I don't say anything right now," Tucker said, looking scared.

He swore under his breath. "Okay, Deputy. Get an evidence bag. We'll take the gun into possession, see if it matches the slug found in the deceased. But what we aren't going to do is jump to any conclusions until we have the forensics on this gun. Is that agreed?"

Harp looked satisfied as he bagged the weapon to take to the lab. But when the sheriff was about to send Tucker home, he put up an argument.

"Excuse me, sir, I know he's your brother, but that's reason enough not to let him go right now. He ran nineteen years ago. What's to keep him from running now? The only thing you can do under the circumstances is lock him up until we get the results from the lab," Harper said.

It was all Flint could do not to argue the point. But Harp was right. If it had been anyone but his brother... He met Tucker's gaze. His brother gave him a look that he'd seen on guilty, scared men too many times. "Fine, lock him up."

Harp started to pull out his handcuffs.

"You won't need those," the sheriff snapped and looked at his brother again. "I'm sure Tucker wants the test results as much as we do, so he'll come along without any trouble." His brother looked numb.

"It's regulation, sir," Harp said, digging in his heels.

Flint gritted his teeth. "Fine, read him his rights and take him in. But I'm warning you, Harp, you will not parade him through town. Take him straight to the jail. I'll meet you there."

Flint would have preferred to take his brother in himself, but if the gun turned out to be the one that had killed Madeline… Not to mention, he had to get to the saloon. There would be an explanation for all of this. Tucker didn't kill Madeline, of that he was certain. Still, as he watched Harp put his brother into the back of the patrol SUV, he felt sick to his stomach.

He stepped over to the rig and motioned for Harp to put down the back window for a moment. "Don't say anything. I'll see you at the jail as soon as I can."

Harp revved the engine and Flint was forced to step back as the deputy drove away with Tucker handcuffed in the back seat.

Billie Dee noticed that Darby's pickup was gone as she pulled into the back of the Stagecoach Saloon. She'd come by to get a recipe that she'd left in the kitchen this morning, one she wanted to experiment with at home.

The only vehicles were several patrons' rigs out front, the SUV that Ashley Jo Somerfield drove and Mariah's motorcycle, which she hadn't driven since she'd gotten pregnant.

As she entered the back door into the kitchen, she walked toward the front of the saloon. Ashley Jo was waiting on a table of six. There were several regulars at the bar and another table of two.

"Where's Darby?" she asked when Ashley Jo rushed back to the bar to get one of the regulars a beer.

"The hospital," she said, sounding winded.

"The baby?"

She nodded.

"Darby left you here alone?" Billie Dee couldn't believe he would do that.

"He said his brother Tucker was on his way, but I haven't seen him yet."

"Don't worry, I'll help. Tell me what you need done."

"That couple over there wanted chili."

Billie Dee smiled. "I have it covered." She hurried back down the hall to the kitchen where the chili had been turned on low since she'd left earlier. There was just enough left for two more servings.

The babies were on the way. She couldn't help but be excited. She felt like part of the Cahill family and had since the first day she'd come to work here.

Gilt Edge, Montana, seemed at the end of the earth when she'd driven her old car through town. She'd planned to keep going on, no place in mind up the road, just making the best of this autumn part of her life as she could.

But as she was leaving, she'd spotted an old stone building with the sign Stagecoach Saloon and Café. Something about the place had drawn her. She'd pulled in and shut off her loud, complaining car engine, thinking she'd have lunch, then get on her way.

That's when she saw the sign in the window. She'd laughed since she'd been looking for a sign of where she should stay for a while—at least as long as she'd dared. The sign in the old stagecoach window wasn't the kind of sign she'd been expecting.

But there she was, outside an old mining town in Montana looking at a sign that read Cook Wanted. She didn't know what could be much clearer than that. She'd hired on and stayed.

She served the chili and refilled water glasses. Behind the bar, she began washing dishes when Flint came in through the back door. He looked upset. Her pulse leaped. *Please, don't let it be bad news about the baby*, she said in a silent prayer.

"Is it Mariah?" she asked quietly.

He shook his head. "No, I just heard. She's fine. Lillie's fine. They're both at the hospital, both in labor."

Billie Dee had to laugh. Lillie had said that she and Mariah were going to have their babies together. Apparently she'd been right. "We can handle things here if you need to get back to the hospital," she said to the sheriff.

Flint touched her arm, giving her a thankful smile.

"You look worried." She hadn't meant to just blurt it out like that.

"It's Tucker. He's been arrested for murder. It will be all over town soon."

"Murder?" She dropped her voice lower. "Who did he kill?"

"No one. But he was in possession of a gun that I suspect killed Madeline Dunn, the woman he was having an affair with. If it turns out to be his…well, it could be bad."

Billie Dee clamped a hand over her mouth for a moment, her eyes filling with tears as she thought of the big handsome cowboy and how happy his family had been to have him home. "I'm so sorry. If there is anything I can do…"

"You're doing it. Just close up here as soon as you can since everyone is going to be at the hospital. Come there as soon as you can. I know they are going to want to see you. I'm going to stop by the hospital, then go see Tucker at the jail."

Ashley Jo had joined them moments before. Now she watched Flint leave. "Was that the sheriff?"

"Flint Cahill, Darby's brother."

"Is everything all right?" Ashley Jo asked.

"Let's hope so."

Flint stopped by the hospital to make sure Lillie and Mariah were doing fine. He spotted his wife the moment he walked in.

Maggie rushed to him. "No babies yet. They're both in labor, though, and their husbands are with them." She hugged him and he held her tight for a moment. Soon they both would be here and Maggie would be giving birth to their first child. He couldn't wait.

"I better get down to the jail."

"Tonight?"

"It's a long story, but Tucker has been arrested."

"No. What did he do?"

Flint wished he knew. "Harp pulled him over for speeding and saw a gun on the floor of the cab..." He met his wife's gaze. "It could be the gun that killed Madeline Dunn."

Maggie shook her head. "I'm sure he didn't do it. You said he loved her. Probably still loves her."

The sheriff nodded, but he kept remembering the day his older brother had walked into his office ready to give himself up for Madeline's death. Tucker had been as shocked as anyone to learn that the coroner at that time believed her death to be an unfortunate accident.

"He's carrying a lot of guilt over her death," Flint said. "He's been trying to find her family. I thought it was just about getting closure. Now I'm not so sure."

"That's the doctor going into Mariah's room. I have to go," Maggie said. "I don't want to miss this birth. Oh, no, it looks like the nurse is looking for the other doctor on call for Lillie." His wife smiled. "Two babies are about to come into this world. Didn't Lillie say they would give birth together?"

Flint laughed. "If anyone can make something like that happen, it's my sister."

"She can't hear about Tucker," Maggie said.

He nodded. "I'll check back in a little while." With that, he left and drove to the jail, dreading what he feared Tucker was going to tell him.

Tucker was awake, lying on the bed, staring up at the ceiling. He'd been trying not to think about the trouble he was in or how bad it might get before it was over. He sat up when he saw Flint.

"Did you get your one call?" his brother asked.

He shook his head. "I wanted to talk to you and I knew you were busy. Did Lillie and Mariah have their babies?"

"We should hear soon. You need to call a lawyer."

Tucker nodded. "It's my gun. I saw the scratch on the grip. But you know I sold it before I left."

"So how did it end up in your pickup?"

He shook his head. "Don't you think I've been asking myself that? Someone had to have put it there and I can think of only one reason why they would do that."

Flint raked a hand through his hair. "What are you saying?"

Tucker looked into his brother's eyes, gray eyes so like his own. "Someone wants me to go down for her murder."

"It might not be the gun that killed Madeline," Flint said, clearly clutching at straws.

"If it's mine, then it's registered to me. If it matches the slug you found embedded in her skull…" Tucker looked away. "You were right. I shouldn't have gone looking for her family. Stirring up the past must have rattled someone." He told his brother about the notes that had been left on his pickup and where there were now.

"Don't worry. I'll find out who killed her. In the meantime…"

"I can't stay behind bars," Tucker said.

"It's the best place for you right now. Anyway, it will be up to a judge to set bail, if you are allowed bail at all. This is a homicide. I'm afraid there is nothing I can do. Harp was right. You leaving all those years ago… It doesn't look good. The judge will think you're a flight risk."

Tucker swore. "I didn't kill her."

"I know that. I want you to call a lawyer in the morning. If you need some names—"

"I will take that one call now," Tucker said, getting to his feet.

Flint glanced at his watch and frowned. "At this hour?"

He nodded. "Just give me my phone. I don't even have to get out of my cell."

Flint looked worried but he left to return with the phone. "I'll give you a minute."

The moment the sheriff stepped away, Tucker called Kate.

CHAPTER SEVENTEEN

"You jump bail and I'll come after you myself," Kate said as they drove away from the jail the next morning.

"You know I won't do that. I appreciate your father pulling whatever strings he did."

She shot him a sideways look as she drove. "So what's this about a gun?"

He related what had happened. "The gun is mine, but I sold it before Madeline was shot."

"Let me guess why you sold it."

He nodded. "I gave the money to Madeline."

"Of course you did. Did you happen to tell her where you'd gotten the money?" Kate groaned as if she already knew the answer. "You didn't happen to mention who you sold the gun to." She shook her head at his expression. "So she knew and she probably told whoever she was working with so they could go steal it. Perfect."

He sighed and leaned back into the seat to close his eyes for a moment. "Can you turn left at the next corner and pull over?" He opened his eyes to see her staring at him as if he'd lost his mind. "I'm not mad or going to make a run for it. I need to talk to the person I sold the weapon to."

"Then you won't mind if I come along?"

"Why not?" He motioned to a parking place and she slid into it and cut the engine before reading the sign on the office door next to where they were now parked. "You sold it to a lawyer?"

"My best friend." He opened his door and climbed out.

Kate quickly joined him in front of the business. "I'm confused."

"Welcome to my world." He pushed open the door for Kate and followed her into the outer office. Like before, the receptionist's desk was empty.

He went straight to the open doorway into Jayce's office. His friend was on the phone, but seeing Tucker, he quickly got off.

"Tuck?" Jayce glanced at the woman with him as he rose to his feet.

"Kate Rothschild," she said.

"She's an investigative reporter for a big deal New York City paper and daughter of Clayton Rothschild, Montana congressman," he said to save time.

Jayce's eyes widened a little before he took in Tucker. "I heard you'd been…arrested?"

"The pistol I sold you years ago turned up in my pickup," Tucker said. "I was hoping you could tell me how that happened."

Jayce looked sick as he motioned them into the chairs and fell back into his own. He shook his head as if he was as confused as anyone in the room.

"Let me tell you what happened," his friend finally began. Tucker waited patiently, reminding himself that Jayce was a lawyer who was good with words and probably just as proficient with stretching the truth. They'd once been closer than brothers. But that was a long time ago. "The gun I bought from you was stolen only days later."

"Stolen?" He couldn't help being skeptical. "You reported it to the sheriff, right?"

Jayce looked down for a moment before he shook his head. "No."

"I was still in town then. You didn't bother to mention it to me, either?"

He met Tucker's gaze. "I'm going to be honest with you. When it happened, I thought you did it."

"What? Why would you think that?"

"Okay, my first thought was that you'd found out that we set you up with Madeline. You had every right to be angry. I figured I deserved you taking your gun back. It's why I never said anything."

"So where was the gun? You hadn't secured it?"

Jayce shook his head. "It was at home in my bedroom."

"Not locked up."

"No. You saw me put it in my desk drawer that day. I forgot about it. I think I expected you to come back for it at some point. You know, offer me money once you were flush again. The saddle is still around somewhere."

Tucker walked to the window. "You have no idea who took the gun, who even knew you had it?"

His friend groaned. "It wasn't as if it was loaded and just lying around."

"You must have mentioned the gun to someone."

Jayce looked away. "I might have mentioned it to the guys. I was worried about you. It wasn't like you to sell your gun and your saddle. But they wouldn't have taken it."

"So anyone could have taken it since I'm sure you didn't lock your house," Tucker said, already knowing the answer.

"Come on, this is Gilt Edge, Montana. No one locks their doors."

He shook his head. Had he mentioned to Madeline that he'd sold his gun and saddle—and to whom? More than likely. Back then he'd thought that he would be introducing her someday to his best friend—once they there married. He'd been such a fool.

Jayce's family lived in the country. Anyone could have gotten into the old farmhouse without being seen since both of his parents had jobs in town back then.

"I'm so sorry," Jayce said. "This whole thing has gotten so crazy. I wish I'd never gotten you involved. When Flint stopped by to question me this morning, I told him I thought you'd taken the gun."

He looked at his friend. "I didn't take it, but whoever did is trying to frame me for Madeline's murder."

"*Murder?* I thought she drowned."

Tucker shook his head. "Someone put a bullet in her skull. The lab work isn't back yet, but I'm betting it was with my pistol."

Jayce looked even more upset. He raked both hands through his hair. "Tuck, I'm so sorry. This is all my fault. I should never—"

"It's water under the bridge," he said, coming back from the window. "So to speak. I have played right into someone's hands. But it looks like I could use a good lawyer."

"Absolutely," Jayce said, pulling himself closer to his desk to reach for his rotating file. "I know some great ones—"

"I want to hire you."

"What?" He froze. "No, Tuck, you need one who specializes in homicide litigation."

"I need someone who believes that I didn't kill Madeline."

Tucker had Kate drive him back to the ranch, where Flint had brought his pickup.

"What now?" she asked as she parked next to his truck.

He turned in the seat to look at her. "You go home until you hear from me."

"You can't be serious."

"Damn it, Kate, it's too dangerous. You can't keep digging into this." He told her about the notes—quoting the lastest one that threatened her before he opened the door to climb out. "They already killed one person. You think they won't kill to stop you? Thank you for springing me, but go home," he said and walked off toward his pickup.

She threw open her door and went after him. Catching up to him at his truck fender, she grabbed his arm and spun him around to face her. "They're scared. We got too close. But now we have to find them. Otherwise, you could be going to prison for murder."

"You think I don't know that?" he demanded. "But you're not getting the whole picture. They are through warning us off."

She let go of his arm. "What does that mean?"

"These people are dangerous. They are through screwing around. They're getting serious. We already know that they killed one of their own. You think they wouldn't kill us?"

She felt a chill ripple across her flesh. She hugged herself. "They aren't stupid enough to kill either of us. Why frame you if they planned to kill you?" She shook her head. "Like you said, they aren't stupid. They've been getting away with all of this for years, possibly. And they definitely aren't going to kill me."

He stared at her as if stunned by her words. "You think you're bulletproof because of who you are?" He let out a bark of a laugh. "You're more naive than I thought."

Kate felt tears sting her eyes. "Is that what you think?" She turned away for a moment. Had he just been indulging her since they'd met?

Tucker swore. "I didn't mean that. I just want to keep you safe," he said behind her, his voice low, intimate.

She felt a shiver skitter across the bare skin at her neck. Turning, she found him standing within inches of her. She felt her lips part, saw his gaze go to them. Even before he reached for her, she knew he was going to kiss her. And she knew it would be like no kiss she'd ever experienced.

He dragged her to him, wrapping her in his arms against his hard body, the kiss demanding. She felt his frustration, his need, the heat of his desire, all so much like her own. She opened to him as he deepened the kiss, losing herself in the feel of his mouth on hers. His tongue teased hers and she could imagine his mouth on her breasts. Her nipples hardened, aching at the thought. In his strong arms, she wanted nothing at that moment but this man.

Tucker ended the kiss as quickly as it had begun. "I'm sorry." His gaze locked with hers. She could see that he was breathing as hard as she was. All the powerful emotions she was feeling shone in his gray eyes.

"I'm not sorry," she managed to say as she tried to find solid footing again.

He shook his head. "I'm on bail for murder," he snapped. "Unless I can find out who really killed Madeline, I'm going to prison, probably for life."

"I'm not going to let that happen."

He shook his head. "And I'm not going to let you get killed because of me."

"Well, I'm not going to stop looking for Madeline's family. Now I have more reason than ever to find out who she was working with. I *can't* stop. I won't stop until you're free."

He dragged off his Stetson and raked a hand through his hair. His gaze on her was dark with emotion. "When are you going to realize how dangerous this is?"

"Don't you think I've known since I buried my brother?"

"This is different."

"Is it? I was the one who found my brother hanging from that beam."

His handsome face contorted with pain. "Oh, Kate. No. I'm so sorry. I had no idea."

She looked away, fighting tears, not wanting him to see the rawest of her pain. "I won't quit, Tucker," she said, her voice breaking. "I lost my brother. I can't let them take you, too."

He stepped to her, taking her shoulders into his hands. "You are the most stubborn woman I have ever met. Can't you see how worried I am about you?"

"I'm worried about *you*," she said, smiling through her tears. "We either do this together, or I look for the Dunns alone. Your choice."

He let out a curse. "I don't want you doing anything without me. You hear me?"

She nodded, ignoring the fact that Tucker could be locked up again for Madeline's murder and then she would be on her own. Even though the sheriff would be racing to find the real killer, she knew he, too, had been hitting a blank wall. No one seemed able to find Melody and her brother, K.O. Dunn.

She could feel the clock ticking. Her fear for Tucker was much greater than her fear for herself and whoever was framing him. She was sticking with this man to the end, whether he liked it or not.

One look in his eye, and she knew he was sticking with *her*.

Tucker looked into Kate's green eyes and knew there was no stopping this woman. He'd been kidding himself if he thought he could keep her from going after a murderer.

He checked his phone and saw that he had several texts. "Want to go meet my new nephews?" he asked Kate. "My sister and sister-in-law had their babies."

She smiled, nodding.

"We'll swing by the hospital on our way."

"On our way?" Kate asked. "I'm going wherever you are if I have to follow you. Or I'll find K.O. and Melody on my own." A breeze stirred her hair. She'd pulled it back, but several tendrils of her dark hair had escaped and now framed her striking face.

He was still shaken by the kiss. What had he been thinking kissing her like that? Wasn't he in deep enough? Had he thought that a kiss would bring her to her senses? If anything, he'd made matters worse because now he wasn't about to leave her to her own devices. He cared too much and that alone was a huge problem.

The day seemed so normal. Sun shining, blue sky, a light breeze that smelled of pine. Gilt Edge was alive with people going about their business. It seemed so strange that he was facing a murder charge and was falling for a woman who made him crazy with worry, even crazier with desire.

He could feel her waiting and knew she wasn't bluffing. "I think we should go back to Clawson Creek."

Kate looked as if she hadn't expected that. "Why?"

"Just a feeling. I know everyone said the family cleared out almost twenty years ago. But Tammy said people had seen lights on out at the house." He shook his head. "I want to check it out. We don't have anything else to go on, so why not?"

"Let's take my car," she said. "I'll drive. You look like you could use some sleep. I suspect the jail cell didn't have a memory foam bed."

He smiled. "Not exactly." He might have argued about her driving, but she was right. He hadn't gotten much rest last night. They climbed back into her SUV. He tried to tell himself that nothing had changed between them. But it was a lie. That damned kiss.

CHAPTER EIGHTEEN

"How long before we know if the DNA matches?" Billie Dee asked anxiously. Now that they had Ashley Jo's DNA, all they had to do was compare it to her own. Finally she would have the answer she so desperately needed.

"You'll have to be patient," Henry said, handing her the DNA swab kit.

She swabbed the inside of her mouth and stuck the swab into the plastic container, and he sealed it.

"I know someone so it shouldn't take as long as it does normally—at least for a preliminary test," he said. "What if it isn't conclusive?"

Billie Dee shook her head. "It will be. What other explanation is there? She looks like me at that age. She's the right age. She has a Texas accent that she tries to hide. One look at her hands and you can tell that this is not her regular gig. She has to be my daughter."

"I just don't want you to get your hopes up."

Too late. Her hopes were already up. But still she felt anxious. What was she hoping for? If Ashley Jo came here looking for her, then why hadn't she said anything to her?

"I know you think I'm foolish. Just because she resembles me when I was that age…"

"You're not foolish. If there isn't a match, at least now we will have your DNA should it come up in the future."

Billie Dee smiled at him. Henry was so kind. "You don't think I'm terrible for giving up my child?"

"Of course not."

"You haven't asked why I did."

He met her gaze. "I figure you'll tell me if you want to. Otherwise…" He smiled. "I told you. Nothing can change the way I feel about you."

"I fell in love with an older man."

"You don't need to do this," he said.

"I do. I don't want to have any more secrets from you."

He smiled at that. "Does that mean no more reason not to marry me?"

"It just might."

"Then by all means, shoot."

"He lied to me from the very start. He wasn't just married. He was involved in some serious illegal business."

Henry looked worried. "The Mob?"

She laughed. "Worse. He was a connected oilman. He still is. It wasn't until I realized that I was pregnant that I found out he was still married. He and his wife were separated. She apparently had the money. They had an agreement. As long as he didn't flaunt his affairs, it was fine.

"But the deal was that he could never divorce her. And he certainly couldn't have a child by another woman. He and his wife couldn't have children, as it turned out."

Henry shook his head as if he knew what was coming. "She found out about the baby."

Billie Dee nodded, her jaw tightening. "She wanted to pass the baby off as her own. She put pressure on her husband. When buying my baby didn't work, they threatened me with all kinds of things if I didn't go along with it. I was twenty-six, a child compared to these people. I thought once I made it clear I wasn't giving up my baby, they would back off."

"They didn't."

She shook her head. "I didn't realize how powerful they were. For no reason that made sense, I was kicked out of my apartment, lost my job… Suddenly I was broke, homeless, pregnant with the child of a man who I realized could and would do anything he wanted to destroy me."

"They had you right where they wanted you. I take it you had no family who could help you."

She shook her head. "My parents were dead. I was raised by my grandmother, who had passed away that year."

"I'm so sorry. Anyone in your position would have made the same decision."

She smiled over at him. "I didn't give them the baby."

"I know you didn't," he said with a laugh. "Backed into a corner, you're going to come out fighting."

"I left, found a pastor who had preached when I was a child. He'd retired but he helped me. I knew I couldn't keep her. I would be too easy to find, too easy for him to have me locked up in some institution while he and his horrible wife raised my child." She shook her head. "I had to find her a good home. I also had to find a doctor who would say I'd lost the baby."

"But what a terribly painful choice."

"It was best. I contacted the man, told him I'd lost the baby and needed money. He didn't believe me."

"So you had the doctor confirm it."

She nodded. "Then, months later, I gave birth to a precious little girl." Her eyes burned. She'd shed so many tears over the years she would have thought they'd dried up. "I never met the family, but the pastor told me they were a wonderful couple of some means who'd desperately wanted a child."

Henry rose to pull her into his arms. "I love you so much,

Billie Dee. As horrible as the things that have happened to you are, they've made you the woman you are today." He let go of her to drop to one knee. "Say you'll marry me," he said, drawing the small velvet box he'd been carrying around for months from his pocket. "Whatever we find out, it won't change anything between us."

She looked into his handsome, caring face and, nodding, watched him slip the ring onto her finger.

As he got to his feet, his face broke into a wide smile. "You have just made me the happiest man alive."

Billie Dee looked at the huge diamond on her finger. "How did I get so lucky?" she asked and met his gaze. "I love you, Henry Larson. I can't wait to marry you."

Kate was doing her best not to act like the kiss had meant anything. But her heart was still pounding, and as she started the car, she realized she was trembling inside.

After their visit to the hospital, she could tell that Tucker wasn't up to talking. Thankful for that, she turned on the radio and let the front of the SUV eat up the miles on the lonely two-lane highway. As she drove, she tried not to think about what she'd had to do to get Tucker out on bail. Her father had been furious with her.

"I've begged you to put this behind you and now you've gotten yourself involved with…" He'd waved a hand through his hair as if he couldn't go on.

"Tucker Cahill was a victim of the woman—just as Clay was."

"My son is dead. Can't you let him rest in peace?" he'd demanded.

"I'm the one who can't rest. Does that matter to you?"

Clayton Rothschild had looked at her and all his anger had seemed to run out of him like water down a drain. "I'm sorry. I know how you looked up to your brother, how close the two of you were."

"Then back me on this, Dad. Let me finish what I started."

"By getting this...cowboy out on bail?"

"Yes."

"Kate, he's wanted for *murder*."

"He's being framed."

Her father had groaned. "That's what they all say."

"I'm telling you he's innocent. You trust my judgment, don't you?"

"Most of the time," he'd said, but she had seen that he was weakening. "What is this man to you, Katherine?"

"A man who needs justice as much as I do," she'd said.

But as she drove toward Clawson Creek, she knew it was so much more than that. Against her better judgment she was falling for Tucker Cahill. The thought terrified her since she knew firsthand that he wasn't over Madeline. That he might never be over the memory of the woman. But tell that to her heart.

Deep in thought, she'd lost track of time and was surprised when she saw the sign for the turnoff. She glanced over at Tucker, having almost forgotten he was there.

The cowboy took up too much space, exuded too much maleness, to forget him entirely. He'd fallen asleep, but as she slowed, he sat up, looking troubled as she drove into Clawson Creek. Last time they were here he'd come along for the ride, not really caring what they discovered. This time was more serious. His life was on the line.

She drove right through the town that had she blinked, she would have missed it. But she didn't blink, and as she passed the lumberyard, she saw a woman come out of the huge barnlike building where the lumber was stored. Carly Brookshire stood in the shade and watched them go by before turning back inside.

As they passed the bar, a man was standing in the doorway. He, too, watched them go past. Kate marveled at what
made entertainment in a place like this.

And then they were through town. A few deserted falling-
down buildings blurred past and a junkyard with rusting cars,
the new cemetery and then rolling hills broken only by open
prairie. She took the first dirt road to the right. On the way,
she'd texted Tammy for directions and was surprised how
close the house was to town.

Tucker stretched. "Thanks for driving. I did need to sleep.
If I didn't thank you for getting me out of jail—"

"Not necessary." She interrupted him. "Anyway, I got you
into this. Remember, you didn't want to find Madeline's accomplice."

"I'm a big boy." She could feel his gaze on her. It warmed
her more than the sun coming in the window. "I figured if
they left me alone, I'd leave them alone."

She looked over at him. "So why didn't you put up more
of a fight last time we were here?"

He chuckled. "Maybe I like your company. Maybe I get a
kick out of seeing you in action. I never thought turning over
a few anthills would get me thrown in jail, though."

"Actually, it was jail you were worried about the first time
we came up here. I guess with good reason. But we're going
to find Melody and K.O. and put an end to this. I promise."

He didn't look convinced. His brow furrowed, his gray eyes
dark with worry. "I couldn't bear it if anything happened to
you because of me."

"You forget. I was neck-deep in this before we met. They'll
have to kill me to stop me."

"That's reassuring," he said and looked out the side window.

They passed a couple of abandoned barns and were now on

the back side of Clawson Creek. Suddenly, the house came into view.

Tucker let out a low whistle. Kate had figured Tammy had exaggerated the size and prosperity of the house. Apparently she *had* known how rich some sultans were.

The Dunn place sat back off the road on a hill, overlooking a creek bottom and within sight of town. It was big, rambling and surrounded by a rock wall, just as Tammy had described.

But the years had made the place less of a fortress. Trees had grown up next to the rock wall, making access to the house much easier. In other places, erosion had washed out a section of the stone fence.

Still, it made Kate wonder why the wall had been needed in the first place. What had the Dunns been protecting inside those walls? The domineering father's three girls? Or were they more worried about keeping people out so they didn't know what was going on inside?

As Kate turned onto a narrow dirt road, Tucker could see the back side of Clawson Creek. Why would Kell Dunn build here of all places?

He glanced at the creek choked with tall cottonwoods below the house. The water was already running high this close to the Belt Mountains and spring runoff. He wondered if this was where Madeline had learned to swim—and perfected the trick that would later betray her? Then he reminded himself that she hadn't drowned that night. Someone had been waiting for her downstream and killed her. Had the murder been premeditated? Or had there been a confrontation? He doubted they would ever know.

Kate slowed. "Tracks," she said in a whisper as if she might be heard by someone other than him. "Someone has been down here and recently."

He sat up straighter and eyed the large house. Last night,

lying on the cot in jail, he'd known he had to see where she'd lived. The house appeared abandoned at first glance but then he saw the hem of a curtain flap in the breeze from an open window.

"Someone is still living here."

Kate shot him a glance as the road access ended with a chain across the road.

"That's odd," Tucker said.

"What?"

"Someone installed that barrier," he said. "The chain across the road is padlocked to metal posts set in concrete. That is not the sort of thing the family would have done if they left in a hurry. And what was the point, if they were never coming back?"

"So you think someone has been using the house," Kate said. "Do you think they're here now?"

"I don't see a vehicle, but whoever drove in here has a key to that padlocked chain blocking the road," Tucker said, pointing to visible footprints in the fine dust. The vehicle tracks continued up the hill to the house.

Kate parked, blocking the road, and reached for her purse. He beat her to it, pulling the pistol out and sticking it in the waist of his jeans and covering it with his shirt.

She gave him a look that told him not to play hero. "If you get caught with that gun—"

"A gentleman never lets the lady pull the trigger," he said.

The look she gave him softened. "Who says I'm a lady?"

"Who says I'm a gentleman?" He opened his door, watching the house as he climbed out. He heard Kate exit the SUV, as well. He would have preferred that she stay in the vehicle until he searched the house. But he'd come to know the woman well enough to know that wasn't going to happen.

"At least stay behind me," he whispered as she joined him. He felt her hand on his back for a moment.

"What choice do I have?" she whispered back. "You have my gun."

The walk up the road only took a few minutes. Tucker stepped over some of the fallen rock wall and reached back for Kate. She took his hand and scrambled over.

"Is it just me or does this feel…spooky?" she whispered as she joined him on the inside of the wall.

He was looking up at the house. "I always thought Madeline was poor. Whoever built this house had money."

"So why a life of crime?" Kate asked. "Maybe it was only a game. Something for amusement. But then again, Tammy said the father was cheap and that they didn't have enough to eat."

Tucker shook his head. "I think Madeline might have lied about a lot of things." But that night on the bridge, he'd sensed a desperation in her that had been real. She had been scared. That at least had been honest emotion.

Kate said nothing, no doubt skeptical when it came to his perceptions dealing with the woman. He couldn't blame her.

They climbed the rest of the way up to the front porch with its towering brick columns. The wood on the porch had weathered but had held up well in the climate. The boards groaned under his tread, though.

He stopped to remind himself how dangerous these people could be. If one of them was inside, he or she might have already spotted him and Kate. The two of them could be walking into an ambush.

Moving to the door, he expected it to be locked. He tried the knob. When it turned in his hand, he felt his heart thump even harder. If someone was staying here, why leave the door unlocked? True, hardly anyone in rural Montana locked doors. Also, who in their right mind would come out here if they'd heard of the Dunns?

Still, he couldn't help feeling anxious. That feeling that they were walking into a trap even stronger as he turned the knob and the door swung open. A dry musty smell escaped along with the faint scent of a recently cooked meal.

Still listening, Tucker quietly stepped into the dim light of the once-mansion-like house. He could feel Kate's hand against his back. The living room was only partially furnished. Everything was covered with a thick coat of dust, including the floor. On the walls were places where it appeared several large crosses had once hung.

There were no photographs or paintings or other decorations anywhere he could see. The place had an austere feel to it. He still couldn't imagine the woman he'd known growing up here.

He looked down and saw no footprints. Whoever had come up the road hadn't come in through this doorway.

"No one can live here," Kate whispered as she peered around him.

He chuckled under his breath. "This from the girl who was raised on a huge ranch outside Helena?"

Her hand disappeared from his back and he felt her move away. "It is easy to think I grew up privileged, but not everything is about money."

He knew she was right and felt contrite, especially since it had been her father's money and influence that had gotten him out on bail. Heading for the kitchen, he wished he could take back his words.

The kitchen wasn't much better than the living room. Everything was outdated, but it was easy to see that at one time the furnishings had been expensive.

"I'm going to check upstairs," he said. "Wait here." He didn't give her time to argue. He took the stairs three at a time as quietly as he could. The upstairs had been divided into a half dozen small bedrooms. He saw only two bathrooms and had to wonder what it must have been like for Madeline growing up here with two sisters and a brother.

True, nineteen years had passed, but still it wasn't how he'd pictured the house Madeline had grown up in. Then again, as Kate had said, having money didn't mean that it had been a happy home. Or that any of that money was accessible to the four children.

He found no one, but it was clear that one of the bedrooms was being used. There was an old mattress pulled up on the floor along with some stray blankets. He was about to take a look in a duffel bag he saw in the corner when he heard a vehicle engine.

Hurriedly he took the stairs, actually thinking Kate might be where he'd left her. He really was a fool. She was in the kitchen holding a butcher knife.

"Unless you plan to cut bread with that…" he said.

"I thought I might have to rescue you." She dropped the knife back in the drawer. "Did you hear that?"

He nodded and motioned her toward the back door. "I think we better see who it is." But before they could reach the door, the vehicle engine revved from behind the house. By the time he stepped out onto the porch, all he could see was a cloud of dust as the driver of the vehicle made a hurried U-turn in the dirt behind the house and tore off the other way.

"My SUV is blocking the road," Kate said. "So there must be a back way out."

"That would be my guess." He hurried out, but the land dropped away rapidly just yards from the rear of the house. All he could see was dust settling. There was no way to go after the person in the vehicle even if they could reach Kate's SUV in time. They couldn't get past the chain across the road.

"Stay here while I run back upstairs for a few minutes to check something."

"Only if you give me my gun." She crossed her arms over her chest, grit in her expression.

He ground his teeth as he looked from her to the settling

dust. "Fine." He pulled the weapon from his waistband and carefully handed it to her. "Try not to shoot anyone until I get back."

She smiled. "I'll be right here if you need me."

"You honestly know how to shoot that?"

"No, I just carry it in my purse for the extra weight." Kate made a face. "I'm an excellent shot, I'll have you know."

"I hope I never have to call you on that." He turned and ran back up the stairs and down the hall to the room with the mattress on the floor.

The duffel bag was navy and fairly new. He carefully unzipped it, glad the person who'd just left hadn't had time to take it with him or her.

What he saw made him draw back. Money. A dozen stacks of hundred-dollar bills. And under them were clothes. Women's clothing. He moved the money aside. It wasn't just women's clothing. It was the sexy stuff that Madeline had loved so much. Silky and new in black and a deep rose color, also her favorite. A scent drifted up from the clothing. That now-familiar gut-wrenching smell of Madeline's jasmine perfume.

CHAPTER NINETEEN

Kate walked around the lower floor of the house, the gun in her hand. There wasn't much to see. The only tracks led back to the kitchen. She followed them straight to the gas stove. There was something thick and red spilled next to one of the burners and it looked fresh.

She tried a burner. At the sound of spewing gas, she quickly turned it off and noticed a matchbook. Picking it up, she saw that only a couple of matches were left. As she started to put it back, she saw that the matchbook looked fairly new. There was the name of a bar on one side, but it was difficult to read in the dim light. On the other side someone had written *K.O.*

Glancing out the window, she saw a propane tank. Well, that explained the stove working, she thought. But that spilled red blob caught her attention again. Sticking the tip of her finger into it, she brought it to her nose and sniffed.

Spaghetti sauce?

Smiling, she wiped her hand clean with a napkin on the counter as she heard Tucker come back down the stairs. He headed straight for the front door. She pocketed the matchbook and followed him.

One look at his face and she knew something had happened in the house that had shaken him. "Want to talk about it?" she finally asked as they walked toward her SUV parked down the hill.

He looked over at her as if he'd been lost in thought. "I found a duffel bag in the house with money and women's clothing in it. Some of the items were in Madeline's favorite color and they smelled of her perfume. Did I mention that the notes I've been getting left on my truck also smell of her perfume?"

Kate didn't know what to say. Worse, his words made her feel sick inside. No, he hadn't mentioned that. But she could tell that it upset him. This was just another reminder that Madeline was still part of Tucker's life even after all these years. The man had been snakebit, as her father would have said. Nothing could ever get Madeline out of his thoughts or his heart. No woman certainly could ever best Madeline—alive or dead.

But she was dead and Kate felt as if she needed to remind him of that. "Everyone knows how close identical twins tend to be—they wear matching clothes, have the same hairstyle, marry the same kind of men—even when they weren't raised together. So triplets must be the same way."

He nodded but she could tell he was having his doubts.

"She's *dead*. But it seems someone wants you to believe she's still alive," Kate said. "They're just fooling with you."

The sound of a rifle shot pierced the quiet spring air. The bullet whizzed past to kick up dust from the road bank next to them. Tucker grabbed her, throwing them both off the side of the road into the thick foliage beneath the cottonwoods along the creek. Another bullet smacked into the trunk of a tree just inches from them.

Tucker dragged her deeper into the underbrush next to the creek. He put out his hand. Without a word, Kate handed him her gun. They stayed crouched down in the shelter of the trees and waited.

She listened, terrified that whoever had taken the potshots at them would be descending the hill after them at any moment. The breeze stirred the new leaves. Sunlight flickered down. Tucker seemed just as intent on the hillside above them—and keeping her tucked down out of the line of fire.

At the sound of a vehicle engine starting up, she held her breath. Her fear was that whoever had shot at them would be coming down the road. But after a few moments, she realized the sound was dying away in the distance.

Still, they waited as the sun moved across Montana's big blue sky. Until it began to get cold down by the creek. Until Tucker finally rose and reached for her hand.

Tucker was still shaken hours later. He looked at the mug shot his brother handed him and felt a jolt of surprise. The man looked nothing like he'd pictured him. But he'd been a good-looking twenty-two-year-old when he'd been arrested, apparently the one and only time.

"This is K.O. Dunn?" he asked his brother.

"Kevin Oyler 'K.O.' Dunn," Flint said. "He'd be more than twenty years older now."

Tucker handed the photo to his brother Hawk. His brothers had gathered at the ranch after he and Kate had come back from Clawson Creek. It had been Flint's idea after hearing what had happened up at the Dunn place.

Flint hadn't wanted to talk about this at the sheriff's office, hoping that no more people knew about it than necessary since Tucker wasn't supposed to even leave town—let alone continue investigating.

Kate was upstairs. Tucker had insisted she stay at the ranch. When they'd reached the house, she'd gone up to get a shower while he talked to his brothers.

He'd filled his brothers in on what had happened at the old Dunn house up by Clawson Creek.

"This guy doesn't look like a killer," Hawk said as Cyrus took the mug shot and made the same observation his brother had.

"Killers often don't look like killers," Flint said, taking the mug shot back. "But you also don't know it was K.O. who took those potshots at you and Kate."

"Maybe it was his underwear you found in the duffel bag," Cyrus said and laughed.

Tucker shot him a withering look, but before he could protest Hawk said, "Do you think whoever it was shooting was trying to hit you? Or were they after Kate?"

He'd asked himself the same thing. "The shots were close enough he could have been trying to kill us both. Or warn us off."

"You're assuming it was a man," Flint said as Tucker rose to walk over to the window. He was having trouble sitting still. That had been too close of a call today. "Is it possible that the driver of the first vehicle you heard didn't go far and walked back?"

"It's possible," he agreed as he looked out over the ranch and the lights of Gilt Edge in the distance. He'd always loved this view. Darkness had turned the pines to ebony. Behind them, the lights of Gilt Edge tinted the night sky with faint gold.

"It's why I brought Kate here kicking and screaming," Tucker said, turning back to his brothers. "She's so damned independent." Flint and Darby nodded, no doubt thinking of their own wives.

"Maybe now you'll stay out of the investigation and let me do my job," Flint said.

"I wish it were that easy. You don't know Kate. She's even more determined to find these people."

"I'm going to have to arrest you both, I guess."

"On what grounds?" Tucker said. "You can't stop Kate from looking for the Dunns. And as long as she is determined to find them, I can't let her go alone."

"She's going to get herself killed and you locked back up in jail," Flint said. "I doubt her father will bail you out again if that happens. You want her death on your conscience?"

He couldn't bear the thought of losing this woman. That he'd gotten that involved with her in such a short time scared him almost as much as flying bullets.

"The only way I can stop her is to hog-tie her in the barn, and even then, it would take some mighty tough rope."

"Then talk her out of it. Surely she realizes now how dangerous it is."

"You really think the Dunns took a shot at you?" Cyrus asked.

"I won't know until K.O. and his sister Melody are found," Tucker said.

"You still think her brother was forcing her to get money from men?" Flint asked.

Tucker had been more sure before he'd seen the mug shot. "Or maybe the father, I don't know. The fact that there were three identical sisters…"

Hawk shook his head. "If it was the brother, he had the perfect setup. Three sisters he could manipulate to do whatever he wanted and no one would know for sure which one they were dealing with."

"So you can't even be sure you were always with Madeline? Is that what you're saying?" Cyrus asked. "That is…creepy."

Tucker hated to admit that it could be true. It would explain why Madeline was often…different toward him. "We won't know until we find the one that is still alive."

Something in his tone made Flint's head jerk up. "Do not tell me that you're thinking it might be Madeline."

"They all share the same DNA, right?" Hawk said. "So there is no way of knowing who you found in the creek."

"Do you know if Madeline ever broke her leg?" Flint asked Tucker.

"No, why?"

"Sonny said that the left leg bone down at the morgue had an old fracture."

"So there might be a way to tell which of the Dunn sisters was found in the creek," Hawk said.

"And which one is still alive," Cyrus added.

Tucker swore. He'd convinced himself that Madeline was dead and he wanted to leave her that way. He felt Flint watching him.

"I have a BOLO out on Kevin Oyler Dunn," the sheriff said. "We will find him and clear this all up once and for all."

"I hope you're right," Tucker said and glanced toward the stairs as if he expected Kate to be standing there, listening.

From her hiding place, Kate had listened to the discussion going on downstairs. She didn't even feel remotely guilty for eavesdropping—especially since she had often been part of the topic of conversation.

She'd taken a quick shower, wrapped her hair in a towel and, pulling on the sweats Tucker had given her, sneaked to a spot where she could hear what was going on downstairs.

Earlier, as she was stripping down to shower, she'd felt the matchbook in her jeans pocket. In the bathroom light, she could easily read the name of the establishment printed on it. Hell Creek Bar, Garfield, Montana. The matchbook wasn't dusty like the rest of the house, making her believe that it had been brought into the house recently.

She'd thought about showing it to Tucker, but she'd instinctively known he would turn it over to his brother the sheriff. She was so close to finding the rest of the Dunn family, so close to finding the Madeline look-alike, that she didn't want anyone to stand in her way. If the Gilt Edge sheriff called the sheriff in Garfield County or, worse, showed up in Hell Creek—wherever that was—he could spook the Dunns off.

No, Kate couldn't let that happen.

After they'd been shot at, Tucker had insisted they go back up to the house. She knew what he was looking for. In the room upstairs, the duffel bag was gone along with any sign of the woman who'd been staying there.

While Tucker had gone out to see if the shooter had left any tracks, Kate had looked around the room. A mattress on the floor. The dust was disturbed where someone had settled in for a while. On the run? Or had they come back for something?

As she started to leave the room, she saw that the mattress had been moved during the person's abrupt departure. The dust on the floor was smeared. And at the edge of the mattress was a small white piece of paper.

Squatting down, Kate had pulled out a receipt from the Hell Creek Bar. The bill had included two burgers, one beer and a cherry cola. So who'd enjoyed this meal?

She'd noticed more handwriting on the back of the receipt like she had on the matchbook.

I think these two might be who you're looking for.

Was whoever was staying here looking for K.O. and Melody, too? It certainly appeared that way.

Intrigued, she'd realized that Garfield County wasn't that far from Gilt Edge. But first she had to make Tucker believe that she'd gone to bed after her shower, so exhausted from today's near-death experience that nothing could keep her awake. She *was* tired but also energized. She would find the last remaining Dunns.

She suspected one of them had been staying at the former house near Clawson Creek and had taken the shots at them earlier. Whoever it was had cleared out. Headed for Hell Creek? That would be her guess.

As she heard the sheriff leave and the brothers say their good-nights, she tiptoed back to the bedroom where Tucker had insisted she spend the night. It was right down the hall from his, he'd pointed out—as if that was necessary. She'd already gone into his room and found her gun, but she hadn't taken it. That would be too much of a tip-off.

She climbed into bed, sweats and all, and pulled the quilt over her. In the darkness she waited, knowing Tucker would check on her. A few minutes later, the door opened a crack. She kept her eyes closed and concentrated on her breathing. The door closed again.

Kate lay perfectly still, waiting. She hated to do this to Tucker, especially after she'd told him she wouldn't do anything without him. But after hearing what the sheriff said about locking him up if he left town again, she had no choice. Once she found the Dunns and cleared him…

The ranch house grew quiet. Still, she waited as the moon peeked out from the clouds and millions of stars glittered outside her window. Soon.

Tucker couldn't sleep. He lay on the bed fully clothed, listening. Earlier he'd peeked into the room where Kate was apparently sleeping. If he hadn't seen her head of dark hair splayed across the white pillowcase, he would have suspected she'd already sneaked out. The woman was impossible. He'd practically had to throw her over his shoulder and haul her into the house tonight to keep her from going back to her hotel room.

"You can't really believe that one of the Dunns is going to abduct me from my hotel room," she'd argued.

"No, I suspect they will grab you when you leave it, because we both know a near-death experience isn't going to stop you."

She'd met his gaze with a steely one of her own. "I've told you from the beginning what I planned to do. Nothing has changed."

But everything *had* changed. Madeline had been murdered, he'd been framed for murder and someone had shot at them. Whoever it had been was willing to chance killing them both. Or kill Kate and somehow make Tucker look responsible for another young woman's death?

He heard a floorboard creak. Then another. "I knew it," he said under his breath. He got up and moved quietly to his door to listen.

Sure enough, he could hear someone sneaking out. He really doubted it was one of his brothers. They were old enough that they no longer had to sneak out of the house in the middle of the night.

Swearing under his breath, Tucker eased open his door and peered out into the dim light of the hallway.

Kate took another step. The floorboards groaned under her feet. That was the problem with old houses, she thought an instant before she was grabbed from behind.

An arm came around her waist, picking her up off the floor. At the same time, a large hand clamped down over her mouth to stifle the scream fighting to get out.

"Going somewhere?" Tucker ground out next to her ear.

Apparently he didn't expect an answer since his hand was covering her mouth. He half carried her back to his room, finally removing his hand from her mouth when the door closed behind them.

"Are you crazy?" he demanded, keeping his voice down. "Sneaking out of here in the middle of the night, knowing someone who wants to kill you is out there?"

"We don't know that for a fact," she said indignantly. "We were trespassing yesterday. Anyone could have taken those warning shots at us."

"*Warning* shots? That's what you've now convinced yourself they were?"

"They missed us."

He cursed and turned away for a moment as if trying to get his temper in check. "Where were you going?" he demanded when he turned back to her. She could see him gritting his teeth, his jaw muscles bunching. Even angry he was unbearably handsome.

"I know you think there is something wrong with me for continuing to look for the Dunns." He gave her a look that confirmed it. "I've never been this close before in finding out who was behind the con that resulted in my brother's suicide. I can't stop now no matter what. I owe it to my brother."

He shook his head. "You owe it to your brother to stay alive. Where were you going?" he asked again.

"Garfied County, Montana."

"Garfield?"

"I found two things at the Dunn house. I would have told you sooner," she said quickly. "But I was afraid you would tell your brother the sheriff."

"Damn straight."

He raked a hand through his thick dark hair, making her wish those were her fingers. She shook off the thought, blaming it on lack of sleep.

"You can't leave again or you'll be arrested."

"What did you find?" His voice was low, intimate.

She looked around, seeing that she was in his childhood bedroom. There was a cowboy bedspread on the twin bed next to the window and an indentation in the spread where he'd been lying minutes before he'd grabbed her out in the hallway.

"A matchbook and a receipt for two burgers, one beer and a cherry cola at a bar." She told him what was handwritten on the back of each.

"So from that you're convinced that K.O. and Melody are in Garfield County?"

"At the Hell Creek Bar."

"Talk about a leap." He raked his hand through his hair again. "So you were going to drive there tonight?"

"I wanted to be there first thing in the morning when the bar opened," she said. It wasn't like she hadn't thought this out and she said as much.

Tucker let out a bark of a laugh. "You consider this thought-out? What if they just ate there on their way somewhere? Forget that. Garfield County isn't a place most people drive through on their way somewhere else. Okay. Why not? Let's go."

"You can't go with me."

"Well, you're sure as hell not going alone."

"Tucker." She stepped closer and reached up to cup his cheek in her hand as she looked into his gray eyes. "I'm so sorry I got you involved in this."

"I was already involved, remember."

"But you wanted to stop. You have to stop now. I don't want you thrown back in jail. You aren't responsible for me. You can stay here and I can—"

He took her hand from his face, but he didn't let go of it. He dragged it over to his mouth and pressed his lips to the palm for a moment. She felt her blood fire. Had he pulled her over to his childhood bed...

"I'm going with you," he said, his voice husky with emotion. "You'll probably get us both killed before I get locked up again, but it's better than worrying about what trouble you've gotten yourself into. Anyway," he said, his gaze lifting to hers. "We're a team, right?"

She couldn't help but smile. "That's us, one of the great detective couples. Like Nick and Nora."

He mugged a face. "More like Bonnie and Clyde."

"Emma Peel and John Steed."

Tucker laughed. "Shaggy and Scooby Doo."

Kate laughed, too. He let go of her hand and suddenly the air around them grew heavy. Her pulse jumped as their gazes locked, and for just an instant, she thought he might take her in his arms and kiss her again.

Instead, he took a step back, saying, "If we're going to make it there by morning, then we'd better get going. I'll leave a note for my brothers."

"We're going to find the last of the Dunns and end this," she said.

"That's what I'm afraid of." He looked up from where he was writing the note at the small desk next to the bed. "And then what, Kate? If they don't kill us, of course. You going to kill them?"

She said nothing as she retrieved her gun and he went back to his note.

CHAPTER TWENTY

They stopped in Grass Range at the café for breakfast as the sun was coming up. Tucker watched Kate put away a huge plate of eggs, hash browns, bacon and toast. He'd never seen a woman eat like she did—and yet every curve on her body couldn't have been more perfect.

"What's to the east besides Jordan?" she asked as she finished the last bite.

"Not much. Mostly badlands. Garfield County is one of the least populated in the state. Well, in the top ten, anyway. A lot of counties out this way have less than a thousand people." Was that really what she wanted to know? Often he wasn't sure what went on in that mind of hers.

As he looked into her face, though, he felt the pull that had left him off balance since the first time he laid eyes on her. This woman was such a contradiction. A privileged rancher and congressman's daughter. An award-winning journalist. A sister determined to get justice for her brother. An independent woman hell-bent on finishing what she started even if it got her killed.

But it was the vulnerable side of Kate that played hell with his heart. Those moments when he saw the pain and the toughness that tried to counteract it. No woman could be stronger or more terrifying, he thought as he looked at her now. This was the kind of woman a man fell hard for. The kind a man spent a lifetime loving.

"Did you tell your brothers where we were going?" she asked as she pushed her plate away and he signaled the waitress for their check.

"So they could tell my brother the sheriff?" he asked.

"It crossed my mind."

He chuckled and shook his head. "It would have been the smart thing to do. I know Flint is working day and night to find the Dunns."

"Can he really throw us in jail for interfering in the investigation?"

Tucker sighed. "So you were eavesdropping last night. I should have known. I'm sure he could, but your father would bail *you* out."

She looked away. "Maybe not."

"They're only trying to protect you."

"I don't want to be protected," she said, turning again to meet his gaze. She lifted her chin, stubbornness making her blue eyes glitter.

"Did you ever consider the fact that your parents have already lost one child? What if they lose you, too?"

"My brother was the chosen one," she said. "Anyway, my parents would forge on blindly. It's what they do. Stiff upper lip. Head in the sand. They are both good at pretending ugliness doesn't exist in their rarified air."

"Seems their daughter is a lot like them."

Anger flashed in her eyes. "I am nothing like them!" she snapped a little too loudly, making the other people in the small café turn to look at her.

The waitress came out to give them their check. Tucker paid and the waitress left them alone again.

Kate lowered her voice. "How can you even say that?"

He smiled at her. "The forging ahead blindly. It just rang a bell when it came to you."

"It's not blindly. I just don't let anything stop me."

Except for a bullet, he thought. But then, that was why he was on his way to Jordan, Montana, looking for possible murderers. He was just as crazy as she was since, if he got caught, he'd be behind bars again. Flint had let him off once. He wouldn't again, he thought as they walked out to his pickup. But that was the least of his problems.

Earlier the sun had been shining to the east—over Jordan. But now dark clouds hunkered on the horizon, warning of a storm on its way.

But it would be nothing like the storm brewing back home when Flint found out that they'd taken off. He'd know they were after the Dunns. There would be hell to pay—if they survived whatever might be waiting for them.

Flint couldn't believe it when he got the call from Hawk.

"Appears they took off in the middle of the night," his brother told him. "Tuck left a note. They took his pickup. Her SUV is still in the yard so I would imagine they'll be back."

"The note. What did the note say?"

"Just said he and Kate had gone and not to worry."

"Not to worry?" The sheriff let out an oath under his breath. "What is it about this woman? I swear, when it comes to women, Tucker doesn't have the good sense of a rock."

"This one's different," Hawk said. "He was a rutting teenager back when he fell for Madeline. Kate... Well, she's special."

"Not you, too." Flint hung up. He'd been trying to find the last two Dunns—Melody and K.O. While Kevin had

been arrested when he was twenty-two, he hadn't had any
other run-ins with the law since.

Nor did it appear that either one of them were gainfully
employed, which he took to mean that they were either running cons or they were being paid under the table so they
didn't have to declare their income.

Right now they were like ghosts. Flint had to wonder
what they were running from. At first he'd thought it was
the discovery of the skeletal remains in the creek—a sure
sign of guilt.

But he couldn't find a record of them for almost the past
twenty years. How had they lived underground all that time?
Or was it possible they weren't even still alive? He had a call
in to a hospital in Wyoming about a patient who'd been admitted whose brother matched K.O.'s description now out
on the wire.

Neither had gone by Dunn, though. But since it was about
nineteen years ago, Flint thought it might be a clue. The
patient had been a young blonde woman with severe brain
trauma, so he knew he could be barking up the wrong tree.
But it was the only tree he had right now.

If they were hiding out, the fact that Tucker and Kate had
been rattling cages looking for them had probably forced them
to go even deeper underground.

The question wasn't why had Tucker and Kate taken off in
the middle of the night? It was where had they gone? One of
them must have found a lead to the Dunns. And hadn't called
him, he thought with a curse. Tucker had always been stubborn, wanting to do everything on his own. Just like all the
Cahill men, he thought. What a bunch they were.

But he suspected that Kate Rothschild was even worse.
He thought about putting out a BOLO on the two. But his
brother was already in trouble with the law. Tucker didn't
need that kind of attention. Once he found him, though, Flint

was going to lock him up and maybe Kate, too. He knew now it was the only way to keep them out of his investigation and keep them both safe.

His cell phone rang. He was hoping it was Tucker. It was Maggie. He quickly picked up, always pleased to talk to the woman he loved.

"Why don't you come down to the hospital for lunch?" his wife said. "I'm at the hospital. These babies are so adorable."

Deputy Harper Cole resented that he hadn't been one of the deputies put on the Dunn case. He was the one who'd found the shell casings that went with the slug in the woman's skull.

"What are you doing here on your day off?" the sheriff asked as he passed Harp in the hall.

"Just picking up my check." Which was true. But he was also here to pick up whatever information he could. He heard Flint say he was going out for an early lunch and if his brother Tucker called, to patch him through at the hospital.

Marsha was in the break room where she always hung out before her shift. She was a gossip magnet. If anyone knew what was going on at the sheriff's department, she did. She's the one who'd told him about Tucker Cahill's relationship with the deceased.

"What do you know about the Dunns?" Harp asked quietly as he took a seat at her table.

Marsha smiled and leaned forward as she filled him in. He was disappointed to realize that there wasn't much new.

"So Misty Dunn killed herself within days of her sister being murdered on the river," Harp said. "And the other one? Melody? The sheriff thinks she is with her brother, K.O., somewhere? There still aren't any leads?"

Marsha shook her head. No news made her sadder than it did him. "Imagine three identical young women. I suspect the men never knew which one they were with."

Harp nodded. "Or which one is dead. They all have the same DNA."

"But they all didn't have a broken leg that healed years ago," Marsha pointed out.

Unfortunately, that information wasn't worth anything unless he could find K.O. and Melody and find out which of the girls had broken her leg. It was the only way to make a positive identification on the bones that were found in the creek.

He stood up. "I'm going up to Clawson Creek and doing some snooping around."

"I thought it was your day off," Marsha said.

"Keep it on the q.t.—just between the two of us."

She gave him a wink. "Call me later."

Harp promised he would. In his car, he called Vicki and told her where he was going but not to tell anyone.

"Harp, be careful. This family sounds scary."

He chuckled. "I can handle myself. You just take care of you and our son. Don't worry. If anyone can find these con artists, it's me," he said confidently. "I'm going to make you proud."

"You always have."

He thought about her last words as he drove to Clawson Creek. The problem was that he *hadn't* always made her proud. Last year he'd done something he shouldn't have and he'd stupidly confessed it to her.

But since then he'd turned his life around, he reminded himself. He was becoming the man he never dreamed he could be. Even his father, the mayor of Gilt Edge, was proud of him. It was more than he'd ever had before. He was a husband, soon to be a father, a deputy who was helping solve cases. He was somebody—not just the mayor's worthless son.

On the outskirts of Clawson Creek, Harp slowed. Someone in this town knew where the Dunns had gone. All he had to do was find that person and convince him or her to talk.

★ ★ ★

"Where's this bar we're looking for?" Tucker asked as he drove his pickup into Jordan, Montana. Dark storm clouds blotted out the sun. The wind had picked up but so far it hadn't rained. He looked for the main street of this small isolated town, hoping he hadn't left the county—and faced going back to jail—on a wild-goose chase.

The area had become infamous some years ago because of a band of antigovernment militia who'd moved in and bucked the system, causing a standoff. Montana had become a hideout for the lawless—just as it had back in the Old West.

"Pull into that gas station," Kate said. She jumped out and ran in the moment he stopped. A few minutes later, she hurried back out and slid into the passenger seat again. "It's north of Jordan. Some place called Hell Creek."

He shot her a look. "Hell Creek. How appropriate."

As he drove through the tiny town of Jordan and headed north into rugged Missouri Breaks Country, he could understand why the Dunns might have chosen this area. It was miles from any other town, seriously in the middle of nowhere.

The landscape could have been that of the moon with towering spires of stone, deep gullies, wind-and water-scoured hillsides of eroded dust and stone. This had once been the home of dinosaurs, their bones still being excavated from the sides of the rugged bluffs.

The most visitors this area received came for Fort Peck Lake to fish or camp in the summer months or ice fish in the winter. In between, he doubted few people passed through except on their way to somewhere else.

They drove north for some miles, the dusty road getting rougher as they went. Not far from the lake, they saw several structures against the skyline. The first was a small gas station and convenience store with four rustic cabins behind it. The old-looking place sat on a rise overlooking the vast rugged country. Farther up the road sat the bar. Everything looked worn and seedy under the dark clouds overhead.

"Hell Creek Bar," Kate said, looking around as if expecting to see the Dunns.

In the distance, Tucker thought he could see a slice of blue water where the marina must be. Around back was an old motel that looked as if it had been turned into permanent living quarters.

He pulled into the bar, next to the four pickups parked out front. "This is just a suggestion, but from the looks of this bar—"

"I'm not going to walk in and shoot anyone," she said as she opened her door and was out before he could finish his lecture.

"That might be your best bet actually," he said to the empty pickup. With a sigh, he followed, noticing the way she had a hand gripped over the top of her purse. He swore under his breath, but given how rough the bar looked, it probably wouldn't be the first time it had seen gunplay. After all, this *was* Montana.

He caught up to Kate at the door. She'd hesitated as if hearing the raised voices coming from inside. It wasn't even noon and it sounded as if a lot of patrons were already hammered.

Pushing open the door, he stood back to let her enter like any well-trained gentleman. Cool, dark air, thick with the smell of stale beer, rushed out. Old cigarette smoke still lingered in the furnishings as they stepped in. Montana bars had been smoke-free for some years now, except for Native American casinos, but in a lot of them, you couldn't tell.

All the noise seemed to be coming from the back where a group of men were standing around a pool table, a game in progress.

Tucker steered Kate toward the bar stool closest to the door. The bartender extracted himself from the goings-on at the pool table and made his way toward them. When he was within a few yards, Tucker recognized Kevin "K.O." Dunn from his mug shot. He was older but had one of those boy-next-door faces that never seemed to change. His hair was still blond but longer. The thing that couldn't change was those eyes. Madeline-blue eyes, as Tucker now thought of them.

"It's him, isn't it?" Kate asked and reached into her purse.

CHAPTER TWENTY-ONE

As Harp drove into Clawson Creek, he spotted the bar and the café. Both had vehicles parked out front. Noting the time, he pulled into the café for a late breakfast.

A waitress in her late teens with the name tag Crissy came over with a menu and a glass of water as he sat down. As she fumbled out her order pad from her apron pocket, he got the impression she was new at this. But definitely eager.

"Just passing through?" she asked, curiosity shining in her dark eyes.

Harp opened the menu and chose the Prairie Wagon Special, which came with bacon, two eggs, hash browns and a side of flapjacks. He closed the menu and smiled up at her. "Coffee. Sugar and cream and advice."

Crissy had been scribbling but looked up, her painted eyebrows arching. "Advice?"

"If you wanted the dirt on a family from here, who would you ask in this town?"

The girl giggled and looked back toward the kitchen to make sure the cook wasn't paying any attention. "Depends on who you're asking about," she said, lowering her voice.

"Why don't you put that order in and then come back?" he suggested.

Grinning, she swept off to the back, returning a few minutes later. She looked excited. "So who do you want to know about?"

"The Dunns."

"Oh, them." She sounded disappointed. "No one cares about them anymore. They left town a long time ago."

"But your parents would have known them."

Crissy nodded. "My mother said they were scary weird."

He could hear the cook back in the kitchen scraping something with a spatula and grease popping, but he could also tell that the girl was worried about getting caught.

"Why did your mother say that?" he asked.

She looked toward the kitchen. "The one that killed herself?"

"Misty?"

The girl nodded. "I heard one of the sisters pushed her down the stairs."

"So she didn't kill herself."

The girl shrugged.

"Did your mother go to the funeral?"

"Wasn't one. The Dunns were in league with the devil. They didn't believe in funerals." The bell tinkled in the back and Crissy took off to get his food.

Harp turned to watch the cook questioning her before she returned with his food.

"You get in trouble with the cook?"

She shook her head, but it was clear she had. "Not supposed to visit with customers," she said quietly and headed to the back.

As he ate, he thought about what he'd learned. Nothing yet. Just idle gossip.

As Tucker sat down next to Kate at the bar, he put a hand over hers—and the gun she was holding inside her purse.

He started to say something but noticed that at least she was keeping the gun out of sight of the men who'd resumed their game at the pool table.

"Two beers." He looked to Kate. It was early for tequila, but with her, he never knew. All she did was nod. "Whatever you have on tap."

"You got it," K.O. Dunn said and tossed down two napkins before turning to walk down the bar to draw the drafts.

"Be cool," Tucker whispered.

"You know me."

"That's what has me worried. I don't want you killing an innocent man."

She scoffed at that as K.O. came back down the bar and placed a full glass of beer on each of the napkins.

"Anything else I can get you?" he asked.

"Actually, there is," Tucker said. "I was wondering if you've been back to Clawson Creek recently."

Instantly wary, K.O. asked, "Do I know you?"

"I knew your sister Madeline."

The man started to step away.

"I wouldn't do that if I were you," Kate said. "I have a gun in my lap and I swear I will shoot you before you can reach that weapon you have behind the bar. I am one hell of a shot."

K.O. froze. Fear registered in his blue eyes as he turned to look at them. He swept his gaze to Kate and back to Tucker. "You're not the law," he said, studying them. "What do you want?"

"Answers, that's all," Tucker said. "And then we're out of here."

"Who was Madeline working with?" Kate asked.

K.O. looked toward the men playing pool and the crowd of others cheering them on. "You have a lot of guts coming in here like this."

"You don't want the kind of trouble we can bring down

on this place," Tucker said. "This woman sitting next to me, along with being a great shot, is Clayton Rothschild's daughter."

The name registered on K.O.'s face.

"She's also an investigative journalist for a New York City paper."

"He left out the important part," Kate said. "Madeline was a…friend of my brother's. My brother, who killed himself because of her." K.O. looked as if he might try to run. "I wouldn't," she said, shifting on her bar stool. "You'd never reach the door."

"Look," the man said, lowering his voice as he moved closer to them. "That was Madeline's deal. I had nothing to do with it."

Kate shook her head. "I don't believe you. Someone helped her. I think it was you."

"No! You think I would pimp out my own sisters?" the man demanded.

"What about your father?" Tucker asked.

K.O. let out a bark of a laugh that made several men at the pool table turn. He leaned toward them, lowering his voice. "My father would have killed her if he'd known what she was doing, let alone that she'd involved Misty and Melody."

"Did he?"

The man frowned at Tucker. "Did he what?"

"Kill her. A young woman's skeletal remains were found in a creek over by Gilt Edge. We think they're Madeline's," he said. "Are you telling me you haven't heard?"

K.O. swore. "Are they sure it's Madeline?" He seemed genuinely taken aback by all this.

"The sheriff in Gilt Edge has been trying to reach her next of kin," Tucker said. "You're a hard man to find."

Shrugging, K.O. said, "If your family was as cursed as mine—"

"She was murdered," Tucker said.

"Wait, what? *Murdered?*" Again some men took interest in them as K.O. blurted out the last word. He lowered his voice and leaned toward them again. "I thought she drowned."

"We know she was working with someone who was waiting for her downstream," Kate said. "She was shot and buried under a pile of driftwood."

K.O. grasped the bar as if in shock. "You're sure she's dead? All this time?" He let out a laugh.

"There something funny about that?" Kate asked.

"Why do you think I've been hiding out all these years?" the man snapped. "You don't have any idea what Madeline is like."

"Where can we find Melody?" Kate asked.

The man looked wary again. "How should I know?"

Kate shifted to remind him no doubt of the pistol in her lap. "Tammy Holden thought you and Melody were…together."

K.O. didn't like the implication. "Watch what you say about Melody. She's had it worse than anyone in the family." He looked up and met Tucker's gaze. "If you're looking to get even for what Madeline did, you're barking up the wrong tree. Melody had nothing to do with it."

When the front door of the bar opened letting in a shaft of sunlight and a gust of wind, everyone turned to see who was coming in. Silhouetted in the doorway was a woman with long blond hair. As she started to step in, Tucker saw her face and gasped. Madeline.

After Harp walked around town, talking to anyone who would give him the time of day, he finally ended up at the bar. It was relatively quiet with only a couple of old-timers at one end of the bar and a wino-looking man at the other end.

He took the bar stool next to the wino, ordered a beer and struck up a conversation. The man looked at him bleary-eyed until Harp offered to buy him a drink. He and Ray became best buddies after that.

"So what's the deal with the Dunn family?" he asked.

"Kell Dunn was a prick," the man said without hesitation.

Harp laughed, glad to have someone finally telling him what he really thought. "And the son?"

"K.O.?" Ray shrugged. "Not a bad kid."

"Okay, what about the girls?"

"There was something wrong there, spooky to see three of 'em looking like carbon copies." Ray shook his head. "Kell and his crazy wife dressed them alike for years. Those girls were his pride and joy." The man chuckled. "His downfall, too."

"What do you mean?"

"They scattered like rain the moment they were old enough. Broke him. Add to that his financial ruin."

"What about Misty Dunn? I heard she killed herself."

"Did she?" The man laughed and took a long pull on his drink.

Harp blinked. "What are you saying?"

"Half the people in town think Kell killed her. She apparently was his favorite."

"And the other half of town?"

Ray rubbed his grizzled chin for a moment, studying himself in the mirror behind the bar. "That it was one of the sister's done it. Never seen a body put into the ground that quickly. Buried her in the old cemetery before she was even cold."

Harp frowned. "I heard they didn't have a funeral."

"One of the girls came into town for wood for the casket. That's how cheap Kell was. If you get them in the ground soon enough, you don't have to have the body embalmed."

Harp thought about that for a moment. "You know where

I can find a shovel?" Ray just happened to have one in the back of his truck.

"I'll get your shovel back to you." Harp handed him a ten.

"No hurry." Ray started back into the bar after giving him instructions to the old cemetery. "I should warn you. People say that piece of land is haunted." The old wino looked toward the sinking sun. "I'd dig fast if I was you."

Once at the cemetery, Harp almost changed his mind. The sun seemed to be disappearing fast, casting long shadows through the gravestones and the trees that bordered the cemetery.

But still he got out, grabbed the shovel and headed in through the weed-choked path. As he did, he noticed that he wasn't the only one who'd been here recently.

On a hunch, Harp followed the fresh tracks in the dust right to Misty Dunn's grave. He took in the graves and markers. The mother was buried here and apparently the grandmother. So where was the old man buried? Or was he still alive? Ray had said the family cleared out right after Misty went into the ground.

No wonder people thought it was suspicious. No one had seen any of them since, from what he'd been able to find out. Very odd.

With the day cooling down from the waning sun, he went to work and hadn't dug far when the shovel hit something solid that made a loud thump and sent a shudder up his arms. That alone spooked him. Weren't bodies supposed to be buried six feet deep?

He began to dig faster. Harp felt his excitement increasing. Everyone in town had told a different story. But what they'd all been saying was that something was wrong about Misty's death—and burial. He needed to know if Misty Dunn was in this wooden box. Pushing away all his fears of the dead, he shoveled faster.

His shovel struck the wood again. It had rotted over the years. That's why he should have known better than to jump down onto it. The wood held for a moment, then collapsed under his weight. He grabbed for earth, repelled by the thought of falling onto the body.

Bracing himself for the worst given the odor rising up out of that coffin, Harp managed to balance on one edge. He peeled back a piece of the rotten wood top. Hot, sweaty and filthy with the fine dirt, he tried not to think about haunted cemeteries or the dead all watching him dig up a body.

As he peeled the wood back and looked down at the mummified face, a cry of revulsion escaped his lips. He stared into the dark holes where the eyes used to be, a chill running the length of him just moments before he heard a sound behind him and the scrape of the shovel being picked up off the ground.

His cell phone rang. Vicki. He pulled it out. Saw the text. Vicki was having the baby.

The flat of the shovel blade caught him in the side of the head. Harp fell face-first onto the rotten coffin. He felt his legs drop down onto the body inside. He tried to get up, but as he did, he was knocked down as a shovelful of dirt struck him in the back. Struck by another shovelful of dirt, then another, he couldn't breathe from the weight of it. A shovelful of dirt landed on his neck. His face slammed into the edge of the coffin, and just before the lights went out, he thought he heard the sound of a vehicle.

Kate saw the blonde's gaze lock with K.O.'s an instant before the woman spun around and tore out of the bar. Tucker seemed too shocked to move. Kate grabbed her purse, slid off her bar stool and went after the woman.

She caught up with her before Melody Dunn reached the

street. "Melody?" She grabbed her arm and spun her around to face her.

Shock made her let go of the woman's arm. She stared into Melody's blank blue eyes, her heart pounding. Behind her, she heard the bar door bang open. Tucker and K.O. joined them. Several other men came out, as well.

"Go back inside," K.O. ordered the men. "I have this under control. *Now!*" He dropped his menacing tone at once as he saw how upset his sister was. He reached for her hand. "It's all right, Melody. No one is going to hurt you."

"I wanted a cola." She choked out the words like sobs in a little-girl voice. "You said I could come in and have a cola as long as I was careful and didn't go out into the street."

"You did great. I'm sorry you got scared. Come on back inside. I'll get you a cola. You can sit in your favorite booth and drink it while I talk to these people."

Melody turned empty blue eyes on them for a moment. "A big cola with lots of ice and a cherry. Don't forget the cherry."

"I won't. I'll make it just the way you like it." He looked at Kate. "I'll be out in a minute." With that, he ushered his sister into the bar.

Kate's gaze shifted to Tucker. He looked as if he'd been hit by a truck. Melody Dunn was beautiful and clearly damaged. Kate had seen that the moment she'd looked into the woman's eyes.

K.O. came back out looking like a whipped dog. "I hope you have what you came for. You know now why I'm protective of Melody."

"What happened to her?" Tucker asked.

"A car accident shortly after we left Clawson Creek. The doctor says she has the mind of a five-year-old." K.O. looked up, grief in his eyes. "Like I said, my family is cursed."

"Why *did* you leave Clawson Creek the way you did?" Kate asked.

"I had to get Melody away from Madeline." His voice broke. "I didn't know what happened to Madeline and Misty. My father had made some bad investments and lost everything. I would imagine he left because creditors were chasing him. I didn't know what happened to Madeline and Misty."

"Inside the bar, when you heard that the woman we believe was Madeline had been murdered, I got the feeling that you suspected who might have done it," Kate said.

"I told you. I wasn't involved in my sister's...business."

"But you knew about it," Tucker said.

"I knew she conned men out of trinkets, yes."

"You also knew about the water trick she pulled," Kate said.

"Madeline was like a fish when she was little. She loved water and climbing trees and doing crazy things. Nothing scared her. We were the ones who were afraid of her. Our father said she'd been chosen by the devil. He tried to exorcise the evil out of her." K.O. shook his head. "If anything, it only made her worse."

"What about Misty?" Tucker asked.

K.O. shook his head. "I hadn't seen her before I left with Melody, but I knew she would do whatever Madeline told her to do. I couldn't save her, but I thought I could save Melody." He looked like he might cry. "Instead, I almost got her killed."

"So Misty could have helped Madeline with her cons?" Kate prodded.

"I suppose so," he said. "Look, Madeline was very persuasive. Who knows what she talked anyone into."

Kate looked over at Tucker, wondering at how persuasive Madeline had been.

The door of the bar opened. Melody stuck her head out tentatively. "I ate the cherry. It's all gone." She sounded close to tears.

"I have to go," K.O. said. "I'm coming," he called to his sister. "Go wait for me and I'll bring you two cherries."

Melody broke into a huge smile, making the years vanish and giving Kate a glimpse of what Madeline had looked like when Tucker had loved her. Beautiful but also damaged. She wondered if that was a combination that her brother had also found irresistible.

The door closed. The wind picked up some trash along the front of the building and sent it whirling into the air.

But Kate hardly noticed. She'd seen Tucker's expression when he'd looked at Melody as if he was seeing Madeline. She felt her heart break for him and for herself.

Thunder rumbled in the distance. The bruised sky had darkened ominously. "Just one more thing," Tucker said. "We were at your old house outside Clawson Creek yesterday. Someone took potshots at us."

"It wasn't me. I was here all day. You can ask around. Why would you go there?" K.O. asked, sounding horrified. "I haven't been back to that house in almost twenty years. You couldn't get me to go back there, even at gunpoint."

"Did Madeline ever break her leg? Her left leg?"

K.O. frowned. "No, that was Misty. Madeline pushed her down the stairs. Why are you asking me this?"

Tucker swore under his breath. The body in the creek wasn't Madeline's. It was *Misty's*. Was it possible? Was Madeline still alive? "If Misty was the one who broke her leg, then the body in the creek is hers—not Madeline's."

Kate couldn't miss K.O.'s shock. All the color drained from his face. He took a step toward the bar, then another. He looked as if he wanted to take off running and never stop. But he had Melody waiting for him.

He hesitated at the bar door, looking back at them for a moment. From inside came Melody's plaintive call to him. He seemed to take a deep breath and entered, the door closing behind him.

Kate looked at Tucker. "It wasn't Madeline in the creek?"

"My brother told me that one of the leg bones had an old fracture. I think there is a good chance it was Misty on the bridge that night, not Madeline."

She shook her head, reeling from the implications. Tucker looked as if he'd been coldcocked with a bat. "But we saw Misty's grave at the old cemetery outside Clawson Creek. If the woman in the creek was Misty, then who is in that grave?"

CHAPTER TWENTY-TWO

Thunder boomed closer. The temperature dropped. Lightning splintered nearby. Before Tucker could move, the sky seemed to open. Huge droplets of rain swept down like bullets.

Only moments before, he'd been rooted to the ground, his head spinning. Of course that had been Misty on the bridge that night. The fear. The hesitation. Not Madeline. Not the woman who'd conned him for so long before getting her sister to finish it on the bridge.

Goose bumps had rippled over his skin. To think that Madeline might be alive… The duffel bag in her old house. The perfumed notes. She'd been trying to tell him all this time to back off.

The rain brought him back to earth with a jolt.

He and Kate made a run for his pickup, both getting soaked before they could slide inside and slam the doors. The storm, which had been hanging over them ominously since this morning, now roared around them. The raindrops turned to sleet and then hail before his eyes.

Gale-force winds rocked the pickup as hail pinged off the hood and cab. "I've heard about storms in this area," Tucker said, having to yell to be heard over the racket. "But I've never seen anything like this." He glanced over at Kate. She looked just as good soaking wet as she did dry.

"I've never seen anything like this, either," she said, staring out at the storm. But he could tell she was more shocked by what they'd just learned.

"This could be a problem." Tucker watched water run down the center of the dirt road they'd just driven in on for a moment before starting the pickup's engine.

"What do you mean?" Kate asked, looking over at him.

"These roads turn to gumbo. We need to get out of here— if it isn't already too late." He backed out, but the moment he pulled onto the already-muddy road, he realized it *was* too late. The top layer of dust that had churned up on their way to Hell Creek was now greasy slick. The tires fought to find purchase. "I'm just hoping we can get back to that convenience store."

The drive was less than a half mile, but the pickup was all over the road as he tried to get there. By the time he pulled into the convenience store gas station, the tires were thick with mud. It was clear they weren't going any farther until the road dried back out.

"We're not getting out of here until the weather changes," he told Kate as they sat in the truck, waiting for a break in the rain to go inside. The hail had stopped. Now the rain fell in a torrent, running like a river into every low spot and pooling on the road. Low clouds scudded past on a wind that rocked the pickup.

"How long will that be?" she yelled over the noise of the pounding rain.

"Once the sun comes out, the gumbo will dry hard as concrete. Until then, though, we're here."

"Do you want to talk about it?" Kate asked after a few minutes of nothing but the hammer of the rain on the truck cab.

"No." But he knew that wouldn't stop her.

"Is it true? Is Madeline alive somewhere?"

"I don't know. But I suspect she is."

Kate shook her head. "She could be the one buried in Misty's grave." She sounded as if she was hoping that was true.

Neither of them spoke as the rain pounded the pickup with no sign of letting up.

"I think we should make a run for it," Tucker said as he saw another vehicle fighting its way up the road. "You can stay here, but I'm going to see about getting us a couple of cabins until we can drive out of here." He opened his door and ran, with Kate at his heels, of course.

Kate stood in the center of the small cabin and shivered as she watched Tucker get a fire going in the woodstove. Not long after they'd entered the convenience store, two pickup loads of fishermen had shown up. The owner of the place had given each group one cabin of the three she had left and told them to make the best of it because, according to the weather, it would be a day or two before anyone was getting out of there.

As they were headed through the rain to their cabin, another truck had pulled up with a boat on the back covered in mud. Looked like the two fishermen would be waiting in their truck, Tucker said. "We're lucky we got a cabin. Don't worry, you can have the bed."

She looked at the bed now. A double that sagged in the middle covered with a worn comforter.

"Not your usual accommodations," Tucker said now as he caught her looking at the bed. The fire flickered in the woodstove, spitting out the promise of heat.

"I can rough it with the best of them," she said, taking offense.

He laughed. "You roughing it with the best of them, huh? Guess we'll see about that since we're stranded here for a while. I'm going to run over to the store and get us something to eat before those fishermen clean the place out. You want anything in particular to eat?"

She shook her head, just imagining what the small out-of-the-way convenience store might offer. "I'm not hungry."

It was true. The only thing she wanted was sleep. She'd been all worked up on the way here, excited about the possibility of finally putting an end to her search. Now, though, after meeting K.O. and Melody, she felt confused and simply tired. *Madeline might be alive?* Wasn't that what she'd hoped, that she would get the chance to confront the woman?

But that was before she met Tucker. Before she started falling for him. Now she never wanted to hear Madeline's name ever again.

"I believe K.O. that he wasn't working with his sister," she said, feeling the need to talk about it rather than think or, worse, cry. "But I got the feeling that he had some idea of who might have killed her. Killed Misty, I guess." She looked at him.

"Kate, I don't have any answers. I need to call my brother so he can look into it."

"He'll arrest you. And maybe me, too."

Tucker said nothing for a moment. "You sure you don't want something to eat?"

She shook her head. As Tucker left, she moved to the bed, pulled back the covers and glanced at the sheets. He was right. She was used to nice things. The sheets looked worn and pilled with noticeable bumps, but she didn't care. Kicking off her shoes, she started to climb in when she realized that her jeans were too damp to sleep in.

Hurriedly, she discarded them, laying them across the chair next to the bed before diving under the cold covers. A fire crackled in the woodstove, but the cabin was still freezing.

She closed her eyes, willing herself to fall asleep so she didn't have to think.

But of course that didn't happen. She kept seeing the expression on Tucker's face when he saw Melody. No, she thought, when he saw an image of Madeline in the woman's innocent face. When he realized the body in the creek had been Misty's—not Madeline's—and that Madeline might be alive. He was a man besotted and, as far as she could tell, always would be.

She squeezed her eyes tighter, feeling the heat of her tears. She couldn't hold them back. Turning her face into the pillow, she cried until the sheets began to warm up and so did she. Her emotions spent, she let exhaustion take her.

Tucker came into the cabin, his arms loaded with enough junk food to last them two days at least. It would probably take that long to get out of here once the storm moved on.

He looked around as he started to put the bags down, thinking Kate must be in the bathroom. But the door was ajar. Then he saw her jeans tossed over the chair beside the bed.

Quietly, he put down the bags he carried and moved toward the bed. She was so slim and the bed sagged so badly that he hadn't even noticed the slight lump in the middle. He smiled down at her, enjoying this peaceful Kate. She looked like a woman without a care in the world—if you didn't notice that the skin around her eyes was red and puffy. She'd been crying.

He felt his heart break and wanted to scoop her up in his arms and hold her and tell her that everything was going to be all right. But he had his doubts about that. At least now she was just dead to this world and quickly regretted thinking it.

As he stepped away, he felt sick. The remains in the creek were Misty Dunn's. Not Madeline's. He thought about K.O., remembering how the man was with his sister Melody. He agreed with Kate. He couldn't see K.O. as the killer.

The rain seemed to be letting up a little. Stepping outside under the small roof at the front of the cabin, he pulled out his cell phone and called Flint.

"Where the hell are you?" his brother snapped.

"Hell Creek actually."

"Funny."

"Not so much. A storm blew in. We're trapped here for a while. The road out is impassible until it quits raining and dries up." He told Flint what they'd learned. "I thought you could check out K.O.'s alibi, but quite frankly, I believe him. He seems to be his sister Melody's only caregiver. He's very protective of her."

Flint was silent for so long Tucker worried that they might have been disconnected. "So that's the last of the Dunns," his brother said finally. "You told him about Madeline?"

"He was upset, relieved actually, since he was trying to protect Melody from Madeline when he took her out of Clawson Creek. But unfortunately, Madeline never had a broken leg." His brother swore. "The remains found in the creek are Misty's."

"He's sure?"

"He said Madeline pushed her down the stairs and Misty broke her leg. He's sure. I think Madeline is alive. I also think K.O. is afraid of her and will take Melody and hide again. Kate seemed to think he suspected who might have killed Misty, but while he denied it, I think she's right."

"Madeline."

"He's running from her, but I think there is more to it. I think someone else is involved."

"Nice work," Flint said after a moment. "Ever thought about going into law enforcement?"

He hadn't. "If you're being facetious—"

"Not at all," the sheriff said. "You can look into it while you're locked up again in my jail." Flint said nothing for a few moments. "So you'll be back once the roads are passable?"

"I'll call when we leave here. We've hunted over here so I don't have to tell you how bad this kind of mud gets."

"No," the sheriff said. "At least it should keep the two of you out of trouble."

He thought about the woman he'd left back inside the way-too-small, way-too-intimate motel cabin. "You'd think so." He disconnected and stood for a moment, breathing in the cold wet air as the storm moved on and the rain began to slow.

Taking a deep breath, he went back inside, then tossed more wood on the fire and stretched out in the old recliner near the woodstove, praying for the oblivion of sleep. Madeline had made his life hell nineteen years ago. She wasn't finished with him.

Only now, it wasn't just him. There was Kate.

Kate knew it was only a dream because she was no longer in the cabin and yet her heart was pounding. A storm was raging outside. Thunder boomed, making her jump, followed almost instantly by a sharp, blinding flash of lightning. She realized that she was in a house but not one she'd ever seen before. She'd been looking for something, searching, when suddenly goose bumps rose on her arms as the air inside the house seemed to change. Her fear accelerated as she realized that she wasn't alone anymore.

A stair creaked. She looked up the wide stairway to see a dark figure standing there and realized she was now in Madeline's old house. Her blood froze in her veins as the figure began to descend the stairs.

Run! But her feet wouldn't move. It was as if she was glued to the spot, watching something malevolently evil coming toward her.

Her heart pounded so loudly she couldn't hear anything else. She tried to scream, to warn Tucker. Tucker? She'd forgotten he'd been with her. But where was he now?

The figure was clad in all black, including the hoodie that covered most of the face in dark shadow. Kate knew that once she saw the face, she was going to die. On the stairs, a gloved hand reached up and pushed back the hood and she came face-to-face with—

Kate sat up in bed, unaware that she was screaming until Tucker bounded from the recliner next to the woodstove and took her in his arms.

"It's all right," he was saying as the scream died off on her lips. He stroked her hair, murmuring words of comfort. "You're all right. Just a bad dream. I'm here. No one's going to hurt you."

Tucker had seen the terrified look in those wide green eyes and was surprised anything could frighten her. Kate clung to him. Her breathing was raspy and fast as she trembled in his arms. All he could think was that it must have been one hell of a nightmare.

"Want to talk about it?" he asked as she began to relax.

She shook her head and disengaged from him to get up and walk to the window. Parting the curtains, she peered out, her back to him. He could see that it was still raining a little. The sky was lightening but the horizon was still black with storm clouds.

Kate looked so enticing silhouetted against the last of the storm. He wondered how long they would be trapped here, how long he could be in this cabin without doing something they might both regret.

When she finally spoke, he could barely hear her over the crackle of the fire in the woodstove. "What was it about her?" she asked, her voice low as the lighting in the room.

Tucker realized he'd been waiting for this question. Kate was convinced he was still in love with Madeline, would always be, and now that Madeline might be alive... How could he convince her that Madeline had been a fantasy for a teenage boy? Kate... Well, Kate was the real thing. The kind of woman any red-blooded male would die for.

He got up from the bed and moved to where she was standing, her back to him, until he was nearly touching her. He could smell the scent of her shampoo in her hair that fell like a dark river in the firelight.

His heart pounded being this close to her and yet still not touching her. He breathed in the mesmerizing scent, knowing that if he touched her, if he turned her to face him, if he looked into those bottomless green eyes, he would be lost forever.

"Kate?"

She closed her eyes, reveling in the way her name sounded on his lips. She could feel him directly behind her. All her nerve endings tingled at even the anticipation of his touch.

"Kate?" Soft as a caress, the sweet sound sent shivers across her bare skin. That ache at her center intensified, but she didn't turn around. She couldn't bear to look into those gray eyes and know that he could see how vulnerable she was feeling.

Mostly, she couldn't bear to see pity in those eyes. She didn't even want to admit the truth to herself. She'd fallen for a man who was in love with another woman. She'd fallen in love with Tucker Cahill.

Gently, he pushed her long hair aside and pressed a kiss to the nape of her neck. She shivered, a sigh slipping from her lips as he pressed another kiss against her bare flesh before he let her hair drop to her shoulders again.

"You want to know about Madeline?" he whispered so close now that she could feel his body heat.

She nodded, terrified that she might cry again. She didn't want to know what it was about Madeline that had ensnared him so completely. But at the same time, she had to know.

"Madeline had only one thing going for her," he said, his voice so soft she had to lean back a little to hear him. "She knew how to drive a teenage boy crazy. A grown man would have seen right through her amateurish seduction."

Her chest tightened. She ached with longing. This man... She'd never felt such need. Desire ran like a wildfire through her veins, making her legs weak and her heart thunder in her chest.

"She used sex as a weapon," he whispered against her ear, sending a shiver through her. If he didn't stop... But she felt as if she might die if he did. "Not knowing any better, I thought it was love. Now, because of you, I know the difference."

His large warm hands settled on her shoulders before he slowly turned her to face him. She felt her heart leap to her throat. His gaze locked with hers. "Kate." And then she was in his arms, burying her face in his shirt.

"Oh, Kate."

"Oh, Kate." He repeated the words, a man surrendering. All the fight was gone. As well as all the reasons this was his worst idea yet. All his good intentions. He'd let this woman get to him. As hard as he'd tried to hold her at arm's length, she'd knocked down the barriers he'd built after Madeline.

He'd promised himself that no woman would get too close again. That he would never trust that much. That he wouldn't, couldn't, love with that heart-opening intensity that could leave him devastated once again.

But he hadn't counted on meeting Kate Rothschild. She charged into things with so much courage and determination that he'd found himself in awe of her grit. Kate, who'd spent nineteen years planning retribution for her brother. Kate, who was as vulnerable as him—and hated it equally as much.

"Oh, Kate," he said again as he gently lifted her chin to look into those green eyes. Their gazes locked. Her breathing quickened along with his. He could no longer lie to himself. He thought he'd loved Madeline. Now he knew what real love felt like. What he felt for this woman standing before him in nothing but a T-shirt and pale pink underwear.

He'd tried to keep her at arm's length but couldn't. He'd wanted this from almost the first time he'd laid eyes on her. The hours they'd spent together had been pure torture. The woman made him crazy and breathless and aching inside for more. He wanted her like he'd never wanted anything before.

Desire spiked through him as he thought of what he wanted to do to her, with her. The scent of her, the feel of her bare skin against his lips, against his tongue, against his own naked flesh.

He dropped his mouth to hers, taking possession of her with a demanding kiss. She answered in kind, both of them clinging to each other as if caught in a gale-force wind. He swept her up and carried her to the bed. He knew once he made love with her he would only want to do it again and again. He wanted her completely, in every possible way, forever.

That alone should have stopped him. This woman could do more than break his heart. And yet, the longing in him was a force of its own. He lowered her to the bed and looked down into those eyes. "You sure about this?" he asked, his voice husky with desire.

Her gaze locked with his, she pulled him down into a kiss. He gave in to it, feeling as if he was on a runaway train. There was no getting off this wild ride, even if he'd wanted to.

CHAPTER TWENTY-THREE

The wind blew all night. Not that Kate noticed. She'd been wrapped up in Tucker—quite literally. Now, lying on her side, spooned against his warm, hard body, she didn't want to move. But she'd awakened to the sound of her phone. She'd turned it to Vibrate and left it on the small kitchen table three yards or so from the bed. The phone danced across the worn Formica top and finally came to rest.

It was the eighth time the phone had done that since she'd awakened. Her mother calling? Her father? Peter? Could be any one of them. Whoever it was they were quite insistent and that's what worried her.

Tucker stirred behind her and pulled her even tighter against him. She lay back, warm smooth flesh to warm smooth flesh, wishing she never had to move from this position. She smiled as she felt the familiar representation of his desire. It stirred a need that she'd thought sated after everything he'd done to her last night. As if she could get enough of him.

Her phone went off again.

Tucker lifted his head to look at the table. "Is that your phone?"

"It is. I'm afraid something has happened. I probably should check it."

"Hmm," he said, lowering his head to her shoulder, where he began to leave a trail of warm kisses across her skin.

She moaned, closing her eyes. Never in her wildest dreams had she ever imagined that making love could be like this. The men she'd known had always been polite, tentative and boring as if they had a script to follow.

There had been nothing tentative or scripted about Tucker Cahill. He'd taken her with a wanton abandonment the first time. She'd clung to him, crying out with each release until gasping for breath, her nails digging into his back, and him arching in a howl of pleasure before collapsing with her in his arms.

The next time, he'd explored her body as if he needed to know every square inch of it—and the exact spots that made her crazy with desire. They'd laughed and played most of the night, with her exploring his body as well, until it felt as if they'd always known each other this intimately, before they'd collapsed into an exhausted satiated nightmareless sleep.

"I have to get that," Kate said as the phone began to vibrate again. She rose from the bed. The cabin had cooled down after the woodstove had gone out. She rushed naked to the table, scooped up the phone and dived back under the covers, making Tucker laugh and pull her into his warm body again.

He held her as she checked her phone, kissing the nape of her neck and following her spine downward. "It's my mother." Her heart was in her throat as she listened to the voice mail. "Oh, no."

"What is it?" he said, sitting up to look at her.

"My father's back in the hospital. This time it sounds seri-ous," she said as she turned to look at him.

Without a word, he got up to go to the window. "It looks like the wind has dried things out." He turned. Since the

woodstove had gone out during the night, the only warm spot
was in the bed under the covers where she now lay naked.

She saw desire burn like quicksilver in his gray eyes, then
dim as he said, "I should get you home as soon as possible.
But if you stay naked like that much longer…"

She nodded, as disappointed as he was that they had to leave
here. She got up and padded across the icy cold floor to re-
trieve her clothing. Out of the corner of her eye, she watched
Tucker pull on his jeans. She wanted to lay her palm against
the warm skin of his back, but she knew what would happen
if she did. He was right. She needed to get home. She hurriedly dressed in the freezing-cold cabin, praying her father
was all right.

"So how does it work?" Billie Dee asked, trying not to get
her hopes up after what Henry had told her. For so long she'd
believed she would never see her daughter again.

"You can go online and send in your DNA, letting her
know you want to find her," Henry said.

"But what if she doesn't want to see me?" she asked, her
voice breaking.

"Tex, she wouldn't have put her DNA into the system unless she wanted to find you."

She nodded, tears blurring her eyes. "It's so…scary. I've
prayed that someday I would find her or she'd find me, but
what if she can't forgive me?"

"Would you tell her who her father is?" Henry asked.

"He's still a powerful oilman in Houston. His wife died.
He's remarried to a younger woman much like his first wife."

"You don't have to tell her," he said.

She got up and walked around the kitchen, her fear growing. "I don't know what to do."

"You don't have to do anything right now. You can think
about it," he assured her. "It's entirely up to you."

She turned to smile at him. "I don't know what I would do without you."

"You'll never have to find out."

Harp opened his eyes, surprised and confused to find himself in a hospital bed. For a moment he thought it was last year when he'd almost died after doing something incredibly stupid and that his whole year of working to prove himself had all been nothing but a hopeful fantasy.

So when the sheriff walked in, he hadn't known what to expect. Flint had wanted to fire him from day one. The only thing that had kept him employed was the fact that his daddy was the mayor.

"How are you feeling?" Flint asked. He sounded concerned, more concerned than he had in the past, that was for sure.

Harp licked his dry lips. The sheriff poured some water from a pitcher by the bed into a cup with a straw and handed it to him. He took a long drink before handing it back.

"What happened?" he asked, his voice froggy.

Flint grimaced, a familiar expression the sheriff used when Harp had done something that wasn't according to protocol. "You don't remember?"

He held his breath, feeling his career and all his dreams slipping away.

"You dug up a grave on your day off," the sheriff said.

Harp let out the breath with a sigh of relief. It wasn't last year. It hadn't all been a dream. He'd saved the day a few times since then. He wasn't a total screwup. Also, his memory was coming back. "Misty Dunn's grave," he said. "I just had this feeling…"

"Turns out that your instincts were correct."

"It wasn't her body in the wooden casket, right?"

Flint smiled. "No, it wasn't. It was her father's. According to the coroner, he'd been murdered. Sonny sent the slugs to the lab but he's betting they will turn out to be from the same gun that killed the woman we thought was Madeline. Turns out the bones found in the creek were Misty's."

Harp frowned. His head hurt. "So someone killed the old man, and everyone thought it was Misty's body in the grave… Wait, why would anyone do that?"

"The popular theory is that Misty was the woman Tucker met on the bridge that night and Madeline was the person waiting for her downstream. They possibly argued, and Misty ended up dead. But how did she explain what had happened to Misty when Madeline went home? Maybe another argument ensued, the father is killed and buried in the old cemetery and everyone is told it was Misty who died. No one sees Kell, the old man, and the family has left. No one knows the truth." Flint looked at him. "Until you decided to dig up Misty's grave."

"How about that," Harp said. "So where is this Madeline I keep hearing so much about?"

"That's the million-dollar question," the sheriff said.

"We have to find her," Harp said, trying to sit up. "She's the only one who can clear your brother."

The sheriff gently pushed him back down. "You aren't going anywhere. The doc says you're here at least until tomorrow. You have a nasty bump on the side of your head. Fortunately, no concussion, though the blow must have been enough to knock you out."

"Wait, how did you find me?" Harp asked, surprised he wasn't still lying in that grave. He now remembered the feel of the dirt being shoveled over him. The thought made him shudder.

"Some old man named Ray said he met you at the bar. He got worried about you when you didn't return his shovel and drove out to the cemetery."

"I remember hearing the sound of a vehicle."

"Ray must have scared your would-be killer away and saved your life. He took his shovel back. Said if you need it again, to let him know."

Harp smiled, glad the sheriff was finding the humor in this.

"Once Ray called the sheriff you were brought by helicopter to the hospital here in Gilt Edge. By the way, Tucker found K.O. and one of the sisters, Melody."

"Is that who hit me and knocked me into that grave?"

The sheriff shook his head. "They were miles away. We're looking into who attacked you while you were grave robbing."

Harp heard the chastisement in his boss's words. He should have known a lecture was coming. "Probably should have let you know where I was."

"You think?"

"But then again, you would have tried to stop me," Harp said.

Flint nodded. "Something about protocol, yes." But he smiled. "Good work, Deputy. Now, get some rest. Vicki is outside in the hallway and anxious to see you."

"You tell her I'm a hero?" Harp joked.

"I figured you'd take care of that yourself," Flint said, but he was still smiling. "I thought you'd like to meet your son."

After Tucker dropped Kate at her SUV on the ranch, he showered and changed before calling the sheriff's department. His brother answered as soon as the dispatcher put the call through.

"Are you headed back?" Flint asked.

"I'm at the ranch. I'd come down to the sheriff's department but—"

"I'll be right over."

Good to his word, Flint pulled up not five minutes later. Tucker met him downstairs in the living room. He hadn't seen

Hawk or Cyrus, both apparently out working on the ranch. He felt guilty that he hadn't done an honest day's work since he'd been home.

"I called over to Hell Creek Bar," Flint said without preamble. "Both K.O. and Melody cleared out this morning."

That didn't surprise him, though he had wondered if maybe K.O. was tired of running. What bothered Tucker was who exactly Madeline's brother was running from. Was it her? Was she that evil? Or was there more to the story?

"By the way," Flint said. "Where's Kate?"

He told him about her father being admitted to the hospital. "She's gone to Helena."

"I have news," Flint said after they'd sat down in the living room.

Tucker listened, not surprised that Deputy Harper Cole hadn't found Misty Dunn in that grave up north. "It was the father?"

"Murdered. Slugs were found in the coffin as if he hadn't been dead when he'd been put in there and was finished off."

"Tell me it wasn't my pistol," he said.

"The slugs match your pistol, but that's the good news," Flint assured him. "You had no reason to kill Kell Dunn. Also, you have an alibi. You were still on the ranch before the Dunns buried who they said was their sister Misty. Apparently whoever had killed the father thought his body would never be found."

Tucker couldn't believe this. "What do you mean *whoever*? Who was left in that house? K.O. and Melody had already cleared out. Misty was dead. The way I see it the only person left was Madeline."

"Except Madeline couldn't have killed her father, built him a coffin, put him in it and buried it at the old cemetery all by herself."

"So there has to be someone else involved." Just as Kate

had been saying all along. The mysterious accomplice that she was determined to find.

"You sure K.O. didn't stick around long enough to help Madeline?"

Tucker shook his head. "I honestly believe he's afraid of her."

"Sounds like he has good reason."

"How are you going to find her?" Tucker asked.

Flint met his gaze. He looked upset. "I think she's going to come looking for you—that's why I'm going to lock you up. If Kate comes back still determined to play detective, then she's going behind bars with you."

"I like the sound of that," Tucker said.

"Not with you. Just in the same jail." His brother gave him the eye. "Something happen in Hell Creek?"

"I'm in love with her."

Flint lifted a brow. "That was quick."

"Not with this woman. She's…" He shook his head. "She's so much that I can't even list all the things about her that drive me crazy, that make me laugh, that make me want her like I've never wanted anything or anyone in my life. She's… everything."

His brother laughed. "You do have it bad. That's another reason you should be locked up for a while."

"Flint, if you really want to find Madeline Dunn and end this, then you have to let me go. Like you said, she will find me—but not if I'm locked up in jail. Also, you can't prove I left the county."

"Are you serious? You called and told me—"

"I was drunk."

His brother rolled his eyes. "If we're right, then Madeline already tried to kill you once. You know what this woman is capable of."

He nodded. "But she doesn't know what *I'm* capable of. I

used to be putty in her hands and her sister Misty's, as well. I've grown up. You need to let me do this."

"I can't lose you again," Flint said. "You don't know what you're asking."

"I do. It's my neck on the line. Madeline tried to frame me for murder. She'll show herself with me free and you know it. Otherwise, why would she come forward?"

His brother raked a hand through his hair, a gesture all the brothers shared, he realized. "You see her, you even get a glimpse of her, you call me. Is that clear?"

"Absolutely. I have your number on speed dial. But there might be one problem."

"Kate," Flint said.

"She can't be in the picture. Right now she's in Helena at her father's bedside."

"The moment she heads this way, I'll have her picked up."

Tucker hated to do that to her, but he had to know she was safe. And now more than ever, he wanted this over. He couldn't live without Kate. But first he had to deal with his old girlfriend.

CHAPTER TWENTY-FOUR

As the batch of brownies came out of the oven, Billie Dee made a plate to take into the bar to Ashley Jo. She didn't know how much longer she could wait for the DNA results. Every day being around Ashley Jo, she saw more of her daughter in the young woman.

Picking up the plate of brownies, she fought to get control of her emotions as best she could and walked out to the bar.

Ashley Jo was busy cleaning a table of four that had just left.

Billie Dee took a seat at the bar, her knees knocking. "I thought you might need a treat," she called to the young woman.

"Brownies? The smell coming out of the kitchen was about to do me in," she said as she finished washing the table and returned behind the bar with the dishes and cleaning supplies.

Billie Dee watched her wash her hands and dry them. She'd always heard that you can tell a lot about a person by their hands. She realized Ashley Jo's weren't the hands of a professional bartender or barmaid. Far from it. They were manicured, not red and chapped from being in water all the time. While Ashley Jo had learned how to make drinks and serve them, she hadn't been doing this long.

"These look wonderful," the young woman said. She picked up a brownie but, before taking a bite, said, "Are you all right?"

Billie Dee started. "Sorry, woolgathering. How are you today?"

The young woman met her gaze as she took a bite of the brownie. She swallowed and grinned. "Billie Dee, these are amazing. Can I get your recipe?"

"Ashley Jo, there's something I've been meaning to—"

"I forgot to tell you." She reached in her pocket and brought out a folded piece of newsprint. Wiping her hands on a bar rag, she unfolded what appeared to be something she'd torn out of a magazine.

"It's a cooking contest," Ashley Jo announced. "When I saw it, I thought of you. You don't have to actually cook. You just have to send in a recipe to win. I thought your chili would win hands down."

Billie Dee couldn't help being touched. "That is sweet of you, but I couldn't—"

"Are you kidding? The way you cook? You will win this."

"That is sweet of you, really. Ashley Jo, I can't help but notice that when you get excited your Texas accent comes out. It makes me a little homesick. You said your father was in the military, but you must have spent quite a bit of time there to pick up such a distinct accent."

The young woman froze for a moment, then laughed. "You caught me. I thought I hid it so well... So much for that fancy finishing school my mother sent me to. But then again, you're from Texas so of course you recognized it. Like I said, I was a military brat, but I'm Texas born and bred. Leave it to you to spot it. Between the fancy finishing school and university—"

"Where did you attend?"

"Texas A&M. Go Aggies!" She let out a nervous laugh. "I

thought I'd gotten rid of my accent. Guess no one can get all the Texas out of a person, huh."

"Where in Texas were you born?"

"San Antonio. I'm sure you've been on the river walk there."

"I have." *San Antonio.*

"How about you?" Ashley Jo asked conversationally.

"Houston."

"I have friends from there. I love the old part of town. Can I get you something to drink?"

Billie Dee shook her head. "So what brought you to Gilt Edge?"

"I could ask you the same thing."

"I was just traveling through."

Ashley Jo smiled, a look in her eye that Billie Dee couldn't quite read. Was that a wariness? "Another thing we have in common. Unfortunately, I never learned to cook, though. I was hoping you might give me some pointers. I know you don't have much time, like, to give lessons, but I was wondering…"

"I would be happy to," Billie Dee said. "Any morning, just come by the kitchen before your shift or on your days off. Up to you."

"Thank you. I'm excited and probably hopeless when it comes to the kitchen, but it will be fun spending time with you," Ashley Jo said. "Since we seem to have so much in common."

Billie Dee smiled but wondered about that. What had Ashley Jo really come to Gilt Edge, Montana, hoping to find? Certainly not cooking lessons. But she had seen the young woman eyeing Cyrus Cahill. Maybe she'd come looking for a cowboy…?

Tucker wasn't one to sit around and wait. He never doubted that he'd be seeing Madeline again, now that he knew she was alive. But he also figured she wouldn't be coming alone. Madeline was the kind of woman who had a man doing her bidding for her—just as he suspected she had nineteen years ago.

Had it been Madeline who'd been waiting for Misty downstream that night? Or had Madeline sent the other person Kate had been looking for all these years?

Tucker walked into his lawyer's office, right past the empty receptionist's desk, as he followed the sound of raised voices.

He pushed open Jayce's office door and stopped—just like the conversation did in the room in front of him.

Cal, Lonny and Jayce all turned abruptly. He shouldn't have been surprised to see Jayce in his office with the two men. After all, the three of them had been best friends back in high school. So why had it sounded like they'd been having a heated disagreement?

More to the point, why did Tucker sense they'd been talking about him?

"I'm curious," he said as he looked into their surprised and guilty-looking faces. "Do you have a receptionist, Jayce? I've yet to see anyone sitting out there."

"She's on leave. To go back to college for a few months. I promised to keep her job for her."

"That was awful nice of you."

Cal let out a snort, making him think that Jayce had something other than the young woman's education going on with his receptionist.

Jayce rose. "Come on in. We're through here. Cal and Lonny were just leaving."

Cal looked as if he wasn't finished, but he took his cue and said, "Come on, Lonny. I guess we better get back to work."

Lonny didn't even give him a look as he passed, but Cal gave a quick nod and the two were gone. Tucker closed the door behind them.

"What's going on, Jayce?"

His friend shook his head and sat back down.

He couldn't help asking, "You still want to represent me, don't you?"

"Of course. What makes you ask that?"

"Just when I came in..."

"The guys." Jayce sighed. "You know what gossips they are. There's a lot of stories going around."

"Like what?"

Jayce motioned to a chair across from his desk, but Tucker declined with a shake of his head. "Your leaving nineteen years ago has people speculating that you killed her and ran. Now you're back. Your brother is the sheriff. Madeline is nothing but bones..."

Tucker nodded. "They really think I killed her?"

"She was holding you up for money. The whole jumping-into-the-river thing, that sounds like someone planned to blackmail you for years."

"I don't believe I mentioned her jumping in the river," Tucker said, his stomach sinking.

Jayce's eyes widened in alarm. He swore under his breath. "You must have. How else would I know that?"

"My thought exactly."

His friend held up both hands. "Easy, Tuck. It isn't what you're thinking."

"Maybe you'd better tell me what it is you think I'm thinking. Or maybe just tell me what you and Lonny and Cal were arguing about."

Jayce looked away for a moment. "We were arguing about how stupid it was to fix you up with Madeline."

"I thought we already agreed on that. There something new I should know about?"

"Lonny. That's how I knew about her jumping in the river or the creek or the lake after pretending she had a baby."

"Lonny?"

"He'd gone through the same thing with Madeline."

"And you still set me up with her?" he demanded, afraid he was going to reach across the table and thump Jayce at any minute.

"I had no idea. Not until all this shit with you went down. Lonny just told me. Only he went to Rip and Rip handled it so nothing ever came of it."

Tucker studied Jayce for a long moment. "So Rip knew how to find her, how to…handle it? And Rip was how the three of you found out about Madeline to begin with, right?"

"I know. Lonny should have spoken up, man. He shouldn't have let you walk into that, especially after he knew how bad it could get. But you know Lonny."

Yes, he did. Lonny had obviously carried more resentment than any of them had known during high school.

Tucker turned to leave.

"Wait, that's it?" Jayce asked behind him.

"I'll be back. Let's just hope your story checks out." He slammed out of the lawyer's office with every intention of going straight over to Rip's body shop even though he figured Cal and Lonny were probably there and it might get ugly.

But as he reached his pickup, he saw that the truck was sitting at an odd angle. He swore as he bent down and saw that his right front tire had been cut. He glanced around, wondering who could have done this. Cal? Lonny?

Swearing, he opened his pickup to get out his tools but stopped short. The sweet scent hit him first. Jasmine. Then he saw the dusky-rose-colored teddy hanging over the bottom of his steering wheel.

His gaze shot up. He'd half expected to see Madeline standing on the curb laughing. But as he looked around again, he didn't see her. But he suspected she was somewhere watching him and enjoying this.

He hoped she enjoyed watching him change his tire. For

the time it took him, he cursed her black heart, telling himself he couldn't wait until they met again.

Kate left her father's hospital room feeling a little better than when she'd arrived. Earlier he'd looked so pale. He'd always been a large man, but it was as if he'd shrunk in that big white-sheeted bed with all those wires and tubes running from him.

But his color was better and the doctor had assured her he was resting peacefully. This time, he really had had a heart attack.

"He's going to have to make some changes in his lifestyle," the doctor had told her mother before Mamie had to leave for a social engagement she couldn't cancel.

"Don't worry," her mother had told the doctor. "Kate will be joining her father in Washington, DC. She'll see that he slows down, won't you, dear?"

Kate had said nothing as she'd watched her mother leave. Now, as she walked toward the exit, she just wanted to go home and get some needed sleep. She'd tried to call Tucker but his phone had gone straight to voice mail. She'd left a message updating him on her father's condition and telling him she was going to stay a few more days.

As she came around a corner in the hallway, she almost collided with her father's personal assistant.

"I feel as if you've been dodging me," Peter said. "You've been to see your father?"

"He's better. I was just headed home to get some sleep."

He raised a brow. "What's going on, Katie?"

She grimaced at the use of her father's pet name for her. "Peter, I don't want to get into this here in the hospital hallway."

"Fine, let's go to dinner. But you can't expect me to—"

"No dinner. Like I told you, I need sleep."

"Yes, I can see that. Any reason you haven't been getting enough, Katie?"

"My name is Kate. My father calls me Katie..." She took a breath and let it out. "Peter, I thought I made myself perfectly clear the last time we talked."

"I'll make a dinner reservation for tomorrow night because I haven't had my say yet," he said, pulling out his phone.

She groaned, not wanting to sit through a dinner with him. Nor did she want to get into it here in the hospital hallway.

"Katie—excuse me—*Kate*, your father's heart attack isn't a good time to make any big decisions."

"Thank you for that expert advice. But, Peter, if this is about me going to DC to work for him—"

"Your head is in the wrong place right now."

"Oh, I think I've never seen things more clearly," she snapped. "You seem to think that we have some kind of... arrangement that is leading me to DC and to you as if my marrying you is some political deal you've made with my father. But we don't."

"It's what your father wants. It's what *I* want. You'll see things differently once we're in DC together. And once we're engaged." He started to go down on one knee, but she grabbed him and pulled him back up, amazed he would try this again.

"Listen to me," she said, lowering her voice and looking around to make sure no one was watching. She'd spent her life in the public eye. Her father didn't need any negative publicity right now.

"We are not a couple. We will never be a couple. I'm in love with someone else." There, she said it.

"That cowboy from Gilt Edge?" He laughed. "That's ridiculous, Katie. This is just some romantic fantasy that will quickly grow old. Like I said, you aren't in the right frame of mind right now. Once you get over this silly quest of yours… Wait, where are you going?"

Kate had let go of him and now started past him for the elevator. "I'm not going to change my mind," she said over her shoulder.

"At least let me walk you to your car."

"Don't bother." As she reached the elevator, she changed her mind and took the stairs down the few floors, anxious to get out of the hospital and away from Peter and the demands her father had been making on her for years. She'd felt she couldn't let her father down because she was all he had with her brother, Clay, gone.

Once past the outer door, she took a deep breath of the late-evening air. She was angry at herself because Peter's words made her question herself. Her father wanted her in DC with him. He'd always said that was where her future career was waiting for her. A part of her had been excited about the prospect. Until she'd met Tucker.

Could she be happy in Gilt Edge as a cowboy's wife?

She couldn't believe how foolish that thought was. She reminded herself that Tucker was still in love with Madeline, who might be alive. Also, it wasn't as if she and Tucker were at a place where she should even be thinking about being his wife.

Kate started for her car, telling herself she was too exhausted to even think, let alone plan her future with so much up in the air. The visitors' part of the lot was empty this late at night. She hadn't realized it was so late or so foggy. The streetlights cast an eerie glow in the fog that now blanketed the city.

As she walked toward her SUV, she couldn't help still being angry with Peter. How dare he try to tell her when she should make decisions. Her father would be fine. Her mother… Well, Mamie always managed somehow. But things had changed.

Not for her parents. She doubted either of them could change even if they wanted. But Kate wasn't the old Kate who'd stayed around, believing she had to fill in where her brother should have been.

When the time came, she'd decide what she wanted to do. Right now all she could think about was Tucker curled up in some warm soft bed. She hurried toward her SUV, anxious to reach home and her own bed. It surprised her. All these years of planning her retribution… She still wanted justice for her brother, but it was no longer the force that drove her each day.

What she wanted now was Tucker. The memory of being with him… For a moment she was back in that cabin, the fire crackling in the woodstove, her body wrapped in Tucker's strong arms.

She'd been so lost in her thoughts that she hadn't paid any attention to the footfalls behind her until this moment.

The steps had quickened and were now right behind her. She spun around, thinking it would be Peter. The moment she realized it wasn't, her hand went to her shoulder bag, but not quickly enough. The blow to the side of her head dazed her.

As she groped for her gun, her purse was jerked away. She struggled, kicking and fighting, as a second man came out of the trees and grabbed her from behind. Her lips opened, but her scream was muffled as a large hand clamped over her mouth. Like the first man, he wore a ski mask over his face.

"What you got in here you want so bad?" the first man asked. "What's this? *A gun?*" He sounded shocked and offended that she would even think about pulling it on him.

"I could use some help here," the second man said as she struggled to get free with every ounce of her strength.

"All right, all right." The first man, the larger of the two, stepped forward and jabbed her arm with a needle. She fought as if her life depended on it because she had a bad feeling it did. But the drug was too powerful and so were the men.

As her body went limp, the darkness closed in and all she could think was, *Tucker. I need you.*

CHAPTER TWENTY-FIVE

Once Tucker's tire was changed, it was late, but that wasn't going to stop him. Now more than ever, he wanted to talk to Rip. This was all about Madeline, but there was more than her involved. He didn't think it was a coincidence that after he'd told Jayce he was going to talk to Rip, he'd come out to find his tire cut.

So who had Jayce called? Madeline? Or her accomplice? How deep was his old friend in all this?

The body shop itself was dark by the time he got there, but a light burned in the apartment upstairs. Tucker parked and got out. Gilt Edge wasn't the kind of town that had a dangerous neighborhood. But there were good and bad areas in town. The good had neat, well-kept houses and yards. The bad had piles of junk, broken-down cars, dirt yards often with at least one big barking dog.

Rip lived in the large apartment over the shop just as his parents had until their divorce when only his father had lived there until his death. Tucker remembered Rip's father as a disagreeable man with powerful, strong-looking arms and constant grime under his nails. Rip, even as big as he was by junior high school, was scared of his sour and often angry old man.

Tucker walked to the side of the building to where the stairs led up to the apartment. He could hear loud music as he took one step, then another. When he reached the top of the stairs, though, he stopped, surprised to find the music blaring—and the door standing open. All his instincts told him something was very wrong.

Kate felt herself going in and out of consciousness. She woke to the murmur of voices. For a few moments, she didn't know where she was or what had happened. But it came back quickly when she realized that her hands were bound behind her, her mouth was gagged and something had been tied over her eyes.

Lying in the back of a lurching vehicle, her stomach roiling from whatever drug they'd injected her with and car sickness, she fought to not throw up.

"Stop complaining and just let me drive," said a male voice from behind the wheel. She recognized the voice as the smaller of the two men.

"Come on, this is crazy. What are we supposed to do with her?"

"Keep your voice down."

Kate heard the second man's seat squeak as if he'd turned to look toward the back of what she realized must be a van. "She's still out cold. If not dead. What did we shoot her up with, anyway?"

"Stop worrying so much."

"Easy for you to say. I wish I'd never gotten involved in this. If anyone is to blame, it's you."

The sound of the motor drowned out whatever else they were saying as the driver slowed and then turned onto a

bumpy gravel road. The engine roared, giving her the impression the van was climbing up a mountain road.

Her heart pounded, fear making her all the more sick to
her stomach. Where were they taking her? And why had they
abducted her to begin with?

Standing at the open doorway to Rip's apartment, the music
was deafening. Since this part of town was more industrial,
there were no close neighbors. Otherwise, there'd be a deputy here by now arresting someone for disturbing the peace.

Tucker knocked on the open door and knocked again as
loudly as he could. Finally, he stepped in, fighting the urge
to put his hands over his ears.

"Rip!" he yelled at the top of his lungs. "Rip!"

There was no one in the living room area and he couldn't
see into the other rooms from where he stood. He spotted
the stereo, though, and quickly stepped to it and shut it off.

The silence was deafening. He let it sink in for a moment.
"Rip?"

No answer.

Moving toward what appeared to be the kitchen, he called
again. The first thing he noticed was the pizza and beer bot-
tles on the table. It appeared that Rip had had a dinner guest.

Tucker touched one of the cans of beer. It was half-full,
the can still cold to the touch. A good portion of the pizza
was still congealing in its cardboard box, appearing that the
meal had been interrupted.

"Rip?" He listened, but now, with the stereo off, he heard
nothing. Wouldn't someone have come out the moment they
heard the stereo go off? And why so loud? Loud enough to
drown out raised voices? Or gunshots?

He felt the hair rise on the back of his neck as he moved
down the deathly quiet hallway. Tucker knew he had no

choice but to see what was wrong. Because something was very wrong here.

Maybe Rip had gotten a business call and he'd left to go pick up a wrecked car. But he'd seen the wrecker sitting out front as he'd come in. Or maybe they'd gone out back. There was a door off the kitchen that might be an exit from the apartment to the steep wooded hillside behind the shop. He tried to imagine something that would make Rip and his friend leave behind their beer and pizza to go out the back way unless...

Had they seen him coming? Known he was going to want answers? Had Jayce called Rip to warn him that Tucker was on his way? Why else would his tire have been slashed?

"Rip?" The sound of his own voice as he looked into each room was no longer comforting. Ahead, he could see one room at the end of the hall. The door was open. Tucker told himself that if he didn't find anyone in it, he was out of there.

Fighting a bad feeling, he eased on down the hallway. He was almost to the open door when he heard a moan. He closed the distance to the doorway. The first thing he saw was blood, splotches of it on the dark filthy carpet. He hadn't realized it was blood, though, until he saw it smeared on the wall. Next to him was one large handprint in deepening red.

A figure came flying out of a room. Tucker had no time to react. Caught off guard, he tried to duck. Something hard and cold struck him in the head before he was slammed backward. He went down hard as the person nimbly slipped past him and was gone.

As he fought to get to his feet and turned, all he got was a flash of dark clothing as the person turned into the kitchen. He heard the back door open and slam and the thunder of footfalls. By the time he reached the door and looked out, whoever it had been was long gone.

He was fumbling out his phone when he heard the sound

of a moan again from down the hallway. He hurried back down the hallway to the last bedroom—the one the figure had come busting out of minutes before.

Rip lay on his back, one hand trying to hold his guts in from the long gash in his stomach. His eyes were open along with his mouth. Tucker pulled out his phone again and hit 911 as he rushed to Rip.

"Who did this?" he demanded as he grabbed some discarded clothing on the floor and tried to staunch the flow of blood. "Rip? Who did this?"

The big man's lips moved. The word came out on a dying breath. "Madeline."

Tucker felt a chill wrap its icy tentacles around his neck.

Rip grabbed his free hand, but his fingers loosened, his hand dropping to the floor as his eyes glazed over.

"Nine-one-one. What is your emergency?" said a female voice on the phone.

Bound, gagged but no longer blindfolded, Kate was dragged from the vehicle. She stumbled along what seemed to be a rocky path. Still weak and sick from the drug and the van ride, she fought to make sense of where she was and what was happening.

She felt as if she'd been in the back of the van for hours. Her body ached. As she looked around in the darkness, she didn't recognize her surroundings from anything she could see. The starlight was bright, a half-moon hanging over the mountain ahead of them.

That earlier feeling that she'd spent hours in the van came back to her in a rush. This wasn't Helena with its fog and low clouds. But where had they brought her?

She knew her life might depend on knowing where she was being taken. If she had any hope of escaping... Escaping was her only hope since no one knew where she was. No one would be looking for her. Her mother would just assume she'd gone back to Gilt Edge—just as her father and Peter would. While Tucker would think she was in Helena with her father.

She felt a tremor of panic wind through her. She breathed in the night air, trying to keep calm. Pine trees. The air was colder here, too. They were in the mountains. She listened, praying there might be other people around. That if she got the chance to scream, someone would come to her aid.

But she heard nothing but the grunting and groaning of the men as they half dragged her up the mountainside to the flicker of the first man's flashlight. She fought the terror at the back of her mind that she would die here in this isolated spot. That this was the end. That she would never see her family and friends. But mostly, she realized with growing panic, that she would never see Tucker again. He would never know what happened to her. No one would.

The thought was too much to bear that she might never see him again. That she might never get the chance to tell him how she felt about him.

Lost in her grief and panic, she hadn't realized at first what she was hearing. Water. Rushing water. She took another step and the ground seemed to drop out from under her. Kate knew she would have fallen if one of the men hadn't had hold of her. She saw then that she was standing on a precipice next to a waterfall. The rocky land dropped away below her as water roared off the mountain to pool far below her.

The sound of rushing water grew louder as the men dragged her along a trail of sorts. Her heart began to pound harder. She was terrified of water after almost drowning when she was thirteen on a vacation in Hawaii. The sound of the water made her legs go even weaker.

The men swore, forced to take even more of her weight between them. Where were they taking her? Surely not up a mountainside to drown her. She told herself that if they had wanted to kill her, they could have done that anywhere along the drive to wherever they were now, but it didn't help stem the growing alarm inside her.

She was at the mercy of these men. She had no idea why they'd taken her. Worse, what they planned to do with her now.

They stopped near the bottom of the mountainside and she could make out what appeared to be several concrete structures. The man holding her up set her down, steadying her. The drugs had worn off some more. She could feel the cold, sense the deep damp darkness around her, as well as the isolation. Wherever they had brought her, there was no one else around.

Something loud made a scraping sound and then she was pushed forward a half dozen yards toward the smaller of the buildings. She was led toward an open doorway. She couldn't see inside the blackness, but when she took a step, she felt a solid floor. The air was colder in there, though. A dank smell rose up, terrifying her.

Kate stopped abruptly, desperate to be back out in the fresh air. She hated cramped places. Worse, cramped dirty, cold, smelly places.

A hand shoved her hard. She pitched forward into the darkness. She fell, landing on her shoulder. A muffled cry escaped her as her cheek scraped against what felt like a rough concrete floor.

"What the hell did you have to do that for?" the larger of the men snapped. "At least untie her. What is wrong with you?"

"You really are of no help," the smaller of the two said. She heard him approach, felt him sawing away at whatever was binding her wrists. Her wrists free, she flexed her hands and rolled over onto her back. Her first instinct was to make a run for it, but she knew she couldn't get past both of them.

She could see both men silhouetted in the doorway, both still wearing their masks.

That was fine with her since she feared that once she saw their faces, they would feel they had no choice but to kill her when they were done with her.

It was the when-they-were-done-with-her part that worried her. What did they want? Why bring her here?

"Leave her," the smaller of the men said. She heard the scrape of the door, closing out even the starlight. Cloaked in blackness, she was alone.

She sat up. Her shoulder hurt, her cheek was scraped, but nothing felt broken. She worked to get the gag untied, happy to spit it out.

Listening, she heard nothing but the faint roar of the creek. Were they gone? Were they just going to leave her here? What if they never came back?

Tears burned her eyes as she pushed herself to her feet. She wouldn't lie here on the floor in the fetal position and wait for whatever they had planned.

The first thing she had to know was what kind of room she was in—and if there was any way out. She wasn't going to die here. She wasn't going to die. Not without putting up a fight.

CHAPTER TWENTY-SIX

Tucker sat slumped in a chair in his brother's office. "Rip definitely said the word *Madeline*. Just like I told you." He'd been over his story a half dozen times already, including why he'd gone there.

"But why kill Rip?" Flint said.

"I have no idea except that Rip was the one who got Madeline to lay off Lonny," he said. He'd related what Jayce had told him about Lonny and how Rip had apparently squared things with Madeline so the blackmail stopped. "I suspect that Rip and Madeline knew each other better than we have been led to believe."

"Rip was killed with a knife and your slashed tire. Madeline?" his brother asked.

He shrugged. "Someone at least wants me to believe that Madeline was behind it. The article of clothing on my steering wheel was a teddy in her favorite color smelling of her perfume."

"But you'd just interrupted an argument between Jayce, Lonny and Cal, with Lonny and Cal leaving just minutes before you found your slashed tire," Flint said, as if he needed the reminder. "If Lonny helped set you up with Madeline... That damned Lonny. I never liked him. He's a whiner... So there is a good chance that they're all involved? Do you trust Jayce?"

"I used to. Now I just don't know." Tucker didn't want to admit it. Jayce had been his best friend since they were boys. But he reminded himself that he'd been gone for nineteen years. People changed. "In some way, I'm afraid they're all involved, Jayce included."

"So any one of them or all of them could have been in on planting your pistol in your pickup."

"Isn't it more likely that Madeline stole the gun? She used it to kill Misty, then her father and then framed me with it. Also, there were two place settings at Rip's table."

Flint nodded. "All true, but Madeline wasn't working alone."

"Maybe she was working with Rip and they had a falling-out," Tucker suggested.

"A definite possibility, if we can trust his dying word. He might have been trying to tell you something about her."

"I think he was aware of how much I already knew about her," he said.

"The lab will run prints, DNA, but all of that is going to take time," the sheriff said. "The problem with murder is that it often leads to another one to cover up the first. Rip was involved with Madeline from what you've said, but... Expecting a call?"

"Kate," Tucker said, checking his phone again. It surprised him that she hadn't returned his calls. "Sorry, it's just that I haven't heard from her. It isn't like her to not get back to me." He thought about what had happened between them at the cabin. Was that why she wasn't returning his calls?

"If you're worried—"

Tucker was, but he told himself he shouldn't be. It was

Kate. Kate, who prided herself on her independence. Kate, who just might need a little space right now.

"I might drive to Helena," he said.

"Tucker, do I have to remind you that you aren't to leave the county? Not to mention, there is a murderer out there."

"There's been a murderer out there for nineteen years."

"But now that person has killed again."

"You don't want to believe it's Madeline because a knife was used," Tucker said, realizing it was why his brother hadn't taken Rip's dying word as seriously as he'd thought he would.

"Women kill in more civilized ways. Usually."

"I suspect Madeline is the exception," Tucker said. "So trust me, I'll be watching for her. But I don't think she wants to kill me. Why bother to frame me? No, I'm more worried about Kate."

He knew it would sound crazy, but he had a feeling that if Madeline—even after all these years—thought that he cared for Kate that she would want to hurt her out of some warped sense of jealousy.

He shook his head. "It still amazes me. They must have been fooling people for years. I doubt anyone could tell them apart. I know I couldn't and I thought I knew Madeline extremely well."

He checked his phone again, feeling himself growing more anxious. It just wasn't like Kate.

"Why don't you call the hospital?" Flint suggested, seeing him on his phone again. "See if you can talk to Kate and relieve your mind. I don't want you taking off. If I have to lock you up, I will."

Tucker held up his hands in surrender. "I'll call, okay?"

"Thank you. I need to get back out to the body shop. I have deputies out there looking for the murder weapon," Flint said. "Go out to the ranch. I'll let Hawk and Cyrus know you're on your way. Otherwise—"

"Otherwise, it's a jail cell. I get it."

"Tuck."

He looked up at his brother, saw the worry and knew Flint wanted to lock him up to keep him safe.

"I'd much rather sleep in my bed than on that cell cot again, so I'm heading out to the ranch. I won't drive to Helena." Not unless he couldn't reach Kate, then nothing could stop him. Flint had to know that.

Kate moved around the building where she was being held, counting off each step. Her fingers skimmed over the rough concrete walls. No windows, but after her eyes adjusted to the darkness, she'd found two places where the moonlight leaked in. One up by the roof, out of her reach. The other adjacent to the door. Both were small slits, nothing she could break through bare-handed.

The building was small and smelled like a locker room. She recognized that smell. A hot spring. Hadn't someone mentioned that there used to be an old hot spring outside Gilt Edge? Was it possible that's where she was? She thought of Tucker, her heart soaring at the thought that they'd brought her back because of him.

That didn't make a lot of sense, she realized. Unless Madeline was involved. Her pulse jumped at the thought. Unless she was bait!

She thought of Tucker and fought tears. Her heart ached so much she could no longer stand. Sitting down, she buried her face in her hands. She would give anything to see him one last time. But if she were right, then it would be the last time for both of them.

Kate knew she shouldn't be thinking like this. But hours had gone by and the two men hadn't returned. She had to face the fact that they might never return. She had to face some other truths, as well. She'd been using her brother's death to keep from living her own life. She'd been so focused on her quest and hadn't even thought about how it would all end. Could she really kill someone? She'd always thought she could kill Madeline, but she wasn't even sure of that anymore.

Not that she was going to get a chance. She'd made a promise to her brother at his funeral. She would get him justice or die trying. If she didn't get out of here alive... It hurt that she wouldn't get him justice. That Madeline and the people she was involved with were getting away with it all. That made her want to scream her heart out.

But she had already screamed until her throat felt like it was bleeding. No one had come because no one was out there. She wondered if she would die here, her bones found like Misty's—so many years from now that she would have become only skeletal remains.

Realizing that she was wallowing in self-pity, she angrily pushed herself to her feet. As she did, she felt something cold and metallic on the floor. A screwdriver. She moved to the door and shoved the screwdriver into the small opening. Some of the old, weathered concrete crumbled to the floor.

Kate began to work faster, encouraged by how easily she had made the opening larger. Fresh air rushed in as she worked. She thought of Tucker and kept digging.

CHAPTER TWENTY-SEVEN

Once Tucker had reached his pickup, he'd started to climb behind the wheel when he saw the new note tucked under his windshield wiper. Like the other time, he looked around but saw no one. Carefully he pulled it out, unfolded it and held it up to the light. As he did, he caught the scent of jasmine. His belly roiled.

It was the same handwriting as the other notes.

You should have left, but since you didn't... I'm waiting for you. Remember our second date? Come alone if you ever want to see Kate again.

His chest aching with a fear that had plagued him for hours, he climbed behind the wheel and drove out of town, headed for the old hot spring. The place had been abandoned years ago, the road up to it privative at best. The original building had burned down in a lightning storm years before he was born.

While still private property and posted with no-trespassing signs, he and his friends had gone up there, anyway. That it might be dangerous had been part of the thrill. It was where he'd taken Madeline on what she called their second date.

The water coming out of the ground was boiling hot, but the pool that formed where it ran into the creek below the waterfall was the perfect temperature, especially on a winter night.

Before he might lose cell phone coverage, Tucker put in a call to Flint. He didn't doubt that Madeline would kill Kate if the sheriff's department showed up in force. But he was no fool.

His brother answered on the second ring. "Tucker?"

"I got another note from Madeline. She says she has Kate. Please, find out if that is true and call me right back."

"Where are you?" Flint asked suspiciously.

"Please hurry." He disconnected and tried Kate again. The phone rang four times before going to voice mail. He'd already left messages but decided to leave another.

"Kate, you're starting to really worry me. Text me just to let me know you're all right. Please. It's urgent."

A text came in right away.

He picked up his phone, praying it was Kate and Madeline was lying. He almost ran off the road as he read it.

How sweet. But your precious Kate doesn't have much time. You'd better hurry.

He started to put the phone down when it rang.

"No one has seen Kate since she left the hospital alone earlier. Her car is still in the lot. Where are you?"

Tucker could see the road to the old hot spring ahead.

"She'll kill you both. Where are you, Tuck?"

It would take his brother at least twenty minutes to get out here. "I'm at the old hot spring." He disconnected as he pulled into the parking area. There were no other vehicles, but that didn't mean that Madeline hadn't hidden hers somewhere and was waiting for him.

He climbed out, telling himself he wished he had a weapon.

But Madeline would expect that. Madeline already had the perfect weapon to use against him—Kate. Somehow she either knew or suspected how he felt about Kate. Which meant she'd been watching him this whole time. Or someone close to him had been watching him.

Tucker realized that he had no idea who he could trust. Or what he was about to walk into as he got out of the truck and started up the mountain to where the boiling water spewed from the ground and joined the creek. He could hear the roar of the water as he hurried up the trail.

Everything he'd learned about Madeline told him that she was a cold-blooded killer. He'd known deep in his soul that she wasn't through with him. She hadn't tormented him quite enough. Now she had the perfect weapon against him—and she knew it.

Kate. Just the thought of her in Madeline's hands nearly killed him. He thought of all the things that made him crazy about Kate, all the things that he loved. Loved. *His* heart ached at the thought of her completely disappearing from his life as abruptly as she had come into it. He couldn't let that happen. He'd die before he would let Madeline take Kate from him.

Kate was exasperating, infuriating, stubborn to a fault, opinionated and impossible. But he loved that about her. Just as he loved her laugh, her smile, the way she cocked her head when she studied him and those bottomless green eyes… He could lose himself in them for the rest of his life. But mostly it was the things that drove him crazy about her that had made him fall for the woman.

How had Madeline gotten Kate up here—if it was true and she had her here? She'd had help. Rip. Or someone who'd been closer to Tucker? He couldn't imagine Lonny or Cal hurting anyone. Well, at least not Cal. And Jayce. Was Jayce capable of murder?

He remembered Jayce's take-no-prisoners attitude in football games. The man was tough when he needed to be. But Tucker couldn't imagine him killing anyone. Not Misty. Not Madeline's father. Not Rip. But he feared that one or all of them were up to their necks in this.

The sky was lightening to the east, he realized as he topped the mountain. It wouldn't be long before the sun came up on another spring day in Montana. His heart clutched at the thought that Kate could already be dead. Madeline could have killed her. He could be walking into a deadly trap with no chance to save Kate—or himself.

In the growing light, he could make out what was left of the old hot spring buildings and pool. Nothing moved below him as he started down the rocky trail. The roar of the creek was deafening. If someone wanted to surprise him at any point, he would be a sitting duck.

Still, nothing could stop him. Madeline would know that. She'd be waiting.

Kate worked the screwdriver into the concrete around the doorjamb. She could see light through the space she'd carved in the crumbling concrete. It surprised her that the sun was coming up. She breathed in the fresh air through the good-size hole she'd made.

She tested the door again. It moved some. Just a little more weakening around the jamb and she thought she could force her way out of here. She kept working harder, afraid that whoever had brought her here would come back once it was daylight.

Still, it made no sense why they'd brought her all the way back to Gilt Edge and left her in the mountains at some old hot spring unless, as she'd suspected earlier, she was bait for Tucker.

She tried not to think about it as she worked. Just a little more, she told herself even though her arms and back ached.

Her knuckles were skinned and bleeding from coming in contact with the concrete, but she couldn't stop. She was going to get out of here. She was going to save herself. Once she escaped.

Kate heard a noise and froze. Over the roar of the nearby waterfall and creek, she heard someone at the door fiddling with the padlock. It was still dark enough that they might not have noticed the hole beside the door frame that she'd carved out. It wasn't large enough to crawl through, so it would probably go unnoticed. At least she hoped that was the case.

But what if it was someone come to rescue her?

She started to scream for help, but something stopped her. It sounded like someone was putting a key into the lock. No one who'd come to rescue her would have a key.

The screwdriver clutched in her hand, she quickly stepped back, waiting for the person to come through the door.

But to her surprise, the sound stopped. She listened, holding her breath, except the door didn't open.

Tucker slowed as he neared what was left of the resort. The place had been a dream. When hot water was discovered up here on the side of the mountain, an energetic entrepreneur bought the land and built one large building that housed the main pool and several smaller ones. He'd planned to turn it into a destination resort.

Instead, that dream went up in flames. After lightning struck the main building and burned it to the ground, all that was left was the concrete pool, which was now filled with green slime and weeds, and the few outbuildings.

Broke and disheartened, the entrepreneur hadn't been able to rebuild and had died a few years later. The place had been tied up in an estate for years, the property near worthless in its present state.

He slowed as he neared a clump of thick pines. Down the

mountain ahead, he could make out the old concrete pump house. Someone had carried off all the pipe works, but the building was still standing off to one side against the mountain. Farther down, where the water pooled, were several more small buildings that had once been the dressing rooms. If Kate was being held here…

As the sun crested the horizon, Madeline stepped out from behind the thick pines, blocking his way. The initial shock of seeing her in the flesh brought him to a halt just yards away. The sound of the creek roared in his ears as Madeline smiled and took a few steps toward him.

The years hadn't been kind to her. While still striking, she looked more like fifty than a woman in her early forties. But there was a fearless confidence about her, something he realized had attracted him from the beginning.

He thought about rushing her in the hopes of taking away the gun she was holding, but he first had to know what she'd done with Kate—and if she was alone. In his pocket, he pushed the button that would call Flint as the last number dialed but worried that his brother couldn't hear their conversation over the roar of the creek.

"I talked to K.O. recently," he said, glancing around.

Surprise registered in her expression before she laughed. "Like I care. My family turned on me. They can all go to hell for all I care. You see anyone else here but you and me?"

"I love your choice of a meeting place. This old hot spring brings back all kinds of memories. Or was it even you I was with?" he asked.

She smiled a smile he remembered too well. A mocking, crooked smile. "You don't know, do you?"

"I was hoping it was your bones in that creek. At least I would have known that you didn't pull this shit on anyone else after me."

"Such bitterness. It was just a game," Madeline said. "No one was supposed to get hurt."

"But Misty got hurt."

She shrugged. "Unavoidable as it turned out."

"Let me guess. She almost drowned that night. I could tell she was scared standing on that bridge. I'm betting she wanted to quit."

Madeline pointed the gun at him as if dotting an *i*. "Give the man a prize. Misty thought she could just walk away. I had already realized she was going to be a problem I would have to deal with sooner or later. She'd fallen in love with Clay Rothschild. Unfortunately, he'd killed himself, but she hadn't known that—yet. So I decided to end it at the creek and blackmail you the rest of your life."

"So you just killed your own sister—one identical to you—in cold blood."

"She tried to grab the gun. I was stronger than she expected." Madeline raised her brows as he took a step toward her. "A lesson you might want to remember." She motioned for him to stop.

He had no choice. "Come on, I don't believe it was a game or you could have stopped. I think it was about the money, the presents, the control over men."

She laughed, also a familiar sound that clawed at his heart.

He wanted to ask about Kate, but he knew that was a mistake. He'd glimpsed Madeline's ego. If she thought the only reason he was here was for Kate...

"Maybe you knew me better than I thought. You were always my favorite."

It was his turn to laugh. "Still trying to con me, huh?" He wondered if the pistol was getting heavy in her hand. He could only hope. But he reminded himself that she'd already killed at least two people with a gun. He doubted she would miss at this range.

"It was just a game at first, but you're right. I liked the trinkets men gave me. I would still have that silver bracelet with the bells that you gave me, but I didn't realize Misty had taken it that night I was to meet you on the bridge. I was otherwise involved so I sent her."

He shook his head. "And she did what you said."

"I might have let her think it would be the last time. Maybe I was hoping she drowned. I don't know. Things had gotten complicated."

"Really?"

"Haven't you figured it out yet? Rip had become our... manager. We began to make a lot of money. Things were picking up, but then Misty fell in love with Clay Rothschild and wanted out. I kept telling her to do me one more favor and then she could run off with Clay."

"You know he killed himself over your...game," Tucker said, thinking of Kate.

"Like I said, things got complicated."

"How could I have ever been fooled by someone like you?" Tucker asked, not expecting an answer.

"I wasn't born that way," Madeline snapped. "Given my parents, I'm surprised I didn't turn into a serial killer."

"Who says you aren't? Misty. Your father. Rip." He said a silent prayer that he wouldn't have to add Kate's name to that list.

Kate listened, but no one came to the door again. She was so close to freeing herself. She knew she was taking a terrible chance, but she had to try. If someone were waiting out there for her, she'd be playing right into their hands.

She began to work frantically with the screwdriver, stopping only once to listen and hearing nothing but the creek. The hole around the door was wide now that the doorjamb was being held only on the one side.

Sticking the screwdriver into the waist of her pants, she gave the door a shove. It moved, making a cracking sound as the wood gave. She shoved again, harder. If the door completely gave way and someone was out there, they might be able to hear it over the roar of the creek.

But it was a chance she was going to have to take. She got a run at it, putting her body into it. The door keeled out but didn't fall. She realized she could slip through it if she kept it pried open by putting her back against the rough concrete.

Her clothing was already ruined, as if that was a worry. She was scraped up and bleeding and ached all over. But she was going to get out of here. Where she was going to go and what she was going to do, she had no idea. She didn't even know how far she was from Gilt Edge.

But at least she wouldn't be caught here when the men came back.

She shoved the door and, using her back against the rough concrete edge, pried it open enough to slip through. The ragged concrete edge scraped her back, drawing blood. She could feel it dampening her blouse, but at the last moment, she managed to free herself.

The door swung back in, almost taking her arm with it. But she was out. She stood for a moment in the dim morning light trying to catch her breath from the exertion and trying to figure out what to do next.

That's when she saw the two figures on the trail up the mountainside next to the roaring creek. A woman holding a gun on a cowboy. Not just any cowboy. *Her* cowboy, Kate thought. Tucker.

CHAPTER TWENTY-EIGHT

"You realize that this has to end," Tucker said. "There are too many bodies, too many mistakes that you've made."

"Seems that way, doesn't it? But it's not over until my last dying breath."

He feared that would be the case.

"You haven't asked about Kate," she said, and there was that smile again, one he'd come to hate.

"The reporter?" He shook his head. "You think that's why I'm here?"

"Isn't it? I saw the two of you in the park."

He smiled. "I'm still the red-blooded American male you seduced all those years ago."

Her gaze ran the length of him. "Too bad we can't go back, isn't it?"

Tucker sensed the change in her. His heart began to pound. She was going to kill him. "So where is Kate?"

"I suspect she's around here somewhere. That was Rip's doing, not mine." She was lying. She knew exactly where Kate was. Or did she?

"Who brought Kate up here if not you? Rip's dead so I know he didn't do it."

Madeline smiled. "Some of your old friends. They'd do anything Rip asked them to do."

Not Jayce. "Cal and Lonny." He felt a surge of hope that Kate was still alive. He still believed Cal wouldn't hurt anyone, not even for Rip. Lonny, though, was another story.

"So they brought Kate up here to lock her in one of the old changing rooms or the pump house. What is the point? You could have lied and said you had Kate."

She shook her head. "She has to be taken care of just like you. You shouldn't have come back. And Little Miss Reporter should have kept her nose out of my business."

Tucker's fear now was that he wasn't going to find Kate because Madeline had brought him up here only to kill him. He could tell by the look in her eyes that she wanted to finish this and disappear again. But only after he and Kate were dead.

In the distance, he thought he heard sirens over the roar of the creek. What he needed was time, he realized as behind Madeline he spotted Kate coming up the mountainside. Wherever she'd been kept, she'd somehow managed to get away. His heart soared. She had something in her hand that caught the light as she sneaked up the trail behind Madeline.

"I have to ask," he said, stalling. "Is Jayce involved?"

She cocked her head at him. "Your best friend?" Her laugh cut him like glass. "That would be tragic, wouldn't it? I guess you'll never know," she said and pulled the trigger.

Kate had found a piece of old pipe about a foot long in the growing light of day. She'd hurried as fast as she could up the trail without making too much noise and warning Madeline. It had come to her that even though she couldn't see the woman's face, she had to be the blonde holding the gun.

She was within yards of Madeline's back when she heard

the gun report. A scream escaped her throat as she saw Tucker fall. She ran the last few yards, coming up behind the woman and bringing the pipe down hard.

But Madeline must have heard her. Or sensed her. She spun around, the blow catching her in the shoulder and arm rather than the head. The gun in Madeline's hand went flying down the mountainside but the woman managed to grab Kate's arm as she howled in pain.

Kate had that split second when she came eye to eye with a woman she had detested for nineteen years. This was the woman who had stolen Tucker's heart. This was the woman who'd broken it.

She swung the pipe again, but Madeline grabbed it, using her uninjured arm. She was strong and threw Kate off balance. But Kate wasn't about to let go of the pipe and give Madeline not only the advantage but another weapon to use against her.

Off balance already, she pulled hard and Madeline fell with her. The two rolled down the mountainside to the edge of the roaring creek. Madeline had landed on top of Kate and now tried to use the pipe to choke her with it. The crazy woman pushed the pipe against Kate's throat. She was screaming something Kate couldn't make out, but she was also winning.

Kate couldn't hold her off much longer. Out of the corner of her eye, she saw Tucker. He was limping and bleeding badly but he was almost to them. Madeline saw him, too, and tried to free the pipe from Kate's grasp.

Seeing that the woman planned to use the pipe on Tucker, Kate fought harder to retain it. But Madeline was strong and determined. She jerked it hard, only succeeding in throwing them both off to the side. Kate felt the water rush up over her, and an instant later, she and Madeline were swept away down the mountainside.

★ ★ ★

The sun had come up, a blazing globe over the mountaintop. The pines glistened in the sunlight and reflected off the moving water.

Wounded but still standing, Tucker stumbled to the edge of the creek as Kate and Madeline were both swept off the mountain into the roaring water. The bullet had torn through his side. His clothing was soaked with blood, but the only pain he felt was seeing Kate's head disappear under the water.

It was as if he was reliving what had happened that night on the bridge. His heart dropped. Nineteen years of seeing it in his nightmares was nothing compared to this. This was Kate. He remembered her telling him that she was terrified of water.

He made the decision in an instant. Trying to get down the hillside to the pool, where with luck she would surface again, would take too long. He could hear the sound of the sirens, closer now. Any minute his brother and the deputies would be here.

But they would be too late.

He had only one choice. He rushed out into the rushing creek and was quickly swept off his feet and pulled under.

Kate tumbled over and over in the water. Something struck her in the back. She fought to swim, but the current was too strong to do anything but ride it out. Pulled under again, she knew if she couldn't breathe soon, she was going to drown. It was just like in Hawaii. Terror filled her. She was going to die.

She fought to the surface only to realize she was still being swept down the mountainside. She saw that the creek dropped straight down into what appeared to be a deep pool at the bottom. She gasped in a breath just before she dropped over the rise. Panic filled her as she fell in a shower of water before plunging deep into the warm pool.

The water was dark down here. Over her head the falling creek water beat the surface into white bubbles. Kate thought of Tucker. She began to swim toward the surface when something grabbed her. *Someone*, she realized as Madeline's hand clamped on her ankle and dragged her down.

Tucker thought he must have blacked out. He opened his eyes to darkness. Bubbles floated around him. Bubbles and blood. For a moment, he floated with the bubbles before he came out of his fugue state to realize it was his blood in the water. And that Kate was in trouble.

He fought his way to the surface to gasp for air.

Where was Kate?

Heart in his throat, he spun around. All around him was water but no sign of Kate. Or Madeline. He was even more aware of his wound and how much he was bleeding. He had to find Kate and fast. He could feel his body weakening.

He'd come to this pool with his friends since he was a boy. He knew it well. After the rush of the creek and the pounding of the waterfall, the pool seemed relatively quiet. Years ago someone had piled up rocks to make this pool. As the creek dropped into it, the pool became deeper and deeper. He could feel the cold water below him on his feet and the spray from where the waterfall hit the pool.

But no Kate. His pulse pounded with fear. What if she was caught under the waterfall? She must not have surfaced or he would be able to see her. It was daylight now; only the mist from the waterfall made visibility difficut.

He dived down. The water was clear but churning white near the waterfall. He caught a flash of fabric, blue like the blouse Kate had been wearing. He caught her arm and pulled, but she seemed to be stuck. That's when he saw Madeline— and she saw him.

Somehow she had managed to hang on to the piece of

pipe she and Kate had been fighting over before they'd gone into the creek. With the pipe clutched in her fist, she let go of Kate and swam for him.

Kate rose to the surface, gasping for air. She took in huge gulps as she trod water for a moment. Tucker. She'd seen him in the water, wounded and bleeding. She could tell that he was weak from loss of blood. She looked around for him only to see Madeline struggling in the water below her with Tucker.

Taking another big gulp of air, Kate dived down to grab a handful of blond hair. She pulled hard, dragging Madeline away from Tucker for a moment before the woman smacked her wrist with the pipe, breaking her hold.

Madeline surfaced but dived again. Kate had no choice. She went after her. Nowhere did she see Tucker. But she had a bad feeling that Madeline knew where he was and was going in for the kill.

Panic filled her as she saw him floating just below the surface, the water around him tinted with his blood—and Madeline, still holding the pipe, heading right for him.

Flint and the deputy scrambled down the mountainside. From their vantage point, they could see three people struggling in the water.

"Stay here!" Flint ordered and, quickly stripping off his weapons, dived into the water. He swam hard across the pool to the last place he'd seen the three and dived.

The water was dark. He rose, unable to see anyone. Still no one on the surface, he dived again. Where were they?

Seeing a flurry of bubbles off to his right, he swam toward it. Tucker. He was floating just below the surface, the water around him discolored from his blood. He grabbed around him. Out of the corner of his eye, he caught movement.

Madeline. She came at him. He put up an arm to defend himself and was struck with something cold and hard. He lunged for her, but she slipped away. He couldn't worry about her right now. His arm ached from where she'd hit him, but he swam to his brother again, grabbed him around his waist and kicked hard toward the shore.

Kate saw Madeline divert her attention from Tucker to strike out at someone else in the water. She drew back, realizing it was the sheriff. As Madeline rose to the surface, Kate did, too. They came up within feet of each other.

Their gazes met across the misty surface of the pool. Kate was surprised to see such hatred in the woman's eyes. She realized what Madeline was going to do before the woman threw the pipe—and easily ducked away. The pipe hit the water and sank next to her.

Yards from them, Flint had pulled his brother to the shore. She could hear Tucker coughing as the sheriff yelled to his deputies. She caught the words *helicopter* and *hospital*.

Madeline looked around, seeming surprised to see three uniformed lawmen. Kate followed her gaze to where a uniformed sheriff's deputy was on his radio calling for help for Tucker. The deputy then headed in their direction, shouting something Kate couldn't hear over the noise of the creek crashing into the pool only yards away.

Madeline shifted her gaze back to Kate as she trod water. For a moment, Kate expected the woman to attack. But instead, she turned and began to swim toward the waterfall. Kate could see what she planned to do. Behind the waterfall, they wouldn't be able to see her. If she got that far, she might be able to get away.

The thought of Madeline escaping was too much for her. Kate swam after her, determined to end this once and for all—just as she had promised her brother.

★ ★ ★

"Kate," Tucker managed to call as he grabbed hold of his brother's wet uniform shirt in his fist and tried to sit up.

"Take it easy." Flint worked to staunch the bleeding. It appeared the bullet that had entered his side had gone straight through. If it hadn't hit any vital organs, he might make it. But he'd lost a lot of blood from the bullet wound and the gash on his head.

"Where is Kate? You have to find her. You have to—"

"She's over there," Flint said as he saw Kate surface next to the waterfall. She turned back to the pool to reach for something. He watched her drag it through the water in a wave of yellow and realized he was seeing blond hair floating on the surface.

"That's Kate Rothschild," the sheriff said to the deputy. "Go help her." The deputy ran over to offer her a hand out of the water. She staggered out and fell to her knees, gasping for air.

"She's fine," Flint told Tucker. "She's just fine." There was a cut on her forehead and he could see that she was bleeding, but Madeline looked much worse.

The deputy dragged the body of Madeline Dunn out of the water and began to do CPR. Even from a distance as Flint watched Kate gasp for breath on the shore, he could see that Madeline Dunn had taken her last one.

He told Tucker the news. "Madeline's gone. It's over. And Kate… She's fine," Flint said as he saw Kate rise and make her way in their direction. "It's finally over."

Tucker shook his head as he watched Kate approach. "It won't be over until I marry that woman."

CHAPTER TWENTY-NINE

"You let Kate get away?" Lillie demanded when she saw Tucker walk into the saloon.

He wondered if it was written all over him. Or just on his face. "You don't *let* a woman like Kate do anything. She's her own person. Comes and goes as she pleases. If anyone should realize that, it's you, little sis. Kate's asked me to give her some time. That's what I'm doing."

It wasn't like he'd had a choice. Flint had told him about Kate going after Madeline to stop her from getting away. Kate, who was terrified of water, had lived on her need for vengeance all those years. Who knew what happened behind that waterfall? All they knew for sure was that Kate had come out alive—and Madeline hadn't.

Kate had stayed by his bedside for days until she was sure he was going to make it. But once he was out of the woods, she'd told him she had to take care of some things back home.

"Marry me."

She'd laughed and looked around the hospital room. "I'm going to pretend you didn't just say that."

"I'm going to ask you again. I'll try to make it more romantic, but I can't promise. I'll keep asking until you say yes."

Kate had smiled at him and taken his hand. "I love you, but I need you to give me some time."

He'd agreed. He'd had no choice.

Lillie gave him a hug now and a sympathetic look before going over to check on her sleeping son, Trask Collin, Jr., or T.C. as he was now called. Her husband, Trask, Sr., was holding his son and cooing to him.

"Amazing what an infant does to a man," Mariah commented as she watched Trask and her husband, Darby, with their sons.

"What will you do now?" Darby asked after smiling at Mariah and handing over his son, Daniel, since Darby had never liked his name, it turned out.

"Hawk and Cyrus told me about some land adjacent to the family ranch. They want to buy it and expand the cattle operation, but only if I will stay and ranch with them."

"Is that what you want to do?" Lillie asked.

"I'm a cowboy," Tucker said. "It's ingrained. I worked all kinds of jobs after I left here, but none that I enjoyed more than being on the back of a horse. However, Flint has made me an offer. There's an opening for deputy sheriff. I've applied to the law enforcement academy and been accepted."

"Congratulations," Darby said. "Two brothers who are lawmen."

"I'll still help out around the ranch if Hawk and Cyrus need me and I'll still get in a saddle every chance I can. I just stopped by to see the babies."

"I was just about to take them back to the kitchen," Lillie said. "You know Billie Dee—she's loving spending time with them. She is going to spoil them like nobody's business. So give them each a quick kiss."

Tucker did as he was told, amazed at how small they were.

He said as much. As he looked down into those precious faces, he yearned for a child of his own with Kate. Soon, he hoped. Soon.

Tucker went by the jail. He hadn't seen Cal or Lonny since they'd been arrested. Both had missed Rip's funeral. Jayce had been there, but Tucker hadn't talked to him.

He knew that Cal had already given his statement to Flint, but Tucker had to know for himself what had led a man he once considered a friend to this point.

Tucker picked up the phone on his side of the thick plastic window. On the other, Cal, dressed in orange, lifted his phone, smiling as if glad to see him.

"I'm so sorry," Cal said. "I never thought any of this was going to happen."

Tucker believed that was true. Cal wasn't one to think about consequences. "Was Rip involved with the con from the beginning?"

Cal shook his head. "He sent Madeline clients, but that was all at first. Then his old man offered to sell him the body shop. Rip decided to go into business with Madeline to get the money he needed."

"She was for that?"

"He might have twisted her arm a little."

"And the other two sisters?"

"The business was booming. Madeline couldn't handle all the clients. She needed help, so who better than two identical sisters?"

Tucker shook his head at Madeline's depravity that she would involve her sisters. "I can't imagine Madeline and Rip as partners but I guess they had a history even before I met her."

"Rip needed the money. Who knows what Madeline got out of it, but the money started rolling in as the sisters targeted bigger prizes."

"Like Kate's brother."

Cal nodded. "Then Clay Rothschild killed himself. Madeline knew what would happen when Misty found out because she'd been trying to quit and Madeline had been promising her she could after just one more job."

"So Madeline killed her sister and left her body to rot under the driftwood at the creek," Tucker said.

"The scam was falling apart. Rip got greedy. Madeline almost drowned one night. She'd finally realized that she was taking all the risks and Rip was taking too much of the money. They dissolved the partnership when Melody and K.O. disappeared. Madeline took off, disappearing, as well. It looked like it was over."

"So which of them had my pistol that they took from Jayce's bedroom after I sold it to him?" Tucker asked.

"Madeline. She'd been planning to use it to blackmail you if you got too close. That time you went looking for her… You almost got too close to the truth."

He had? He'd thought he'd hit a dead end. Maybe if he had kept looking… Tucker refused to let himself go back to wondering what if… "What would have happened if I hadn't left town when I did?" he had to ask.

Cal shrugged. "Rip would have blackmailed you, pretending to be Madeline, I bet. He joked once that he could have owned the Cahill Ranch."

Tucker shook his head, thinking what Rip's good-ol'-boy facade had been hiding. "Rip was as much a monster as Madeline."

His old friend quickly defended Rip. "He grew up poor, working in that shop with his old man who did nothing but put him down."

"That's not an excuse," Tucker said, and Cal reluctantly nodded. "If Madeline hadn't killed him, he would have died behind bars. Rip could have done so much more with his life."

He thought of K.O. and Melody, then of Kate and how badly she'd wanted retribution. In the end, everyone lost. "So how did you and Lonny get involved in all this?"

Cal had the good grace to look chastised. "After we'd hooked you up with Madeline, Rip asked us to suggest other teenage boys."

"Why would you do that?" Tucker demanded.

"It wasn't like they didn't get something in return. Most of them were just pay-and-gos. Only a select few got the whole treatment."

He shook his head. "And what did you get out of it?"

"Rip paid us, but it wasn't for the money." Cal looked even more down in the mouth. "Jayce went away to college and law school, and you took off. It was just me and Lonny left. Being Rip's friend, well, it made us feel special, you know, like we weren't losers."

Tucker actually could understand. Rip had that kind of personality that men like Cal and Lonny would feel the need to be in the man's charismatic shadow.

"Did you hear? Jayce is going to represent me."

Of course Jayce was. They'd all been friends for too long for Jayce to desert Cal now.

"I'm sorry," Cal said. "Rip said he was just playing a trick on you by having us take Kate."

"You knew better than that."

"I guess. But you were already mad at me and Lonny so we thought what the heck. It was stupid, I know. But Rip told us that Madeline was back in town and that if we didn't do what he asked, he'd sic her on us."

It seemed it wasn't just K.O. and Melody who were afraid of Madeline. He said as much to Cal.

"Look what she did to Rip. The judge has got to realize that Lonny and I were scared."

Tucker doubted that would hold much weight with a judge but said nothing.

Cal's voice broke as his eyes filled with tears. "I wish I'd never gotten involved when Lonny suggested fixing you up with this girl he'd heard about."

"Yes," Tucker said, realizing it was strange how things turned out. He wouldn't have met Kate if his friends hadn't set him up with Madeline.

Billie Dee knew the moment she saw Henry's face. He stepped into the Stagecoach Saloon's kitchen and her heart began to pound.

"You got the results," she said in a whisper even though they were alone.

He nodded and stepped to her.

Billie Dee didn't know at that moment what she wanted the results to be. If Ashley Jo was her daughter, then it meant she'd come here looking for her. So why hadn't she said something yet? And if she wasn't her daughter…

Henry shook his head. "Ashley Jo isn't your daughter."

Billie Dee felt disappointment turn her knees to water. Henry grabbed her before she slumped to the floor. He eased her into a chair.

"I was so sure," she mumbled, realizing how much she wanted it to be true. How much she wanted her daughter. Needed her daughter.

"But there is some good news. When I got your DNA I put it up anonymously on an adoption registry."

She looked up. "You were that convinced Ashley Jo wasn't mine?"

"You got a hit, Billie Dee. Your daughter is looking for you. Now it is just a matter of time before she finds you."

"I'm so glad all this nonsense is behind you," Mamie Rothschild said at breakfast one morning after Kate's return from Gilt Edge. "Your father is so pleased that you were left out of all that awful news coverage—and so was your brother. Except for your kidnapping."

"As I've mentioned before, I don't want to talk about it," Kate said and took a bite of toast. It tasted like cardboard. Everything she'd eaten since she'd returned had been tasteless, but she'd known she had to eat to keep her strength up—and also to keep her mother from nagging her.

"Then let's talk about you joining your father in DC," her mother continued cheerfully. "He's tried not to push you, but he's anxious for you to be involved. He needs the help and it will do you good to get out of Montana after…everything."

"I'm not going to work with Daddy in DC."

"Kate—"

"Mother, don't Kate me."

"This last…escapade almost got you killed." Her mother's voice rose sharply. "Not to mention the scandal that could have come of it if some smart reporter had dug up your brother's relationship with that…woman."

"Clay was in love with that woman. Misty Dunn. And she was in love with him. It's why she's dead. She wanted to quit and her sister…" She shook her head. "I've already told you this."

Mamie waved a fluttering hand through the air. "One tragedy after another. It's too horrible to think about."

"Yes, it was horrible that Clay couldn't come to one of us for help."

Her mother looked away.

Kate felt her stomach drop. She stared at her mother's profile. *"He came to you?"* Her words exploded on a ragged breath.

"You won't understand until you have children of your own."

"He told you about Misty?" She couldn't believe what she was hearing.

"Misty? He thought her name was Madeline," her mother

snapped. "Some common woman who had been blackmailing him. He had the gall to ask me for money so the two of them could run away."

Kate stared at her mother in shock. "So you knew how desperate he was."

"Don't use that tone with me. Of course I had no idea that he might…" Her mother shook her head. "You think if I'd given him money that would have solved everything?"

"In the long run, probably not," Kate said. "But—"

"Your father thinks it best if we put this behind us." Mamie rose from the table. "DC. That's where you belong, working with your father and putting all this ugliness—"

"Distance doesn't cure anything."

"How will you know unless you try it?" her mother asked. "You're going to need a new wardrobe. Your father suggested an advance on your salary. I believe he's already deposited plenty into your account so you can buy something sharp for DC." With that, her mother left the room.

Old habits were hard to break. Kate knew that better than anyone. She was a Rothschild. She'd felt the weight of that name all her life. She wondered if her brother had felt the same way and assumed he had. Would he and Misty have been able to make a life for themselves if they'd had the money to run away? Doubtful, since he was seventeen and couldn't even support himself.

She couldn't blame her mother. The woman responsible for all their grief was dead. She shuddered at the memory of battling Madeline in the pool behind the waterfall. All these years, she'd dreamed of coming face-to-face with the person responsible for her brother's death. Had she really believed that she could kill that person? She'd bought a gun, gotten shooting lessons, spent hours at the range until she was ready. But she'd never been ready for what had happened behind that waterfall.

All of it had left her traumatized. She felt as if she didn't know who she was anymore. She'd always felt so strong, so determined, so invincible. When in truth, she'd been none of those at that moment. Was that how her brother had felt at the end?

Maybe her mother was right. Maybe she should go to DC, work for her father. The job had its appeal because it was… safe. She realized that's what she'd lost. That feeling of being safe. Raised in an ivory tower of wealth, she'd felt untouch-able.

She was neither anymore. She'd worn the Rothschild name like a shield only to find out that it was useless against true evil.

Kate thought of her last conversation with Tucker before she'd left Gilt Edge.

"I don't know if this helps, but Madeline told me that Misty was in love with your brother. So much so that she'd tried to quit that night after she jumped off the bridge and met Madeline downstream. Madeline had known then that Clay had killed himself. She knew her sister wouldn't be able to live with his death and her part in it."

"More than likely she was worried that Misty would rat her out," Kate had said. "Thank you for telling me, though." She'd looked toward the mountains. "So it's really over?"

Tucker had nodded. "What really happened will probably never come out. Isn't that what your parents are hoping?"

"Maybe my brother can finally rest in peace."

"What about his sister?" Tucker had asked.

Kate had smiled into his handsome face. She was going to miss this cowboy. "She's going to need some time."

"Take all the time you need. I'll be here."

She had smiled as she'd stepped to him and kissed his cheek. She'd hesitated for a moment, breathing in the familiar scent of him. Closing her eyes, she'd tried to memorize it, afraid she'd forget over time.

He'd drawn her into a hug. Tears had flooded her eyes as she'd put her arms around him, luxuriating in his warmth, in his strength. He'd saved her life in more ways than he knew. "I love you, Kate," he'd whispered into her hair.

"I love you," she'd whispered back. They stayed like that for a long moment before she stepped away.

Leaving the kitchen now, she found her mother in the sunroom having tea and freshly baked cookies. "Come join me. I just spoke with your father. He is so pleased you will be joining him."

"You shouldn't have told him that," Kate said as she took a seat.

"I'll ring for your tea."

She stopped her mother. "I don't want tea or cookies. I'm leaving."

"Leaving for DC already? You haven't had time to get a proper wardrobe. I suppose you can buy something when you get there but—"

"Mother, I'm not going to DC."

"But your father—"

"I'm going back to Gilt Edge."

"Whatever for?"

"For Tucker Cahill."

Mamie groaned. "That...cowboy?"

"Yes, that cowboy. I learned something from all this. It took a while to sort out. But mostly that life can be short and if you want something, no matter how scary it is, you have to go for it."

"You sound like a sports shoe commercial," her mother snapped. "I thought you'd gotten this foolishness out of your head."

"I don't want to follow in my father's footsteps to some DC

political career. I want to wake up in Tucker's arms and listen to the birds outside the window. I want to ride horses into the mountains. I want to have babies with him."

Her mother's lips pursed. "You have no idea what being a rancher's wife is like."

"No, I don't. But I could learn if that's what Tucker wants."

"Well, if you're dead set on this, then maybe you can take Muriel with you."

"Your cook?" Kate laughed. This was so like her mother. "I won't need Muriel. I'm going to learn to cook."

Her mother scoffed. "Why, when you don't have to?"

"Mom, I want a simple life more than I want my next breath. I want Tucker."

Mamie shook her head. There were tears in her eyes. "But you're a Rothschild. You can have so much more."

Kate laughed again. "There is nothing more that I want. I'm going to be a Cahill. That is, if Tucker asks me to be his wife again."

"If you're willing to settle for that kind of life," her mother said.

"Settle? I can't imagine having more than what Tucker has offered me. Love, Mother. Unconditional love."

"From a *cowboy*," Mamie said with distaste.

Kate smiled. "Yes, from a cowboy."

Tucker had just come back from helping his brothers string barbed wire along the new fence when he saw Kate drive up. His heart did that Ferris-wheel drop it always did at the sight of her, making him a little light-headed.

He'd never been so glad to see anyone in his life. And yet, he worried as he watched her get out of her SUV about what she was doing here. Kate wasn't one to leave things up in the air. He'd always known she'd be back. But to tell him she was taking her father up on his offer in DC or...?

She stood looking around as if seeing the ranch for the first time, before she finally saw him standing on the deck. When she broke into a smile, as if as glad to see him as he was her, he took the stairs two at a time to reach her.

But a few feet shy of taking her into his arms, he stopped. "Kate?"

She nodded, tears in her eyes, and closed the distance between them. He drew her to him, hugging her tightly before finally pulling back to look into her face.

"You've recovered?" she asked.

"Good as new."

Kate nodded. "All those wonderful things you said to me when you were in the hospital?"

He nodded around the lump in his throat. "I meant every one. Still do."

"Well, if you should ever ask me to marry you again..."

He smiled and looked deep into those green eyes. What he saw warmed him to his toes and sent his blood into a slow, steady boil.

"You remember my childhood bedroom?" he said.

She laughed. "I didn't really get a good look at it actually."

"No? Well, woman, you're in luck. My brothers are off working so it's just you and me."

"I like the sound of that," she said, smiling as he swept her up into his arms. This time, he took the stairs three at a time.

CHAPTER THIRTY

The wedding reception was held at the Stagecoach Saloon with family and only a few friends.

Kate had insisted they elope. "Otherwise, my parents will demand a huge wedding that would take over a year to plan, and hundreds of guests that neither of us know."

"Are you sure?" Tucker asked. He'd asked her to marry him one day at the saloon with his family all around and Kate had said yes. It was, to that point, the happiest day of his life. "I thought every woman wanted a huge wedding on her special day."

"By now, you should know that I'm not every woman. All I want is to become Mrs. Tucker Cahill and I don't want to wait."

They'd gotten married at city hall with his brothers and sister as witnesses. Lillie and Mariah had planned the reception, as if he could have stopped them.

But he had to admit, it was all perfect. Tucker found himself looking around the noisy room at his family and friends. The conversations jumped from one topic to the next, broken only by laughter or friendly joking. His heart swelled as he realized how blessed he was to have everyone who mattered here, including his new nephews.

Jayce stepped up to him and handed him a glass of champagne. "To Kate and happy-ever-after," his friend said, and they clinked glasses.

Tucker had missed Jayce. He was just glad they'd put the past behind them. Jayce had confessed that he was in love with his former receptionist and going to ask her to marry him when she returned.

Tucker spotted Kate across the room. Kate made his heart hammer, his blood run hot. She was his equal. A woman who could hold her own. A woman who challenged him.

He laughed at the thought. Kate was all that and more. She made him laugh, made him cuss, made him want to take her over his knee. But mostly he wanted to take her in his arms. Just take her.

The passion she ignited in him still surprised him. He'd thought he would never want a woman the way he did her. He'd certainly never planned to give his heart freely, but Kate had stolen his heart from the get-go.

He smiled over at his father. Maybe Ely wasn't so crazy, after all. "Only a damned fool would let that one get away," his father had said of Kate. Tucker smiled. Now she was his wife. His smile broadened as she caught his eye and headed for him.

"Let me see that!" Lillie shrieked as she rushed to Billie Dee and grabbed her left hand. She stared down at the diamond and shrieked again. "Why is this the first I'm hearing about this?" she demanded.

"You've been a bit busy with your son," Billie Dee said.

"Oh, Billie Dee, I'm so happy for you. I knew it. I just knew it. Henry Larson, right? I knew it," she said again before Billie Dee could confirm it. "Oh, you said you were going to find yourself a handsome cowboy, and, boy, did you. Darby! Have you seen this?"

Lillie practically dragged the cook over to the bar. "You have to see this!" Lillie thrust the cook's hand out at him. "Billie Dee is engaged!"

Darby's gaze went from the ring on her finger to Billie Dee's face. He burst into a huge smile. "Congratulations. I've known Henry Larson for years. He's a great guy."

"Thank you."

"So when is the wedding?" she asked, turning to Billie Dee. "You absolutely have to let me help you with it. You can have it here! Isn't that right, Darby?"

"She can have it anywhere she wants."

"We haven't set a date," Billie Dee said. "We want a very small wedding with family only, but since the Cahills are my only family, I want you all there."

From the bar, Billie Dee saw Ashley Jo raise an empty glass in a mock toast and smile before mouthing, "Congratulations."

Lillie noticed her brother Cyrus standing by himself at the edge of the dance floor. Lillie also noticed that Ashley Jo had been giving Cyrus moon eyes all evening. "You should ask Ashley Jo to dance," she suggested.

He chuckled as he glanced toward the bar. Ashley Jo quickly looked away as if embarrassed to have been caught watching him. "What makes you think she's my type?"

"She's female, attractive, single, and I can tell she likes you."

He laughed and shook his head. "Go bug Hawk. It looks like he and Drey need you."

She glanced in Hawk's direction. Why was it that those two couldn't stay away from each other at every event? When were they going to realize that they belonged together? Lillie sighed and said as much to her brother.

"Don't tell me. Tell Hawk."

She thought she just might do that. As she headed for him, Drey said something and stormed off. There was no hope for Cyrus and Hawk, she thought. "What was that about?" Lillie asked Hawk. She hated seeing her brothers upset. She would give anything to know what the problem was between Deirdre and Hawk. They'd been so in love in high school. What had happened to drive them apart? And yet every time she saw them together there seemed to be something going on as if they couldn't keep away from each other.

"Nothing," her brother snapped.

"Hawk—"

"Drey is getting married."

Lillie blinked. "To whom?"

"I didn't ask." With that, he walked away.

Lillie fought tears. Hawk was so stubborn. If he let Drey go, she feared he would regret it for the rest of his life.

Kate wound her way through the crowd, her gaze on her husband. Oh, how she loved the sound of that word on her lips. Tucker Cahill. Her *husband*. Out of the corner of her eye, she saw her father in deep conversation with Tucker's father, Ely. She didn't want to know what that was about.

Her mother was visiting with Maggie, the sheriff's wife. From the animated conversation, Kate bet they were talking about decorating. Maggie and Flint had just moved into their new house and Maggie had been busy furnishing it—a favorite subject of her mother's.

As she reached her husband, he put his arm around her and pulled her close. "I love you, Mrs. Cahill."

She sighed against him. "I like the sound of that."

"There's something I want to show you," Tucker said and, taking her hand, led her toward the back of the building.

"I'm afraid to ask," she said as he led her upstairs. "Tucker, this is our wedding reception," she said, pretending to resist. "Surely what you have in mind can wait until tonight."

He laughed as he opened the door to the upstairs apartment. "Darby and Mariah have moved out. Darby offered it to us until we either buy a house in town or build on the ranch. What do you think?"

"It's cute," she said, taking in the apartment. "Who decorated it?"8

"Mariah and Lillie. You can change anything that you don't—"

"I love it. I don't think I'd change a thing. They have good taste," she said as she walked around looking at the furnishings, the paintings, the window and bed coverings. "It really is perfect. A love nest."

He grinned at that. "One bedroom, which is all we need right now, and a bathroom. With the kitchen and the bar downstairs…"

"This might really work," she said, nodding as she met his gaze. "Billie Dee has promised to teach me to cook. I guess Ashley Jo is interested in lessons, as well. So by the time we get our own place…" She stepped to her husband. "I will be cooking you amazing meals."

Tucker put his arms around her. "I can't wait to see you in our kitchen. Actually, I can't wait to see you in every room in our house."

She laughed. Their gazes locked and he slowly lowered his mouth to hers. The sound of music and laughter worked its way up the stairs as Mr. and Mrs. Tucker Cahill slow danced in their new apartment before going back to their wedding reception and beginning their new lives.

★ ★ ★ ★ ★